THE HEIST OF
HOLLOW
LONDON

THE HEIST OF HOLLOW LONDON

EDDIE ROBSON

TOR PUBLISHING GROUP  NEW YORK

THE HEIST OF HOLLOW LONDON

Copyright © 2025 by Eddie Robson

A Tor Book
Published by Tom Doherty Associates / Tor Publishing Group
120 Broadway
New York, NY 10271

www.torpublishinggroup.com

Tor® is a registered trademark of Macmillan Publishing Group, LLC.

EU Representative: Macmillan Publishers Ireland Ltd, 1st Floor,
The Liffey Trust Centre, 117–126 Sheriff Street Upper, Dublin 1, DO1 YC43

The Library of Congress Cataloging-in-Publication Data is available
upon request.

ISBN 978-1-250-37206-2 (hardcover)
ISBN 978-1-250-37207-9 (ebook)

Our books may be purchased in bulk for specialty retail/wholesale,
literacy, corporate/premium, educational, and subscription box use.
Please contact MacmillanSpecialMarkets@macmillan.com.

First Edition: 2025

Printed in the United States of America

10 9 8 7 6 5 4 3 2 1

For Gabriel and Jago,
who deserve a better world
than the one depicted in this book.
I hope they get it.

THE HEIST OF
HOLLOW
LONDON

PANIC! AT THE SPONSORAMA

Arlo knew it was a stupid idea to intrude on the sponsorama but Drienne could talk him into anything. The Elite League Finals was literally the only party in town this month, she pointed out, and they could check out what tactics their rivals were using and maybe grab some free shit. Arlo could have saved time by agreeing straightaway, but by resisting, at least he got to set terms: Drienne agreed they'd spend no more than two hours in the sponsorama, take care not to break any rules, and then leave and do some actual work for the rest of the night.

The sponsorama covered several blocks to the immediate east of the stadium, a former residential area that had been flattened and turned into a commercial district a decade ago with a view to hosting events like this. Like any sponsorama, it was a fluid space—dazzling, glamorous, intense, and almost none of what you saw was really there. The area's existing buildings had been transformed by projections: logos, adverts, demos, and endorsements swelled from them like growths, mutations. Everything you saw was connected to the Elite League Finals and its commercial partners, and anything not connected to those things was hidden from view, right down to the clothing of anyone who entered. When Arlo and Drienne stepped across the border, their clothes appeared to change into the event's official casualwear. Drienne seemed to be wearing a bright green-and-purple tennis dress with lace-effect trim, while Arlo had a sports jacket and shorts in the same colors and style. The hang and movement were impeccable—you had to move pretty quickly before it became apparent the clothes were just holograms. Drienne tried to outrun her clothes, dashing from one side of the pedestrianized boulevard to another, dodging people who unlike her were permitted to be there. Arlo told her to stop drawing attention to herself.

The traditional global sporting event vibe was present—a mix of inspiration, togetherness, understanding between nations, all that crap. Against his will Arlo felt the need to be his very best and achieve things he could be proud of, feelings he knew came from subliminal triggers embedded in the image washes that covered almost every available surface. He'd never learned the trick of resisting them, unlike Drienne. She often mocked him when she caught him saying something that obviously came from a trigger.

Despite this, Arlo had to admit it *was* fun to be in the sponsorama and feel like they were part of it all. The ELF had arrived in Shanghai two weeks ago, would run through most of June and the first week of July, and Sunglow was the official retail partner of the event: therefore Oakseed employees were obliged to act like it wasn't happening, as if they hadn't noticed one of the biggest events on the sporting calendar was going on right in front of them. It still entirely dictated Oakseed's strategy in the city, of course—all their brand ambassadors were spending the duration of the event aggressively targeting the border of the sponsorama, where they were still permitted to operate—but no one discussed the event itself, or even mentioned its name.

Arlo and Drienne took different paths through the sponsorama, agreeing to meet up when they were done. After twenty minutes, Arlo had managed to bag a free sample of a limited edition flavor of Dapper, Sunglow's leading soft drink brand, a free trial subscription to their Moodboard app (which Arlo would not be able to run on any devices he owned), and a tub of vitamin supplements. He was on the lookout for some food when Drienne ran past him, grabbed his arm, and dragged him toward the exit.

Arlo would later learn Drienne had bombed three major lucer feeds, causing multiple brand violations including changing every Dapper logo to that of M:Pyre, Oakseed's equivalent product. The Officials policing the sponsorama had noticed and were chasing her out of there. There was no reason for the Officials to suspect Arlo, and Drienne could have just left him out of it—but he would never abandon Drienne in a situation like this, even when she'd brought it on herself. You didn't leave your partner in the lurch if things got sticky. It wasn't part of the code of conduct or anything— your loyalty was to Oakseed, not your colleagues—but all ambassadors understood it simply wasn't done.

As Arlo and Drienne crossed the border of the sponsorama, their clothes reverted to their actual appearance. A lot of people were still milling about in the wake of tonight's match, drinking in the local bars, so Arlo and Drienne split up and tried to disappear into the crowd, figuring two people running together were easier to spot than one. As soon as Arlo felt confident he was out of sight, he ducked into an alleyway to catch his breath and listened out for the Officials. He wasn't sure how committed they were to clamping down on this stuff. Technically, it was illegal for two Oakseed-held mades to enter the sponsorama, but prosecuting them probably wasn't worth it: they were only street-level brand ambassadors. The Officials could easily block Drienne's imagery from the feeds she'd bombed, scrub her out of existence, like she was never in the sponsorama at all. Surely they had better things to do? But no, this was wishful thinking: Officials were the worst kind of securit, who defended brand integrity with quasi-religious zealotry, and the ones who got assigned to an event like this would be the worst of the worst.

Arlo felt a gentle but unignorable pressure on the back of his left hand. He straightened the fingers on that hand and his flexible backhand display instantly stiffened into a flatscreen, which displayed a map showing Drienne's location. She'd sent him a distress ping. He reckoned he could get there in a few moments if he ran, so he ran.

A lone Official was beating up Drienne in the middle of the street, taking it at a leisurely pace, barking an incoherent lecture on brand compliance between blows. This attracted plenty of stares from the tourists passing on either side, the ones who couldn't (or didn't want to) pay the jacked-up prices inside the sponsorama: in other words, exactly the people Arlo and Drienne were meant to be targeting tonight. Well, Drienne had succeeded in getting their attention, and she was wearing the new second-wave summer line, at least. Some of the crowd were grabbing images and loops of the incident. The Official who'd caught up with Drienne was the tallest and most muscular of the four who'd pursued them, and Arlo wondered what had happened to the other three: maybe this one wanted Drienne to herself, but it was also possible the others were on their way here, eager to join in.

Arlo quickly removed his shirt and tied it around his waist. Lots of those stupid tall disposable hats they gave out at the games had been disposed of by fans leaving the stadium, so Arlo picked up one that was lying on the ground and put it on. Hoping this made him look like a normal fan, and sufficiently different from the guy who'd just been chased out of the sponsorama, he approached the Official. His legs shook and he hoped she wouldn't think to cross-reference him with any security footage she'd accessed. If she recognized him he'd just have to try to talk her down. His main skill was being charming, so it might work.

"Excuse me?" he said to the Official.

She stopped kicking Drienne and turned to Arlo, irritated. "What?"

Arlo pointed in the general direction of the sponsorama. "I saw some kids back there hacking a Gazbank billboard to make it show clown porn." He was pretty sure Gazbank was still the official financial partner of the ELF. "Maybe you could do something about it? It's disgusting."

The Official fell for it. She lost interest in Drienne and dashed back toward the sponsorama. Arlo looked down at his feet where Drienne was painfully trying to get up.

"Are you okay?" Arlo said, extending a hand toward Drienne.

Drienne batted the hand away dismissively. "I'm fine. She'd only just started kicking me when you got here. She started off by pushing me around, then tripped me up when I tried to run away." She looked up at him properly. "Ha! Why are you wearing that *hat*?"

Arlo removed the hat and tossed it away. It had crossed his mind that Drienne's erratic behavior might be a sign she was having one of her episodes, but as he talked to her now, she seemed herself. "You don't need to go to hospital?"

"Fuck no," Drienne said, clambering to her feet and flexing her limbs to check the extent of her injuries. "I could go for some noodles, though."

They couldn't really afford to go for noodles. Part of Drienne's pitch for invading the sponsorama had been to score free food and save themselves some money. They were so far off target this month, and Oakseed didn't cut them any slack just because the circus was in town. They really ought to be eating basic rations at home, in anticipation of earning absolutely nothing in terms of commission. But Drienne needed a pretext to sit down and recover, and Arlo was hungry, so fuck it. They'd just have to be really, *really* poor next month. Oakseed wouldn't let them starve to death, even if it liked to keep them hungry.

"That was a really, really stupid thing to do," said Arlo while they waited for their food, sipping on drinks: he had a highball, she had a pale ale. This was one of the little contrasts they'd established while working together, feeling it made them distinctive. The thing people always remembered about them in customer feedback was she had a Massachusetts accent while his was from England's

Home Counties. And while they were both tall and good-looking, Drienne was pale-skinned and sharp-featured while he was darker (his donor had South Asian heritage) and had an almost delicate look. He naturally came across as genial and harmless, she had something rebellious about her: when she smiled she always looked conspiratorial.

Drienne shrugged. "Maybe I felt like being stupid." There was still street dust in her wavy orange hair, and blood seeped from a cut above her right eye. The key item from the summer range she was wearing—a fake-distressed workshirt featuring the logos of defunct hailer apps—was genuinely distressed now.

"You could have told me you were going to do something stupid before you did it."

She smiled. "Where's the fun in that, man?"

"They'll report us. They have *no* sense of humor about this kind of thing."

Drienne shook her head. "So what if they do? Everyone does it. They do it to us, we do it to them. It's not in anyone's interest to start a bunch of legal shit over something this small."

"I don't share your confidence, dear."

"*You* won't get in trouble," said Drienne as their food arrived. "You didn't do anything."

"Pardon me for being concerned for my friend. You still haven't said thank you."

"For saving me from the Official?"

"Yes."

"I did say thank you. Didn't I?"

"No."

"Okay, thank you." She laughed. "Can you believe how easily she fell for it? Moron."

"Right, so it wasn't my brilliant ruse that got you out of it, it was the fact she was stupid. I notice *you* failed to outwit her."

"Yeah, well I'm stupid too, as you already pointed out."

"That's not what I said. I said you did a stupid thing."

"People like you and I don't *need* to be clever, Arlo."

"You and *me*."

"What?"

"People like you and me. You wouldn't say 'People like I don't need to be clever,' so you wouldn't say 'People like you and I—'"

"Whatever—what I'm saying is our lives would be much easier if we were stupid, like that Official. Her life is simple. There are rules, and if someone breaks the rules, she beats the shit out of them."

For a few moments they ate in silence. Arlo understood Drienne's actions now: being clever didn't do her any good, so she asserted herself by being stupid. He understood, but that didn't mean he considered it a good idea.

Drienne got a note, which she read from her backhand with a puzzled expression. Then she got her slate out and opened a window on that. Then she cackled loudly. "Well, noodles are on me." She mirrored her display to Arlo's backhand so he could see it too: multiple feeds showing Drienne being beaten up by the Official, all the grabs made by passing tourists. The Oakseed sweepers had already tagged it, highlighted the clothing, and linked it to the storefront. Some of the loops had really nice arty filters, and Drienne looked very beautiful as she took her beating, so it all looked quite constructed, and most people probably assumed it was, if they even cared about the difference between artifice and reality. It hadn't viraled or anything but it was getting around, and meant Drienne would certainly hit her target this week, and management wouldn't take any action against her for her earlier violation, because almost anything was permitted if it made enough sales.

"That wasn't your plan all along, surely," said Arlo.

Drienne just raised one of those dark eyebrows at him and ostentatiously paid the bill.

In a spirit of exuberance at Drienne's accidental success, they hit the clubs, where her success multiplied: people who'd seen the loops in the local feeds recognized her and wanted to talk to her.

She made further direct sales off of that, and Arlo even managed to make some just from being in her orbit (some of the loops had included his heroic intervention, but most people hadn't watched that far before either buying the clothes she was wearing or swiping to something else). They split up for a while, working different floors of a club with a coral-reef theme. Arlo latched onto some dissent among people who were furious about how the ELF had taken over this part of the city, preventing them from going to their usual haunts, and he encouraged them to direct this ire at Sunglow. They were an easy target: a few decades ago they'd been the hipster brand, the cutting-edge nonconformist brand, but today's young people, who'd grown up with them as a dominant presence, saw them as no different from the others, and today's young people were right about that.

For Arlo and his colleagues, Sunglow was synonymous with the accelerated growth experiments in their cloning process, which they'd hoped to patent and sell to the other mega corps, making huge profits. But it had badly backfired, producing a whole generation of mades with genetic flaws that lurked inside them like time bombs, causing them to suddenly, horrifyingly deteriorate. Arlo had only been four years old, still being raised in an Oakseed nursery in England, when his carers told all the kids the unvarnished truth about what was happening to kids in Sunglow's nurseries, the point being to underline how lucky Oakseed's mades were to have been produced by a company that raised them properly rather than trying to cut corners. One particular detail—about the Sunglow mades bleeding everywhere as their skin lost cohesion—stuck in Arlo's mind, and he had nightmares about it for years. (He still wasn't sure if that was true or if the stories had been embellished, but the fact of the experiments was not in dispute, nor that they had failed.)

It was part of Arlo's job to trash Oakseed's rivals, but when it came to Sunglow, he actively enjoyed it, and he had some success in spreading the idea that buying from Oakseed in preference to Sunglow was a protest against the ELF itself. Footage of him saying this made its way to a couple of mid-profile feeds: a lot of people mocked his claim but it was all reach, it was all good. At this rate, he and Drienne might even be able to take *a day off* this week.

Arlo met back up with Drienne around 3:30 A.M, finding her in a corner alcove shaped like the open mouth of a whale. She was drinking directly from a bottle of fortified champagne.

"Steady on," he said, "don't spend it all straightaway."

"Oh god," she said as she poured him a glass, "*I* didn't pay for this."

"Who did?"

"Refugee from the sponsorama, been getting bullied by his boss all week. Just wanted someone to listen to his grievances and revenge fantasies and so on and so forth."

"And he didn't stick around to drink the champagne with you?"

"He stuck around to drink the first bottle but he was already blotto when he got here. When the second bottle arrived, I suggested to his friends they might like to take him home before he did something he'd regret."

"Did he buy anything except the champagne?" Arlo asked, sipping it. It tasted sharp and sour and he didn't really like it, but it seemed to fit the occasion.

"He works at an elite sporting academy out in Guangzhou? I think he said? And they might be looking to move their uniform contract, so I took his card." She produced the card, a brashly designed item with an animated image of its subject on both surfaces. "Do you want to pass it up the chain, or shall I?" They often shared tokens like this if either of them needed a boost—if the connection bore fruit there'd be a commission for whoever brought it in.

Arlo shook his head. "I'm good. You pass it on."

"It's probably bullshit anyway," said Drienne, putting the card in her bag. "How'd you get on? Okay?"

Arlo told her about the rhetorical spin he'd played on the anti-ELF guys, which he knew she'd enjoy. These were always the best times, the closest he ever got to relaxing. Their apartment was full of prompts to go out and work, and when he did go out he often felt sick and miserable and angry he couldn't find more sales and promo opportunities. But if they hit their targets they could grab an hour or two, late on, and act like they were still working, but in their minds they'd clocked off. Often those hours went by all too fast, but sometimes, just sometimes, it felt gloriously languid and unhurried, and he could forget about targets and commissions and kid himself they were real people.

Just as Arlo had started tapping into this feeling, an urgent note rattled his backhand, telling him he had to leave immediately. It would continue to intrude into his senses in every possible way until he obeyed: there was no point trying to ignore it and do something else.

"What is it?" said Drienne. "Where are you meant to go?"

"Doesn't say."

"It's not about our trip to the sponsorama, is it?"

"I don't know, Dree, it doesn't say."

"What *does* it say?"

"I have to go outside, and there'll be a car. That's all. Have you got one?"

"A car?"

"No, a note."

"No."

"It can't be about the sponsorama. They wouldn't talk to me and not you."

"Maybe they want you to dish the dirt on me, and then they'll question me afterward."

"I doubt it's about that." He finished his glass of champagne, noting how much was left in the bottle: he used this information to judge how drunk Drienne would be by the time she got back to the apartment. He'd probably find her cross-legged on the floor, singing along to her animatronic budgerigar again. He wished she'd install some new songs on that bloody thing. There was one called "Maxwell's Silver Hammer" and she sang that every time she got drunk and it drove him insane.

"What could it be about, then? At this time of night?"

Arlo had no idea. Most people, he supposed, would assume it was a family emergency. But Arlo had no family.

In a sense, though, it *was* a family emergency.

Arlo walked out of the club and directly into the company car he'd been told would be waiting. He hadn't expected it to be one of the *good* company cars, but that was exactly what he found: a spacious saloon with reclining seats and a minibar. At first he was delighted, then it struck him they would never send this car purely because they wanted him to enjoy the ride, and after that he couldn't enjoy the ride because he was wondering why they had sent this car. Figuring he may as well take advantage of the facilities, he opened the minibar, which triggered an instruction to drink no alcohol.

"I'm already quite drunk," he told the car. "Is that a problem?"

The car suggested he drink an M:Pyre energy shot to sober himself up.

"Where are we going, anyway?" he asked.

The car ignored him. This was also not reassuring. Arlo tapped his backhand and brought up a map, trying to guess. Their route was taking them up a flyover that went directly through the sponsorama, so the car couldn't possibly be stopping anywhere round here. It drove fast down empty priority lanes, passed over streets thronging with sports fans, still up and enjoying the carnival atmosphere. It occurred to Arlo he didn't even know who won the match tonight. No one in the sponsorama had been talking about it.

The car began to slow, turning and heading down a ramp, before stopping in a well-lit bay—an ambulance bay. He was at a hospital. There was nothing wrong with Arlo's health; if there was, his slate would have picked it up and told him to get it treated. Which could mean only one thing: He was here to be reaped.

It was all over. He'd never go back to the apartment again, never see Drienne again, never hear her singing along to that budgerigar. Those noodles were the last meal he'd ever eat, that champagne was the last drink he'd ever have. The force of this realization hit him and he started to panic and cry.

Two orderlies waited by the door of the car when it opened, poised to grab him. Arlo supposed some people tried to make a run for it when this happened. But what was the point?

CHANGE MANAGEMENT

In the living quarters of Oakseed's intelligence management farm, Loren was trying on clothes. Not real clothes, as the employees here only ever wore standard-issue uniforms. They *could* buy other clothes, but there was no way of cleaning them as none of their quarters had a washing machine and there was no public laundry nearby. Each week the farm's central laundry issued every employee with a set of clean uniforms in the correct size, which might have been previously worn by every other employee in the building who also wore uniforms in that size. Any other clothing that ended up in the laundry would be recycled into a company uniform, so there was little point buying anything else.

Loren was trying on aug clothes. Oakseed had their own software for this, of course, so customers could see how they looked in clothes before buying the real ones—but it was deliberately limited, so people couldn't try aug clothes on and then get shots and footage for their feeds and put the aug clothes back on the rail (so to speak) without buying anything. Loren had modded it so they could do whatever they wanted. Today, what they wanted was to try on a dark green kaftan. Usually they played dress-up with formalwear, set themself up looking sharp as hell, but for some reason today they felt like a change.

Not all change was good. The kaftan didn't suit them at all. You needed to be taller to pull off a kaftan. Loren looked like they'd got caught up in their bedsheets on their way to answer the door. But they liked to try these things. They felt like somewhere there was an outfit that would unlock their true self, the self they were unable to be in here. They just hadn't found it yet.

Like all the quarters in the farm, Loren's were small and not shared. Loren was an assist, and their generation of assists had been engineered to be more comfortable talking to systems than people. They socialized a little with some of the others on their floor, usually on the spur of the moment with anyone whose downtime happened to overlap with theirs, doing nothing more ambitious than going to one of the handful of bars and cafés at the edge of town nearest the farm. But there were often days when Loren exchanged few words with anyone other than the parts of the system they worked with. The farms were designed to be as self-contained as possible, because the megas were insanely protective of their systems and at the same time didn't feel in control of them. They liked to keep them in a regulated environment.

Loren's next shift began at 8:30 A.M. and ran until 12:30 P.M., then they would come back to their quarters and sleep through the afternoon before their next shift at 10:00 P.M. A notification would sound when the start of Loren's shift was five minutes away. Loren never needed the notification because they had a very good sense of time, but they always waited for it to sound before leaving their quarters because it made everything feel orderly. They checked the clock and the start of their shift was seven minutes away. They turned off the aug kaftan, revealing their uniform underneath, and put on their shoes. This took less than two minutes. Once Loren had done it, they stood next to the door and looked at their backhand, their gaze fixed on the top left corner where it said 8:24.

They waited.

The display clock clicked over to 8:25.

The notification did not sound.

Loren could have just left, but it felt wrong to do so when there'd been no sound. They checked their settings, even though it was impossible to turn those notifications off or silence them. They checked if their display was faulty (it wasn't) and checked the rota to make sure they weren't mistaken about what time their shift began (they weren't).

By this time it was 8:27, and Loren was going to be late if they didn't leave now, so they walked to the elevator, took it down six floors, and emerged into the dimly lit, low-ceilinged warren of desks. If you were the sort of person who couldn't shut out their surroundings it was stiflingly claustrophobic, but no one who worked here was that sort of person. Loren walked the thirty-seven steps that took them to their workstation, and arrived while the clock still read 8:30. Usually their station would already be awake when they reached it, having registered their presence in the elevator as it descended. But the station was powered down, and remained so even when they tried to power it up manually.

Loren realized all the other stations on this row were also powered down. They rarely looked at their colleagues' stations, so they hadn't taken this in. But every station was dark, and everyone trying to use them looked as confused as Loren felt.

Loren sat at their station and awaited further instructions. These eventually arrived at 9:13, in the form of a notification on their backhand telling them—and every other employee in the facility—to report to the building's entrance hall.

Back in Shanghai, Drienne was standing at the bar, posing for selfies with an excitable group of pop streamers, when she got the message from Arlo telling her he was at the hospital, and that he wasn't sick. That was all he wrote.

Drienne immediately understood, and went to the bathroom where she spent a few minutes making anxious and despairing noises. Then she pulled herself together somewhat and tried to put it out of her mind, reasoning Arlo wouldn't want her to waste the opportunities that were presenting themselves tonight, and besides, there was literally nothing she could do about his situation. So she cleaned herself up, retouched her makeup, went back over to the pop streamers and recorded some reactions for their channels, then she set the whole thing running as a cross-feed event, instructing her own feed's editor to cut something together from the haphazard footage.

By the time the pop streamers had moved on, Drienne had admitted to herself she had failed to put what was happening to Arlo out of her mind, and she was incapable of doing so. Instead she ordered some shots, which she shared with an off-duty greeter who'd been working over at the sponsorama and needed to take a break from it all. Literally he was the first guy that caught her eye, and she had plans for him. More shots were ordered and drunk, and she listened to him subtext about how relentless it was at the sponsorama, where everything you said was monitored for its fidelity to the event's brand values and given a rating and you were reprimanded for falling below 90 percent.

Ordinarily, Drienne would have enjoyed a good bitching session about such matters, as she had plenty of similar grievances of her own, but at that moment she couldn't focus on the microaggressions that came with being retained by Oakseed because all she could think of was the mega-aggression that was happening to Arlo in some fucking executive hospital. So she broke into a staff-only area of the club with the greeter and fucked him against a cleaning unit, and streamed it. She didn't ask his permission to stream it, but he either didn't mind or didn't notice. It vaguely occurred to her he might be fired for having sex with someone held by a nonsponsor's company during the event; she tried to care, but not very hard.

Drienne knew she'd be reprimanded, not for doing it or for posting the video, but for the fact it wouldn't earn anything—the guy she'd fucked had zero clout, he wasn't interesting, wasn't even particularly hot. The stream would do nothing, in fact it would probably drag her profile down, and might even undo the boost she'd received from her escapade tonight. She didn't fully understand how the algorithm worked, because she wasn't meant to, but there was pressure to maintain a certain standard of content, because if your engagement levels dropped then fewer people saw your stuff so it was hard to push them up again. So what she'd done was a bad idea, especially when she'd just gotten away with blundering into the sponsorama.

She went back to the bar, lined up some more shots, and then did it again with a different guy.

FRANKFURT, SCHENGENIA, 11:14 P.M.

Nadi was in the middle of her fourth straight week of duty at Oak-seed's grocery hall in the old financial district. Earlier today she'd asked the manager if they could change the in-store music to something else, and the manager had told her no, the music was optimal and you couldn't possibly get bored of it because it was dynamically generated so it never repeated. Every piece of music you heard in the store was unique. That was true. But it was unique re-generated pap based on middle-of-the-road hits from two or three decades ago, which in turn were rip-offs of songs from two or three decades before that. So it all sounded the fucking same.

Nadi didn't know why the dynamic staffing system had her running security at a grocery hall. The workforce was profiled in every detail so it could put you on work you were suited to. Or that was the idea. But Nadi was not suited to this, in her opinion. Most of the people you caught stealing would plead that they were starving, and their kids were starving, and they'd never stolen anything in their lives before but they were *desperate*, they'd say before collapsing to the floor sobbing, and they wouldn't stand up and you'd have to drag them away across the hall's shiny floor.

Nadi's colleagues in the security division seemed immune to this kind of thing. Tonight's shift manager was a dude called Cave, and when Nadi had been assigned to this location he'd handled her induction. He'd told her to ignore all that shit. These people weren't *opportunists*. The days when you could covertly slide a pack of spaghetti down the sleeve of your coat and walk out were long gone. Now, if you wanted to steal groceries you needed to disrupt the cameras' pattern recognition. You needed uplifting shoes that canceled out the extra load when you walked over the weight sensors at the door. You needed to prepare and you needed to invest in the equipment. Anyone who didn't know that was stupid and deserved to get caught. According to Cave.

It made the job much easier if you believed this. And Nadi's automatic reaction when she heard the sob stories was *they're lying.* That was her training kicking in. But Nadi had never been good at silencing the other voice that said *What if they're not?* Maybe most of them were lying, but there *were* poor and desperate people in the world. Some of them would inevitably steal from grocery halls. Because Nadi couldn't stop that voice, she found every case painful to deal with and she wished they would put her back on parks duty. In parks you were dealing mostly with lost kids who'd wandered off. Usually you found them and their parents were grateful and you could go home feeling good. Occasionally it turned out they'd been abducted by a pedo, and then you got to kick the shit out of a pedo and she enjoyed that. (Who didn't?)

But the staffing system had stuck Nadi in a grocery hall and left her there. Maybe it wasn't the system: maybe she'd done something wrong and was being punished. Sometimes management punished you without telling you and the punishment would go on until you worked out you were being punished.

The cameras alerted the securits that suspicious activity was taking place. The other securit on tonight's shift, Muller, indicated to Nadi they should both head for the exit and block the suspect's path. The suspect was a teenage girl wearing an unseasonably warm bomber jacket, with her hands shoved in the pockets, trying to keep her eyes fixed on the door. She was pretending not to have noticed the securits heading her way, because she was pretending she had no reason to be looking out for securits. Nadi and Muller blocked the girl's path; she kept her head down and muttered, "Excuse me," trying to walk around them. Muller put out an arm and stopped her.

The girl looked up at Nadi and Muller and tried to seem defiant, but she was scared. She looked like she was more scared than she'd anticipated she would be, now she was face-to-face with the securits. Nadi was used to having this effect on people. Genetic selection, steroid treatments, and training had made her grow up tall, heavy, imposing. Her resting face was a glower. Her body language had hostility drilled into it. Even her straight black hair, bluntly cut to hang at the level of her earlobes, had an aggressive look. People tensed up around her, always feeling the suggestion of violence was in the air. In truth, Nadi rarely used force and rarely wanted to, but she looked like she was impatient to thump somebody. All the time. The only people she met who weren't intimidated by her were other securits. So it was a shame she didn't like them and they didn't like her.

Nadi and Muller escorted the girl to an area by the windows and Muller questioned her about the contents of her pockets. While this was happening an announcement came over the PA system, telling all customers to put down their shopping and leave the hall immediately.

"It just said we need to leave," the girl eagerly pointed out to the securits.

"Not yet," said Muller and told her to take off her jacket.

Nadi looked around. The customers were visibly puzzled by the announcement. But the message was repeated and they all started to move to the exits. And all the staff—the sorters, the stackers, the help—were heading the same way. The music had changed too, morphing into a song with urgent, uneasy tones. The duty manager, a self-important woman called Stefi Vogts, oversaw the exodus. Nadi walked over to Stefi and asked her what was going on.

"We're being recalled," said Stefi, without looking at Nadi. Her focus was split between her slate and the movement of people out of the hall, but even if she hadn't had these distractions, she generally preferred not to look at the securits when talking to them.

"What, everyone?"

"Not you and Cave and Muller. But everyone else, yes."

"Who's going to run the hall?"

"No one. We're closing up."

"Until when?"

"Look," snapped Stefi, "I've told Cave what the securits are to do. Talk to him."

Nadi walked back over to Muller, who was still preventing the teenage girl from leaving. Cave had come to tell Muller something, and Muller seemed confused by it.

"But we haven't searched her yet," Muller said.

Cave shook his head. "Just let her go. We need this place clear."

"But the cameras—"

"For fuck's sake, *it doesn't matter anymore*," Cave said. "Let her go. We've got shit to do."

The teenage girl scrambled for the door and Nadi heard her running down the street, putting distance between herself and the hall before anyone had a chance to reconsider.

Nadi wondered what Cave meant by *it doesn't matter anymore*, but he didn't want to talk, he wanted her to go and find people who still hadn't left. Some of them had missed the announcement because they had their earfeed barriers set too high, and there was a bombed-out dude asleep in the toilets. When everyone else had gone, Nadi shut and locked the doors. To Nadi's knowledge, this hall had never closed since the moment it opened. Which meant its locks had never been used before. They *felt* like they'd never been used before.

Nadi turned to find Cave leaning against a fresh produce display, tossing stoneless peachettes into his mouth and munching them. He hadn't paid for the peachettes. It was the kind of behavior he gleefully reported colleagues for, and Nadi wondered if this was a trick. When he saw her looking, he shrugged and said, "Eat whatever you like. This is all going to waste."

"Why?"

And Cave smirked. He liked knowing things you didn't, and he liked being a prick about it.

Drienne put off going back home to Shaw Apartments, partly because the house mother was probably waiting there to reprimand her about her conduct tonight, partly because the thought of going back to an empty apartment was too depressing. Finally at 6:00 A.M. she called for a car. While she waited for it, she sat on the curb and checked her provisional bounty statement, to find out how much she was going to get paid for these loops of her being assaulted.

She'd heard nothing further from Arlo. She felt grief and anguish for him, but also terror for herself. How would she cope without him? They'd been together so long—he knew about her episodes, he could spot them coming, and he looked after her whenever they happened. He knew how to talk to her and stopped her doing anything stupid, and he always made sure it didn't interfere with her work, so Oakseed had never found out about her condition. She'd never find anyone as good at coping with it as him. Most people wouldn't even try. In any case, she wouldn't get to choose who she was partnered up with, they'd just assign someone to her. She hadn't fully appreciated how lucky she'd been to end up with Arlo.

The car pulled up and Drienne more or less crawled into it. Some company girl was in the front seat already and seemed unhappy her car had been diverted to pick up a drunk. She helped Drienne inside, not through any generosity of spirit but because the car wouldn't be going anywhere while Drienne was still trying to negotiate the step up from the curb.

The door closed and the car lurched away. Drienne groaned and the car warned her that if she vomited on the floor, her account would be docked. The company girl opened the glove compartment and found a receptacle in there that Drienne could vomit into if necessary.

"Thanks," said Drienne. "Who you?"

"I'm Andrée."

"That's like my name! I'm Drienne."

"Yeah," said Andrée, not finding this particularly remarkable, "they're always giving us similar names."

"Your name's like my name the other way round. *Dri*-enne. An-*dre*." Drienne sat back. "They *are* always giving us similar names. It's like . . . they want to be able to tell us apart, but not too much."

Andrée nodded. She looked a little familiar to Drienne, but this didn't necessarily mean they'd met or anything. She might just be a variation on a popular template: Drienne met colleagues who looked familiar all the time. This young woman had slightly wild, wavy hair and smoky eyes, and was disconcertingly slim, even by the standards of brand ambassadors—assuming that was what she was.

Drienne was far too drunk to be able to tell whether Andrée was happy to engage in conversation or was barely tolerating her. But she was also too drunk to care. "Are you new, then?"

"New to Shanghai, yes," Andrée replied. She sounded European—most of Oakseed's ambassadors in Shanghai did, something to do with it matching how the brand was perceived here.

"You live at Shaw Apartments?"

"Yes."

"Brand ambassador?"

"Yes."

"Thought as much," said Drienne, nodding. "They've got more of us than they know what to do with these days."

"Maybe soon they'll be moving a bunch of the old ones on to . . . something new, I don't know."

"Happens to us all. We all get *moved on*."

"Oh sorry—was that really insensitive? Are you about to—"

"No, I didn't mean *me*. I'm twenty-three, I've got a few more years in me yet." A few more years as a brand ambassador, which she hated, before she got moved onto something that would probably be worse. She didn't hate it *all* the time, and sometimes tricked herself into feeling okay—but when she actually *thought* about it, yeah, she hated it. And when she did think about it, she found it hard to stop.

There was no point telling Andrée any of this. Maybe she wouldn't hate being a brand ambassador, and if she did hate it, she didn't have the power to change it. So Drienne decided to change the subject.

"My partner's in the hospital," she said, because at that moment it was the only thing she could think of to say—which was odd, because as soon as she'd said it she could think of lots of other things. She'd had a very eventful evening. But that was the one that leapt to mind when she had to speak.

"Oh, are they okay?"

"Yeah, he's completely fine, perfect health."

"Good."

"No, but that means they're reaping him."

Andrée flinched a little. "Shit. I'm so sorry."

"Thanks. I'm . . . pretty angry about it."

"I know, but what can you do?"

Drienne thought of some of the things she'd like to do, but she had just enough self-control not to mention them out loud. Because if she did any of those things—she probably wouldn't, but there was always a chance she'd snap and stop caring about the consequences—and in the aftermath someone checked back through her recent conversations, someone might decide the new girl was complicit, and she didn't deserve that. Drienne decided not to talk about it again.

NEWARK, DELAWARE, USA, 5:08 P.M.

Kline had been trying to puzzle out what was going on for months, as had everyone else who worked on his floor. They played games like this all the time, looking at patterns in company activity and trying to work out what they meant. But this was clearly bigger, so big they didn't talk about it in the labyrinthine wood-paneled rooms and corridors of the HR offices. They didn't even talk about it on the private channel they reserved for exactly this kind of chat, because even that felt too risky. Instead, they hung out in the coffeehouses and spoke about it in coded language, swapping out the names of people and departments. (One of Kline's colleagues, Atrice, was especially good at coming up with these code words.) It fascinated them all, of course. All of them were obsessed with the structure and operations of the company. This was why they'd been assigned to HR in the first place. All of them were very sensitive to any changes in it, and they'd seen some very big changes recently, but didn't yet know what they meant.

Last year, there'd been some big xec hires from outside the company. That was unusual: Oakseed preferred to promote from within, people who knew the culture. All the megas worked this way, and they were all aggressive in the face of poaching, so big money was involved to bring these new hires onside. Kline felt this break with policy suggested a failure of confidence in Oakseed's culture and a desire to change it, but what direction would they be moving in? Kline and the others profiled the new hires, tried to work out what they added up to; they came up with some theories, but nothing concrete emerged.

More recently there'd been a pattern of new market expansions being postponed, construction of new sites being put on hold, resources being redeployed at short notice. Kline felt the company's marketing had a slapdash look to it of late too: they'd redesigned their famous acorn logo to mark some anniversary, but everyone hated it and Oakseed had reverted to the old one, insisting the redesign had only ever been intended as a temporary thing. At that point, most of Kline's colleagues felt a major acquisition was in the cards, or possibly a merger, though that was difficult to contemplate given the size of Oakseed. Kline had voiced the notion the company might, perhaps, be trying to streamline its operations? Doing fewer things better? The others had shouted him down: Martin, Atrice, and Yules had been especially loud.

Then, a couple of weeks ago, the layoffs began. Entire divisions and regional operations were cut back to the minimum, or closed entirely. Anything that was a loss leader, or speculative, or didn't make a profit but someone high up in the company thought it was cool, was withdrawn. HR processed more redundancies in two weeks than they'd done in the previous two years. Their workload was unprecedented: some of the people they'd made redundant were given temporary contracts to come to HR and help make other people redundant. By this point, everyone agreed Kline had been right after all, the company *was* streamlining its operations. Kline liked being told he'd been right so he didn't say what he actually thought, which was that he'd been wrong and it was much worse than that.

This afternoon, they'd been slapped with a *shitload* of work of a very different order, and it was clear what it meant. Everyone on Kline's floor was in shock, but all he could think was, *I knew it.* He was absolutely kicking himself he hadn't said it. He swore he would never doubt himself like that again, because when it came down to it he was always right, even about something as inconceivable as this.

Andrée was more patient with Drienne at the other end of the journey than she'd been at the start. They'd arrived at Shaw Apartments, a building that looked like a demented space-age castle with turrets of different heights at its five corners. More effort had gone into the finish of its exterior than its interior: its two-person apartments were small and deliberately joyless. But from the outside it looked spectacular—anything bearing the Oakseed brand had to—and it looked all the more spectacular right now, with the sun rising over it.

After they got out of the car, Andrée was the first to notice something was amiss. Drienne didn't notice because she was too busy—first with vomiting into a drain, then with spitting and trying to ascertain whether there was still more to come up. What Andrée had noticed, looking through the nearest entrance arch, was the inhabitants of Shaw Apartments were not in their apartments but standing around in the central plaza. It looked like *all* of them were standing there, and at this hour of the morning that suggested a fire or a security breach.

"What's going on?" Andrée asked as Drienne walked over to join her.

"The fuck?" asked Drienne, dabbing at the vomit spittle around her mouth with a nine-hundred-dollar monogrammed handkerchief she'd stolen from one of the xecs in the sponsorama.

They walked over to the entrance and tried to step inside—and a securit moved into their path. He was two meters tall, hairless and muscular, and his resting face was entirely neutral—securits weren't all based on the *exact* same DNA template, but there wasn't much variation between them. Just enough that they could tell each other apart, really. "You can't go in there," he told Drienne and Andrée.

"We *live here*," said Drienne, waving a clumsy hand at the securit's chestplate, trying to get it to read her id.

"I know you live here," the securit replied. "Or rather, you *did*. You don't anymore."

"Both of us?" said Andrée.

The securit nodded.

"Seriously?" said Drienne. She turned to Andrée. "Look, I know what *I* did, but what did *you* do?"

"Nothing!" shouted Andrée, panicking a little. "What did *you* do?" She turned to the securit. "I'm not with her, by the way. We just shared a car . . . I don't even know her . . ."

"This building is no longer Oakseed property," said the securit, holding up a hand to placate them. "So you can't live here. It's not about you."

"Where are we supposed to go?" said Drienne.

"Wait a sec." The securit consulted a document on his slate. "Lancaster, Pennsylvania."

"*What?*" said Andrée.

"Transport is being laid on."

"But what about all our stuff?"

"It's being boxed up now and will follow you."

Drienne felt quite sober all of a sudden. "This doesn't make any sense. Why isn't this an Oakseed building anymore?"

"I don't know anything I haven't already told you."

"What about the xecs? Are they getting moved to Penncaster, Lansylvania, or is it just us? Are we just going to not *have* a Shanghai staff?"

The securit pointed at a shuttle bay across the street. "Ms., please just wait over there for the shuttle to the port—we really do need to clear this building."

The fight had gone out of Andrée by that point, but Drienne knew there was one more thing she had to say. "My partner won't be here—he's in hospital, they're going to . . . he won't be coming back, so . . . can all his things be sent to me? He'd want me to have them." She knew this sounded self-serving, but there was no one else she could imagine Arlo giving them to. There were a few keepsakes she was keen to have, some things she could make good use of, and the rest she'd sell or pass on to others.

"I'm not dealing with that side of things."

"Can you tell whoever is? It's all in our apartment—it just means packing it all into the same box."

"Your apartment was done already." The securit sighed, nodded. "But yeah, I'll pass it on."

Andrée guided Drienne across the street, commenting that neither of them were dressed for long-haul travel—couldn't they at least let them change their clothes? Drienne agreed, but she kept looking back at Shaw Apartments—her home for seven years, and someone had sold it from underneath her, just like moving figures from one column of a spreadsheet to another. Her life had been broken up and sold for parts while she was out at work. She wanted answers, even if she suspected she wouldn't like them.

THE OPERATIVE WORD

After Arlo's message to Drienne had gone through, his slate's mailbox had been disconnected. He assumed this was part of the process of removing him from the world, isolating him from the people he knew—a reasonable assumption on his part, but quite wrong. He could still see his feed, but he was unaware that major news stories, directly relevant to his situation, were being filtered out of it. If someone told him this was happening, he wouldn't be surprised; such filtering was routine and the parameters shifted all the time. Messages would vanish from their mailboxes, then they might reappear—sometimes altered, sometimes the same. Bookmarks that worked yesterday would go dead or lead elsewhere. Even their own personal media was subject to regular audits and culls. It was something they all lived with, and he'd stopped paying attention to what came and went, what he could and couldn't see, long ago. Wondering what you were missing was like banging your head against the walls of a room with no doors.

At that moment, Arlo believed nothing would be relevant to him ever again. Upon arriving at the hospital, he'd been escorted to a secure room and informed of his donor's condition. (It struck Arlo that being a made changed other definitions: if Arlo were natural, *he* would be the one referred to as the donor, not the person lying ill in a private ward. But Arlo was a made, and had always known this man as his donor, all his life: the term emphasized Arlo owed him a debt, one that was about to be repaid.) His donor had severe internal injuries—Arlo wasn't informed how they'd come about—and his heart, liver, and pancreas were on the verge of collapse, so Arlo's would be needed. No made was ever kept alive after harvesting, even if they'd only had to give up one kidney or a lung: the company considered them suboptimal workers, and it was simpler to freeze the rest of their salvageable parts in case they were needed in the future, and dispose of the rest. (It was rumored they made it into pet food, but Arlo found this unlikely: you don't want to train cats to crave the taste of human flesh.)

Arlo didn't know much about his donor, Joshi Samson. This was not because he was prevented from finding out—indeed, mades were encouraged to learn about their donors and take inspiration from them—but he didn't want to know. He was vaguely aware Samson was xec-class, as most donors were: identified at school (or even from birth) and fast-tracked, big things expected of them. What good could it do Arlo to learn anything about him? They shared DNA and nothing else. Some xec-based mades took pride in the achievements of their donors, as if it reflected well on them in some way, and acted like it made them somehow better than mades who didn't come from a donor, who were based on generated templates. Arlo didn't feel like that at all. His life could hardly have been more different from Samson's. He didn't tell anyone he was xec-based if he could help it.

Yet Samson was the whole reason Arlo was in Shanghai. Even though they'd never met, Arlo was obliged to live within easy reach of Samson, so he would be on hand if he needed to be reaped. Samson was originally from England, and had worked as an undermanager at Oakseed's cyc plant in London before becoming a manager at their printworks in Colchester, so Arlo had been made and raised in a nursery on the southeast coast. Arlo's first posting as a brand ambassador had been in Brighton, but after he'd been there less than a year the printworks had closed down and Samson reassigned to the Shanghai office, so Arlo had to go too.

Fortunately, Arlo liked Shanghai. It was there he'd been assigned to Drienne because they looked good together. Whether
they were personally compatible was irrelevant to the company,
provided it didn't get in the way of their work—but she'd become
the only close friend he'd ever had. He should have taken one last
proper look at her when he had the chance. But then he thought,
Why? In a few hours, his brain would be detached from all the
systems that kept it working; it would die and be turned into mulch
and all the images inside it would vanish.

The securits at the grocery hall in Frankfurt had been instructed
to guard it until they were told otherwise. These instructions
were unnecessary. No Oakseed facility was ever left unattended
if there were securits capable of attending it. In an emergency
someone must *always* stay with the building, even if staff were injured. If the complement of active and competent securits was less
than protocol demanded, their priority was to call for replacements.

Nadi, Muller, and Cave had been there about an hour when
further instructions came in. The duty manager for the area had
decided it didn't take three securits to guard an empty grocery hall.
One of them could be more usefully deployed elsewhere. Cave
chose which of them would go, so of course he chose Nadi, because he didn't like her and he did like Muller. Nadi had noticed
how they spoke and touched in an intimate way when they weren't
on the shop floor. She wondered if, after she had left the hall, they
would fuck while leaning against the fresh produce display.

Nadi told Muller and Cave she'd see them tomorrow and
stepped outside. It was late, but the bar across the street was still
open. The people drinking at the outside tables watched Nadi as
she emerged and Cave locked the door behind her.

Nadi waited on the curb for the transport she'd been told was
coming to pick her up. The drinkers across the street chatted to
each other and laughed. It seemed like they were laughing at her.
This was not an experience she was familiar with.

"What?" she said to them, loudly.

"You're fucked," a young man in a white shirt said, and everyone he was with laughed.

Nadi couldn't understand why this was happening. She could cross the street, she thought. She could go over there and talk to them up close and see if they laughed *then*. But before she did, the transport pulled up in front of her and she boarded it. It seated about twenty people, and it was almost full: it had collected other securits who could be deployed more usefully elsewhere. It picked up two more before heading south, driving sixteen miles, and arriving at the dispatch center. This was the biggest such hub for two hundred miles. It contained precision electronics, foodstuffs, fine-art items, high-end musical instruments, and anything else that couldn't be printed, as well as resale stock. It was always fully staffed around the clock. Nadi emerged to find it being emptied out. Employees gathered in its loading bay. The whole operation was being overseen by securits.

"Glad you're here," a harassed-looking shift leader told the new arrivals. "We've told them to separate into mades and nats, okay? I'll give you all access to the list of everyone who's on shift, and we have to log everyone out. Nats get sent home, mades go into those." He pointed to one of the large road haulers, which were typically used for transporting crates, not people.

"Why are we logging everyone out?" Nadi asked. "Why aren't the exit readers doing it?"

"There's a problem with the readers. I don't have time for questions, this has to happen *now*. And you don't have time for questions either, so if anyone asks you any, ignore them."

Nadi was ushered into the loading bay. She spent the next hour comparing the faces that appeared in front of her to the list. She directed mades toward the haulers. Some of them asked what was going on and Nadi replied she didn't know. When there were no faces left to check, Nadi was told to get on one of the haulers and keep order. She and another securit clambered into one of the haulers to find maybe two hundred mades sitting on its floor, their knees bent to their chests to take up as little space as possible. There was just enough space near the loading doors for Nadi and the other securit to stand and keep watch over them. They closed the loading doors, leaving it almost entirely dark inside. Then the hauler drove away.

Whatever was going on, it did not seem to have been planned very well.

Rumors spread up and down the flight bound for Lancaster, Pennsylvania. Drienne had slept while they'd waited at the port, with Andrée waking her up whenever they had to move from one place to another. Now they were seated together on the flight, and it was Andrée's turn to sleep. Drienne didn't contribute to the rumors, but she did listen to them.

The most common theme was they'd all been sold as a job lot to another company. Opinion differed as to which company it was, or what they would have to do there. Some of the theories were more dramatic, like Oakseed was pulling out of Asia altogether because a war was about to be declared; or they weren't going to Pennsylvania at all, and were in fact headed for one of the Eastern European fiefdoms, where they'd lose even the meager rights they had now. Another said Oakseed had gone bust altogether, just completely collapsed, and everything was in the hands of receivers, including the mades. But that was obviously absurd. Oakseed was far too big to fail.

The first task Kline and his colleagues had been issued was to ensure the company's legal position regarding its employees was secure, and that it had no unexpected obligations toward anyone. (The pension fund was dead in a ditch, which was going to be a disaster with ramifications that would be felt for decades, but nothing could be done.) Next, they got to work destroying records.

Anyone who'd worked in the HR department any significant

length of time had buried their fair share of incidents on behalf of management. Kline could name twenty off the top of his head. They had all "accidentally" deleted data, in the knowledge they'd be the ones to take the fall if there was an investigation—in part, that was what the HR mades were *for*, to give management someone to blame. But sometimes, for a variety of reasons, there were documents they couldn't destroy, spreadsheets they couldn't strategically corrupt: sometimes the absence of a record was more suspicious than just leaving it there for someone to glance at and then move on. Oakseed's obligation to keep such records was about to come to an end. They couldn't destroy *all* the company's data— deleting it properly took time, and there needed to be *some* records to hand over to whoever bought its component parts—but the company had accrued such a vast amount of data, no one was going to look at it closely.

Shortly before 9:00 P.M, Kline and three others were redeployed to generate a database of every made retained by Oakseed, along with vital information such as their work history and ledger position. This was a simple enough task, but the company needed this data to be formatted in a way it had never previously been. Every single made's data needed to be turned into a profile with a positive spin and attractive imagery (or as attractive as possible). Kline and the others came up with a process to create this, ran a sample of records through it, refined it, repeated this a couple of times, agreed the results were good enough considering the deadline was midnight, then left the process running and went to get coffee.

They chatted and joked about the challenges of trying to get the thing to work, but none of them discussed what it actually was they'd produced, even though they all knew it was a sales catalog, and they were all in it.

They came back to find the completed catalog, which now included one other data point: their prices. Of course they all looked through it to find their own price, and Kline was braced for how low his would be. He was old and no one really knew how long he'd be good for work, because he was a first-waver: there weren't any older than him. But that was exactly why it stung. When he'd gone through nursery, all of this was new and exciting. Mades were the future of business and his generation were the first. The whole time they'd been growing up they'd been told how special and important they were, and how they were going to change everything. But generation after generation had followed them. It had become commonplace. In fact, some said using mades for business was now outdated. Kline's batch was no longer special or important, and the number he saw on the screen at the top of his profile reflected this.

Kline looked up his old partner from his brand ambassador days, Ennio. After they'd been moved off the street, Ennio had been assigned to one of the company's golf courses as a caddy. Despite having no transferable skills beyond advising people whether to use a nine iron or a pitching wedge, his price was slightly higher than Kline's, which put Kline in an even worse mood.

Arlo awoke in the early afternoon and realized he was still in the holding room. He had fallen asleep on the large sofa and slept very badly. He turned over and wondered if he might be able to fall asleep again. Yet he was kept awake by a question he couldn't answer: Why wasn't he already dead?

It made little sense to him. He'd been told Samson's condition was severe, the situation was urgent, and the operation would take place very soon. Yet here he was, several hours after arriving, and he had not yet been reaped.

Arlo stared at the ceiling for a while. Before falling asleep he'd felt angry and despairing, but he was not the kind of person who could stay at an extreme emotional pitch for long, and now he was just puzzled. What was going on?

A nurse brought him food, and he wondered if she was a made, like him. A lot of countries were using them in hospitals now—often the corps would sell their contracts on cheaply, and it helped address high staff turnover. He asked her, in Mandarin, what was going on.

"The operation's been delayed," she told him with a pleasant smile, as if this was a regrettable inconvenience and not the sword of Damocles dangling over Arlo's head.

"Delayed, not canceled?" Arlo had dared to hope Samson might already be dead.

"Delayed. He's critical, but stable, for now."

"So what's the holdup?" he asked. "You're waiting for an operating theater to be available?" Arlo found this unlikely, given Samson's xec status—they'd surely find room for him no matter how busy they were.

The nurse shook her head. "We have capacity. There's an issue around his entitlement."

"His medical entitlement? But he'd only lose that if he'd been fired, wouldn't he?"

"I don't know the details, I'm afraid."

"So, *has* he been fired?"

"I don't know. Sorry, I must get back to my other duties."

After she'd gone, Arlo was so confused he almost forgot about the food in front of him—almost. As he ate, it occurred to him that you weren't supposed to eat shortly before an operation, so if they'd brought him food, the delay must be significant. The food was not good, but this realization made it taste that little bit better.

The former residents of Shaw Apartments did end up in Pennsylvania as promised. Drienne never really believed the alternative theories—the company didn't usually lie to mades, it just kept things from them, so it wouldn't have told them they were going to Pennsylvania unless they were. Shuttles took them from the port to a business park, where a complex of Oakseed buildings was connected by walkways; from the outside it all looked very impressive, like a soaring citadel of innovation. Then they were shown into one of its buildings. It was filled with open-plan offices from which all furniture, equipment, fixtures, and fittings had been removed. All the monitors and control pads had been taken off the walls, and even parts of the air-conditioning system had gone. It also looked like the vacs had been taken away before they'd finished cleaning up the mess.

Drienne found it hard to tell how long the building had been in this state, but the atmosphere had a stale quality that suggested it had been shut up for a few days at least. She certainly didn't feel like it had been cleared out for the purpose of giving the mades somewhere to stay. Oakseed just needed to put them somewhere, and this place was conveniently empty. The power had been disconnected, so the mades sat around in a dim, empty office, waiting. It was unclear if anything else was going to happen.

Before too long a pair of bewildered and anxious-looking HR managers from the Delaware office turned up to take charge. They were visibly flummoxed by the lack of facilities, furnishings, and power. They located an old printer and some basematter in the basement of one of the other buildings, and got some of the stronger mades to drag it over to the office where everyone was. By this time, they'd established the solar panels were still fitted to the roof, so they connected the printer and put it to work producing thin sponge mats and blankets for the exhausted mades. It would take several hours to print enough for everyone. The managers assured the mades a food delivery was on its way from the city.

Andrée went to talk to the managers about where all their personal belongings were. Then she came back over to Drienne, who had found a deep windowsill to sit in.

"Well?" said Drienne.

"They know nothing about what's happened to our stuff. Or they just wanted me to go away."

"We're not getting our stuff, are we?"

"I wonder if they just, like . . . sold it all."

"Or sent it all to a cyc plant." Drienne moved her feet so Andrée could sit at the other end of the windowsill.

"I don't know why they didn't just let us pack," said Andrée, cleaning a grimy spot on the windowsill before she sat down. "I hardly own a thing, I could've thrown it all in a bag in five minutes. It would've been easier to let me do it than someone else."

"Maybe they didn't want us to take it. If they're selling us to someone else, maybe they don't want us coming with *literal* baggage."

"You think that's what's going to happen?"

"You heard the rumors about Oakseed collapsing?"

"Yeah, but . . . a company this big doesn't just *collapse*."

"Okay," said Drienne, "but look at this place—what the fuck's going on here?" She peered out through the window across the landscaped grounds, where the lawns showed signs of having been untended for several weeks. "The size of this complex, and it's just sitting here doing nothing?"

"Maybe it's due for a refit."

"Yeah maybe, and maybe it's just a coincidence it's having a refit at the exact same time we need to be shipped halfway across the world and dumped in the care of two guys from Delaware who clearly don't know what the fuck they're doing and haven't been prepared. Maybe it's *all* part of a plan."

"The company messes up sometimes."

"True." Drienne gave up arguing with Andrée and checked again to see if her commission had come in. She hadn't been able to get into her account since she left the club back in Shanghai. Now she found a message saying the account had been closed and the funds in it withdrawn. But to where?

Arlo tried not to get his hopes up, but his mind kept working on the possibility he might not die in this hospital. It was simply too enticing, the thought Samson might not have the right to Arlo's internal organs after all, and *he* might be the one to die while Arlo walked out of this place whistling and clicking his heels. He enjoyed this thought so much he wept slightly, and even if it was a false hope, he may as well take his pleasures where he could get them.

It was past midnight and Arlo had been in the holding room for about twenty hours, and was considering the possibility Samson had not only lost his medical entitlement, he'd done so through some dismal failure—fired for incompetence, perhaps, or embezzlement—when a doctor entered. Arlo's heart leapt. He imagined the words on her lips: he was free to go back to his apartment, back to work. Being in his drab apartment and going to his soul-sapping job had never been a more thrilling prospect than it was at this moment.

"Arlo Rahane?" said the doctor. "Could you come this way, please?"

"Why?" Arlo almost barked at her. He'd meant to ask this in a more measured way: he wanted to know if he was about to be escorted home, or—

"Everything is ready for the operation."

Fuck. Whatever the issue had been, it must have been resolved. Of course it had. Men like Samson always got what they wanted in the end.

Well, there were worse ways to go, he supposed, as he followed the doctor down the corridor. They'd give him anesthetic, he'd go under, and never wake up. No struggle, no pain. He told himself he was ready. It was a lie, but he kept telling it to himself. He could be very convincing when he wanted to be. It was what made him good at his job.

4

FLYING BLIND

Every time another batch of mades arrived at the Pennsylvania complex, from Wellington, St. Petersburg, Cape Town, Santiago, Gothenburg, Montreal, it sank in a little more that all the signs suggested Oakseed had indeed collapsed. The newcomers did all kinds of jobs: supports, itemizers, accountants, janitors, taggers. When each open-plan office filled up, the HR managers opened up another one and ordered more bedding to be printed off and more rations to be delivered, and they contacted their superiors yet again asking for more support. At one point, Drienne saw the HR guys in the corridor outside the office where she currently resided trying to keep their voices down while having a stand-up row with each other.

The managers had been asked time and again for confirmation that the company had collapsed, and time and again they fobbed off whoever asked with some crap about restructuring and rationalization. However, this line was trotted out with visibly decreasing enthusiasm, and Drienne thought if everyone took a turn, maybe they could wear the managers down. So she went over and asked.

"That kind of speculation isn't helpful," replied the HR guy she'd approached, wearily.

And that was when Drienne knew for sure it was true. She went away and tried to work out how she felt about this. Their next situation was unlikely to be better than their current one. The mades had been produced in response to a dramatically declining birth rate and consequent labor shortage. All the megas had invested hugely in them. But global demographics had changed, and the need for mades had become less pressing. Production of mades had fallen by over 95 percent since Drienne was created, and right now none of Oakseed's rivals needed more, or at least not in any great quantities. It would be nice to think the dissolution of Oakseed meant the mades' debts would be canceled and they'd be libbed, but realistically they would be sold to pay the creditors that were always left behind when a company collapsed. And as demand for mades was low, their contracts would be sold cheaply and their lives would be treated as such.

The future was uncertain. But Drienne's sense of inevitability about her life had come close to crushing her many times, and she couldn't help feeling excited by the possibilities opening up, even if most of them were bad. She found herself aching, almost physically *aching*, to talk to Arlo about this. She was forming sentences in her head, rehearsing for a conversation they weren't ever going to have.

For the second time since arriving at the hospital, Arlo awoke and couldn't understand why.

This time he was not in the hospital holding room, he knew that much. He could feel an actual bed underneath him, and he could hear extraneous noise now, unlike the holding room that had been entirely soundproof. But he couldn't see anything. Upon inspection, he found his eyes to be heavily bandaged.

Sluggishly, Arlo thought back to the last thing he remembered: lying on a gurney that steered itself down the corridor and into an operating room. No one had spoken to him; they'd barely looked at him. He hadn't asked what was about to happen, because he'd thought he knew. The doctor who'd come to get him was there, plus another doctor, and an anesthetist drone. Then Samson had been brought in. Arlo had tried to get a glimpse of Samson's face, hoping that if the xec was conscious, Arlo could look him in the eyes—but Samson's features stayed frustratingly out of view, like in a dream. And then the anesthetic hit.

Arlo flexed his left hand; it felt strange without the sheath that housed his backhand. He only ever took the sheath off to clean it and the skin underneath, and always put it straight back on afterward. He raised the hand and pushed up his hospital gown so he could touch his fingers to his chest. He almost expected to find a hole there, to realize he'd been plugged into some life-support device that would do the job of all the organs they'd just removed, because they needed to keep him alive a bit longer, for reasons he couldn't imagine right now. But there was no hole, no incision, he hadn't been cut open, the skin wasn't even tender. He poked at his rib cage just to make sure, then when it didn't cave in under his touch, he moved his hand down to his abdomen and even his genitals. Everything was still where it should be.

It was just his eyes. They didn't hurt, but the skin around them was tight and stiff, and he became aware he was on heavy painkillers, without which they would hurt a great deal.

What the fuck was going on? Had they *just* taken his eyes? There'd been no talk of eyes when he'd arrived at the hospital. Had there been a ludicrous mix-up, and what they'd told him had been wrong, and he was actually just here so they could reap his eyes? He became increasingly furious about this. It was patently a better deal than death, but how did they expect him to *live*? He wouldn't be able to do his job now, and he wasn't trained to do anything else. What would they do with him? But maybe he wouldn't be left blind—maybe he'd been given some cheap substandard eyes reaped from a dead made, while Samson got Arlo's young, fresh eyes slotted into his middle-aged head.

Someone had to come here and explain to him what was going on. So he called for assistance.

Assistance arrived quicker than he expected, in the form of not

just one person, but *two*. He wondered why he merited this level
of attention. They both sounded female. Arlo assumed they were
medical staff but he had no way of knowing. One of them, speaking Mandarin into a translator, asked what he needed.

"Are your painkillers working?" the other one added, sounding
concerned.

"Yes," replied Arlo. He tried to form his next sentence in
Mandarin—not using translators was a point of pride for him. But
he felt too wiped to speak coherently in his second language, and
making himself understood was more important than pride. "I just
don't know what's going on," he said in English.

"The operation went extremely well." This member of staff was
moving around Arlo's bed as she spoke; it sounded like she was
carrying out tests.

"You've been an excellent patient," said the first member of staff
kindly.

Arlo hadn't been thinking of himself as a patient. Patients
come in to be treated; he was a resource to be mined. "What *was*
the operation? Nobody's explained anything to me. I thought I'd
come here to donate back—" He realized he was using the po-
lite language, and for what? "Donate" implied someone with more
than they needed giving it to those less fortunate, and that didn't
describe what was happening here at all. "I thought I was here to
be reaped."

"Didn't anyone explain it to him?" said the other woman. Her
translator didn't put this into English, but Arlo understood the
words.

"I don't think there was time," said the first.

"Right," said the other woman, who seemed to be a doctor. Now
she was addressing Arlo again through her translator. "So yes, that
was why you *came*."

"Yes—they told me he needed my heart, and liver—"

"But Mr. Samson's situation changed, as did yours."

"How?"

"I'm afraid the hospital's code of conduct doesn't allow us to discuss his situation. Patient confidentiality."

There was no point getting angry with the hospital staff over this. "Are you allowed to tell me what you've done to me?" Arlo said, as nonconfrontationally as he could manage.

"Yes! You've been given an eye transplant."

"But there was nothing wrong with my eyes. Was there?"

"No. Their condition was extremely good—wasn't it?"

"Extremely good," the woman who wasn't a doctor agreed. She was on the other side of the bed now, applying a device to Arlo's upper arm. He guessed she was a nurse.

How odd. He'd had those eyes more than half his life. He'd been given the standard operation at the age of eleven, as soon as he was deemed old enough, and at the time it had upset him deeply—which he knew was a common, unremarkable reaction. Everything looked different through the replacement eyes—not *very* different, but still different. The world looked a little washed out, a little colder somehow. The nursery autodoc told him there was no difference, he was imagining it, and if there *was* any difference then the replacement eyes would be superior.

Over the years he'd gotten used to those eyes and rarely thought about it anymore. The idea of having to go through the adjustment process again was dismaying.

"Why do it," Arlo asked, "if my eyes were fine?"

"We weren't furnished with that information. We received the instructions and payment, and all was in order."

"Fucking hell," muttered Arlo. Maybe it was a security issue?

"Your body's responding very well to the accelerated healing program," said the nurse as if he hadn't spoken. "These bandages should be able to come off in sixteen to twenty-four hours."

"So I'm not going to be reaped?"

"No."

"What's happened to Mr. Samson, then? Is he dead?" That certainly qualified as a change in circumstances.

"I'm afraid so," said the doctor. "May I offer the hospital's condolences?"

"You may, but I don't need them. I don't know the guy, I'm just his clone."

"Nevertheless." Then the two women spoke to each other with the translation turned off, too quietly for Arlo to hear. One of them left the room.

"Good news!" the nurse (who was still here) said to Arlo.

"Really?"

"You're well enough to travel and we can arrange for you to be put on the next flight to Vancouver."

"*Vancouver?*"

"That's where we were told to send you after the operation."

"But I live here."

"Not anymore. Have you enjoyed your time in Shanghai?"

Arlo was going to give a sharper answer to this. But he simply said, "It's a very beautiful city."

Loren had been at the Lancaster, Pennsylvania, offices for about eighteen hours. They were dealing with the boredom by playing games of Go in their head. There was nothing to do here except talk to the others, and no one seemed to have anything interesting to say. They were partway through a game when they noticed a team of twenty or so people in dark gray shirts had turned up. One of them spoke to the mades, explaining they were representatives of Rook-Divest, the receivers dealing with the breakup of Oakseed's assets. The woman who said this was clearly unaware that this was the first official confirmation the mades had been given of the company's collapse, and was surprised when it provoked some shocked responses from the mades. Loren felt surprised too: they'd assumed everyone else had worked this out and were resigned to it at this stage. But unrest quickly bubbled up from the crowd, some members of which surged forward, angrily engaging with the receivers.

Loren didn't hear much of the debate that followed, but it

seemed the protesters believed they were being lied to, that Oak-seed hadn't collapsed at all and this was just a fiction to mollify them while the company sold them off. Some said they refused to be sold and demanded to be taken home, back to their jobs. Loren couldn't understand this at all. If Oakseed still existed, why would they take back workers they'd unceremoniously gotten rid of? And surely the fact the mades were being kept in a gutted Oakseed office strongly supported the notion the company had collapsed? Were they just unable to accept the demise of the entity that had made them, housed them, and used them all their lives?

The discussion, such as it was, began to turn violent. Loren made their way to a part of the office that was away from the fighting and resumed their game of Go until it all died down.

They'd forgotten about her.

After escorting the depot mades to the port, Nadi had expected to be allowed to go home. Instead she was told to continue guarding the mades as they waited for a flight, then to guard them on the flight itself. Everyone who gave her these instructions seemed to believe an outbreak of unrest was imminent. Nadi's training meant she considered the implications of every movement: she could look at crowds, sense trouble brewing, and pinpoint it. She saw none of that from the mades, who all looked bewildered and exhausted. Nearly all the passengers slept through the flight, including Nadi.

When the flight arrived in Montevideo, Uruguay, it landed at the airstrip of Oakseed's private resort, the one the xecs used for board meetings and whitepage summits. It was *fancy*. The mades were told they were all going to stay here for the time being. It sounded nice, but wasn't. The suites and chalets were all taken, so the mades were sent to bed down in the sports complex. They slept on the floors of squash courts and in the clubhouse of the golf course. Some HR managers oversaw the allocation of space, so Nadi had asked them when she'd be going back to Frankfurt. They'd told her they didn't know, and in the meantime it would be great if she could continue to watch over the mades she'd come here with, because there was a shortage of securits here.

A made called Edison who had worked at the sports complex as a fitness trainer told Nadi there was a shortage of securits because people had come over from the city and kept trying to break into the resort. Every available securit had been corralled into a militia to keep them out.

"Why are they trying to break into the resort?" Nadi had asked him.

"Because the xecs are here," Edison replied. "They've been here for weeks, working on their plan to save the company. Now they're just here wondering what the fuck to do."

"But what do people want with the xecs? The people who are trying to break in, I mean?"

Edison shrugged. "Answers. Apologies. Revenge."

Later that day, Nadi went out to check that the gates and fences around the sports complex were secure. This was just an excuse she came up with to get out of the building. Observing the mades for any sign of insurrection was exhausting and boring and she couldn't switch off. She walked the perimeter and spent a while looking at the tennis courts. She had never seen a real clay court before, let alone played on one. On the rare occasions Nadi got to play on a real-life court, it would be a low-quality hard surface, poorly maintained, with cracks big enough for mice to live in. She had asked one of the managers if she might play on one of the resort's courts in her breaks, and the request had been rejected without consideration.

Nadi's walk around the perimeter took her past the croquet lawn, which lay between the sports complex and the hotel. She looked up and saw a middle-aged man standing on one of the hotel's balconies. He looked out at the marina and the ocean beyond. He had his hands in his pockets. He wasn't smiling.

He caught sight of Nadi watching him. She gave him the casual salute you were meant to do with higher-ranking employees, the familiar but respectful gesture used by security staff for well over a century.

The man nodded an acknowledgment, turned and went inside.

The next day, the reps from RookDivest turned up and Nadi asked one of them when she was going back to Frankfurt. The guy she spoke to blinked, told her she wasn't, and she should go and join the other mades, because the sales were starting.

5

A FAINT SMELL OF MARZIPAN

Arlo assumed he was now in Vancouver, but how would he know if he wasn't? He had no idea what Vancouver sounded or smelled like and even if he did his senses weren't keen enough to distinguish it from every other city on Earth. The people who'd helped him board the flight had said they were going to Vancouver, the pilot had said at the end of the flight they had landed in Vancouver, but Arlo wouldn't trust he was there until he could see it with his own eyes. He searched for reasons why someone might lie about sending him to Vancouver. It could be a reassuring fiction; he could think of plenty of places he'd be a lot more worried about going to.

The flight had been amazing, except for two things: he couldn't see anything, and he had a bulky carrying case handcuffed to his wrist. He'd been given the case before leaving the hospital and been told someone would take it from him when he arrived at his destination. He hadn't been told what was *in* the case, because no one ever told him anything if they could help it. The chain on the cuff was reasonably long, so he was able to put the case down and had freedom of movement, but he still kept catching the chain on the arm of his seat.

The flight had been first class, or at least he'd been told it was, and he believed it: he'd been seated in a private pod and supplied with audio entertainment, excellent food, and drinks on demand.

A member of the cabin crew who dealt with disabled passengers had guided Arlo through the port and onto his flight, and regularly visited his seat to see if he needed anything. The young man had a beautiful voice, coarse yet warm, and Arlo wondered what it would be like to fall in love with someone and never see their face; to know them only by the sound of their voice, the touch of their hands, the feel of their body underneath yours . . .

Arlo had become prone to flights of fancy such as this since the operation. He'd had little to do in the hospital except think, and for the first time in his adult life he was off the sales carousel; he didn't have to worry about hitting his next target. He now realized how much these concerns had occupied his thoughts, even when he wasn't consciously thinking about them. He wondered if his brain had now reset into its default state and would be like this from now on, or if he'd built up a backlog of thoughts he needed to process, and they were all coming out in a barely filtered gush, and it would calm down after a while.

The flight attendant (the one with the voice) guided Arlo through the port in Vancouver, through border control and security, and into a car that was waiting for him. The attendant bade him goodbye and Arlo tried to hold the voice in his memory.

As the car drove away, Arlo placed the case on his lap and ran his hands over it. Even though it was chained to his wrist, he couldn't shake the feeling someone might have covertly taken it off the other end of the chain and switched it for a different case while it had been resting on the ground. But when he'd been waiting at the port in Shanghai he'd familiarized himself with the shape and texture of the case, including any nicks and dents he could find, and he felt fairly confident the one he had now was the one he'd been given at the hospital.

During Arlo's operation, his slate had performed a full factory reset, and each time he tried to use it, it asked him for authorization he didn't have. It appeared not to know who he was. This was probably a deliberate tactic aimed at making him dependent on the structures taking him from one city to another. He needed the booked flight, the helpful attendant, the car at the other end, because he was unable to arrange such things for himself, so he couldn't change course and run away. But he had no intention of running away. You'd think they'd know that, with all the personality analytics they ran on the workforce.

Having no slate, and no available eyes with which to look out the window, he asked the car to turn on an audio channel. "Something with local news," he told it, in the hope of getting some sense of what the city was like.

Arlo was used to not being able to access whatever he wanted, so he hadn't clocked how limited his selection of in-flight entertainment had been. Other passengers had been able to access the net and news media, but Arlo only had an edited range of music, humor, sport, and discourse channels. So while the world had spent the last two days talking of little other than the collapse of Oakseed, it came as a complete surprise to Arlo to hear a succession of professional commentators, pop streamers, and other celebrities giving their views on the situation and what consequences they expected would follow. When Arlo understood what was happening, he found himself tuning in and out of the voices, reeling away from them as he tried to connect this seismic global development to his personal situation, then latching back onto the voices in the hope of finding new facts that might make sense of it all.

Arlo's mind instinctively resisted the idea Oakseed could fail. The fact of the company had been so drilled into him, had felt so inevitable, so impossible to fight. He knew this was how they wanted him to feel, but that didn't stop him feeling it. Above all, something in him still regarded the company as *his* company, and wanted it to succeed.

Arlo forced himself to think past all this. When he considered it rationally, it was clearly true that Oakseed had collapsed. It explained why he wasn't dead: Samson hadn't been fired, the company simply no longer existed to support his medical entitlement, and the hospital had refused to proceed. Arlo laughed at the thought: if the company had held together just a few more hours, he'd be dead and Samson would be alive. Someone, somewhere had done him a huge favor by calling in the receivers when they did. He wondered who it was and if he'd ever get to thank them.

It didn't explain why he was in Vancouver with someone else's eyes in his head and a case shackled to his wrist. Or if it did, he was still missing some pieces of information that would connect it all up. It was clear Oakseed no longer held him, so he must have been sold to someone else. Someone in Vancouver. He must be on his way to them right now.

He wondered what had happened to Drienne. Until now he'd assumed she'd be going about her life in their old apartment, but that clearly wasn't the case. It was possible he'd never find out, and he hated that thought.

The car came to a stop in what sounded like an underground car park and the engine turned itself off. Had he arrived? Arlo waited a few moments, but nothing happened. He'd assumed someone would be here to meet him.

"Well?" he asked the car. "What now?"

The car didn't reply.

Arlo checked his slate, but it still demanded authorization before it would do anything. He tried to open the car door, but it was locked. Surely whoever arranged all this wouldn't go to all this effort just to let him die in an underground car park. He had literally no enemies; he hardly even knew anyone. And why send him all the way here? You can lock someone in a car just as easily in Shanghai.

Minutes passed.

Then the car door opened.

"Sorry," said a woman in a deadpan, amused drawl. "I meant to be here when you arrived, but I was on a call."

"It's fine," Arlo replied automatically.

"Come on up."

"Who are you?"

"My name's Mia Ostrander. I'm your new holder."

They took an elevator to the twelfth floor. Arlo knew it was the twelfth floor because the elevator had a voice that said so. Mia led Arlo along the hallway, holding his hand lightly. The hallway seemed spacious (judging by the echo), had thick carpets, and smelled faintly of marzipan. They arrived at a door that Mia opened, and then she led him inside.

"Let me take that," she said, lifting the case from his hand. The cuff sprang open and fell from his wrist.

"Thanks," said Arlo as he massaged his wrist where the cuff had been. The skin wasn't irritated—like most mades of his generation, he was equipped with grafts on vulnerable areas that were designed to hamper suicide.

"Can I offer you a drink?" Mia said as she guided him over to a recliner (a very comfortable one, with a rich, authentic leather smell, not that Arlo had ever smelled real leather). By now he was pretty sure what was in store for him. Probably a lot of the brand ambassadors would end up in places like this, becoming fuckdolls for the wealthy. It could have been worse, he supposed. But then, he didn't know what she was into yet. There could be pain, degradation, mutilation, et cetera.

He asked if he might have a green tea.

"Of course," said Mia. "You can take off his bandages now."

Arlo was confused by this until he worked out Mia was talking to a third person, whose presence in the room Arlo hadn't clocked until now. This third person approached Arlo and introduced himself as Darboe.

"Don't worry," said Mia, "he's a registered nurse, not just some guy I picked up off the street."

"Are you sure they're ready to come off?" said Arlo.

"Should be more than ready," said Darboe. Gently, he slid a tool under the bandage by Arlo's left temple, twisted it, and did something else Arlo couldn't identify—and the bandage came free, including the cooling gel sacs that had molded themselves to Arlo's eyelids. He tried to open his eyes but the lids were stuck together.

"Don't force them open," Darboe told him. "Just wait." He daubed gently at Arlo's eyelids with a moist wipe and they began to loosen.

"Now," said Mia, "I have some news for you which will come as a shock, but try to stay calm because it's good news for you in the long run."

"Okay," said Arlo.

"Oakseed has collapsed, it's gone out of business."

"Yes, I heard about that in the car on the way here."

"What?"

"It was on the radio."

"Goddammit, I gave specific instructions—" Mia stopped. "I'm sorry, I asked them not to tell you about the Oakseed situation in the hospital or on the flight because I wanted you to focus on your recovery. I was going to explain it all to you when you got here. So you know?"

"I don't know *how* it happened."

"It's complicated, as I'm sure you can imagine. Right now it's chaos—sites they were renting had to be vacated immediately, other properties have been seized by governments in lieu of tax or whatever. Oakseed have been desperately consolidating all their remaining physical assets on their remaining sites. Everything's for sale."

"Am I the only one you've bought?"

"For now."

"Try opening your eyes," said Darboe.

Arlo gave a small nod, then with trepidation let his sticky eyelids twitch. They parted quite easily. His vision was blurry, though.

"Feel okay?"

"Sore," muttered Arlo. The lids felt bruised, as if he'd been punched in the same place in both eyes with the exact same amount of force, and it hurt to blink, but he hadn't blinked in well over twenty-four hours and he couldn't resist the compulsion to do so.

"That's normal." Darboe held a slate in front of Arlo's eyes and it shone lights into them, making him wince. "This is very good work."

"Shanghai has amazing people for this kind of sensory and neural surgery," said Mia. She was sitting directly opposite Arlo, also in a leather recliner.

"It's healing perfectly."

"Good."

Darboe finished his examination and moved out of the way. Arlo's vision was clearing and he was able to get a proper look at Mia. She was older than Arlo had expected from her voice: he'd imagined her to be about his age, but perhaps, he reflected, we always imagine people to be about our own age if we don't find any cues to the contrary. She seemed to be in her early forties. She was statuesque; she sat with her legs stretched out and crossed at the ankles, and a large, elegant hand was curled around a glass of some thick green juice. She had keen eyes and straight hair worn in a sweeping side parting, which divided her hair into a larger deep red side and a smaller orange side. She wore a shirt patterned in orange and white triangles, red jeans, and no shoes. Her nail polish also matched her hair: left hand and right foot red, right hand and left foot orange. The shades of orange and red were all identical.

In contrast to Mia herself, the spacious apartment in which she stood was decorated in muted colors. It contained a tasteful mix of modern and vintage furnishings. There was no clutter anywhere.

Arlo wasn't sure his eyesight was quite as good as it had been before the operation, but maybe it would sharpen up in time. Which made him want to ask—

"Why did you force me to have this operation?"

Mia smiled. "That's a fair question. Don't forget your tea."

Arlo glanced at the coffee table to the right of his chair and saw a cup of green tea on it. Lettering down the side advertised a local sushi restaurant and featured images of their most popular dishes:

by touching the images and speaking their names you could order them. "Are you going to answer my fair question?" he asked.

"Yes." She looked over at Darboe. "Thank you," she said pleasantly.

Darboe nodded and started packing implements into a black bag that sat on the floor next to the recliner. Mia stood and walked over to him and made arrangements for him to return for a follow-up examination of Arlo tomorrow. While they did this Arlo turned to the window, which looked out on a rich forest unlike any he had ever seen. He wasn't totally sure it was real, and he searched for tells that it might be a screen, moving his head to see if it scrolled true. It appeared to be real.

Darboe finished packing and held out a fist to Mia. She took it in both of her hands and kissed it. "Thank you." Then she returned to her chair and sipped her juice while Darboe left the apartment. When he was gone, Mia made eye contact with Arlo and smiled.

This was it, Arlo thought. She was going to tell him to undress, so she could check out the goods. Probably the eyes were some particular kink of hers, a different color or something like that, she wanted her fuckboy to be *just* how she liked him—

"So you're probably assuming this is a sex thing?" Mia asked. "Middle-aged lady alone in her swanky apartment."

"Well . . . yes."

She chuckled and nodded. "That's understandable. But no, actually I want you to help me steal some money from Oakseed before the receivers get their hands on it."

Arlo laughed. Then he realized she was perfectly serious. "What?"

"Yeah."

"But I can't . . . I've never done anything like that before."

"I know. But you are the *only* person for this job. And I'm afraid you can't say no."

6

EUGÉNIE?

This was a nightmare and she had to make someone understand. It was bad enough where she was before, believing she was a made without rights or options, but now she'd been cut off even from the few points of security she'd had, and it seemed she was to be sold like cattle. Like *cattle*.

She tried to stand and felt dizzy, so she sat back down and tried to calm her breathing.

There might be an opportunity here, she realized. If she could communicate the truth of her situation, perhaps the mistake that had been made so long ago could be rectified. Perhaps she could find her family again. She wondered what they had been told about what happened to her. The memories of her past were dim and shapeless, like something seen through a filthy window, and she felt like the more she held on to them, the more she bent them out of shape. But there was a large, fine house, with high ceilings, and she could feel the emotions in that place: it was full of love, and she'd felt safe there. Outside the house was dangerous.

She'd been outside the house as long as she could remember.

Someone addressed her as Drienne, her hateful made name. She tried to ignore it, but the speaker assumed she just hadn't heard, and said it again.

The speaker was Andrée, the young made who'd accompanied

her from Shanghai. She had a red mark on her face after getting herself involved in the altercation between the mades and the receivers. She'd been at the front of it all, screaming "LIARS!" and hurling herself at the receivers, fists flailing. Andrée wasn't built for fighting, and it had been a stupid thing to do, very typically stupid. You couldn't expect any better.

The mades had calmed down now. There'd been a moment when it seemed like the receivers might be overwhelmed by sheer weight of numbers, but one of the receivers speaking through an amplifier had pointed out to the mades how difficult it would be for them to survive if they left the building, as their accounts had all been closed along with Oakseed, and opening new ones could only be done by their new holders. Which was obvious, but the mades were too stupid to realize it for themselves.

"Fuck off," she told Andrée, who was talking nonsense about something. When Andrée just stared at her, startled, she said it again, louder. Several people nearby turned to look. She glared at them until they looked away.

She needed to find someone she could talk to about her situation. The people who seemed to be in charge at the moment wouldn't do at all. For now the most important thing was not to slip back. She could feel her mind being dragged back into that dim oblivion. She had to remember who she really was. Her name was—

What was her name? God, she was forgetting already. It was . . .

Where was Arlo? He always helped her with this, when she had these occasional blessed moments of lucidity. He held on to all those details about her, like her name—

It would be on her slate. She kept a file of notes about herself for just this reason. She picked it up and opened the storage tree, but the file wasn't there. Of course, the slate had reset itself during the journey here. She would just have to try to remember.

Eugénie? Was that it? It sounded right. *Eugénie Eugénie Eugénie.* The more she said it to herself, the righter it sounded.

Yes. It was right.

Eugénie opened up a new note on her slate and wrote "Eugénie" in it. She lay back on her bedroll and focused on the knowledge that she was Eugénie.

Mia seemed to think Arlo might have heard of her, or that her name might at least ring a bell with him, and he felt dumb for not having a clue who she was. But as she told her story, he realized it was exactly the kind of thing that would have been filtered out. It touched on all kinds of issues he wasn't supposed to take an interest in, or even be aware of.

"I was taken into Oakseed's academy in Richmond when I was nine years old," she told him. "When I graduated they took me on—initially in waste optimization, but I really wanted to be a product designer, and that's when I became the lead on Naildit."

"Oh!" said Arlo. "*You* invented that?"

"Yeah. I mean there was a whole team, but the core concept was one of my magic-hour proposals."

Smart nail polish with easy connectivity to all your Oakseed devices, affordably priced—the kids in Shanghai loved it, went nuts whenever a new limited edition came out. Arlo felt very impressed to be face-to-face with the person who thought of it. "I've sold a *lot* of that stuff."

"Of course you have. And of course Oakseed owns that shit because I was under contract, and I always *knew* that was how it worked. Which is why, when I was twenty-nine, I left to set up my own company, MO. You heard of that?"

"I think so." (He wasn't sure. Probably not.)

"We had a neat line in smart houseplants that could reprocess waste matter, but that's probably not the kind of thing they had you selling."

"I was mostly on wearables."

Mia nodded. "So it was all going great, we were set for an expansion drive, I rejected an offer from Oakseed to buy me out, and they came back with a lawsuit saying they didn't need to buy me out because—you really didn't hear about this?"

Arlo shook his head.

"Okay, so get this: They said anything I created came from my personality, and my personality was shaped by being in their academy from such a young age, *therefore*, even though I was no longer their employee, my intellectual property was still *their* intellectual property."

Arlo took this in, then he said, "Fucking hell."

"Right?"

"That's outrageous."

"*Outrageous* fuckery even by their standards. Don't get me wrong, I do realize your situation is much more horrible, and that's basically what the deal has always been for you—"

"Well, yes."

"—but I still thought it was low to say, 'Hey, we got you when you were nine years old, so that means we own you for life.'"

"So did this go to court?"

"Yeah, and I won."

"Wow."

"And then they appealed, and *they* won."

"Oh."

"And then *I* appealed, and I lost."

"So what did you do?"

"They offered me a job—a very good job, to be fair, *very* well paid—and they figured I'd take it because what else was I going to do? The whole thing was them saying fuck you, you should never have left, and we're gonna make an example of you to everyone else who's thinking about leaving."

"And . . . you didn't? Take it, I mean?"

"I didn't. I retrained in law so I could work on IP cases like this one and maybe undo what happened." She shrugged. "Still haven't hit *that* goal, but I make a living."

"So where does Oakseed collapsing leave all this? Do you get your rights back?"

Mia laughed. "Oh bless you, no. Intangible assets are being sold too, and my personality is registered as a very valuable intangible asset. But this is an opportunity, because Oakseed would never have sold it to me for *any* amount, whereas the receivers will sell to whoever comes up with the money. I have actually lodged a legal challenge asserting I *should* get it back for nothing—it won't stand up, but the process should take at least a couple weeks to play out, which gives me time to find the money so I can buy it."

"And when you say *find* you mean . . . *steal*?"

"Yes. Despite being wealthy by any sane standards I do not have anywhere *near* enough money to buy back my personality. But . . ." She drained her juice, then put the glass on a side table and leaned forward in her chair. "Early on in my career, Oakseed sent me to do model refinement at an office out on the fringes of Europe, finding ways to cut costs and waste in the printing process. And I happen to know a xec at a cycling plant stashed a Coyne with something in the region of eighty million dollars on it in a locker."

"A coin?"

"A Coyne. You never seen a Coyne? I guess you might not." Mia explained it was a type of anonymized, untraceable data storage device, shaped like a large, dulled silver coin about the size of your palm. It had been invented by someone called Cressida Coyne (in fact, she was just one of a team of four, but everyone agreed her name fit the product nicely). It sold itself as a means of freeing oneself from tracking, but after a flurry of popularity it became so closely identified with crime that criminals felt it drew too much suspicion, while the law-abiding felt it made them look like criminals, and it was taken off the market.

"Wow," said Arlo. "Eighty *million*?"

"Uh-huh."

"How do you know this?"

"Because the xec asked me to help him launder it. See, the Coyne itself is untraceable but the money you put *on* it has to be clean, otherwise when you try to spend it, it could connect you back to something crooked. The cash on this one had some new

kind of digital fingerprinting no one could work out; I had a repu-
tation as an original thinker and he thought I might be able to get
around it."

"And did you manage it?"

"No. I had no experience in that area, but guys like him think
if you're smart with design you can manipulate anything. So I
told him sorry, can't do it. He said thanks for trying and if I ever
breathed a word or tried to take it for myself he'd end my career."

"Where'd he get the money?"

"I didn't ask and he didn't tell. There was a lot of shady stuff going down in that part of the company because that's what happens
when you do business in a dereg zone that's desperate for outside
investment. But I do know it's still there."

"*How* do you know? After all this time?"

"The cyc plant's got about a hundred lockers for any valuable
items or precious metals that turn up while they're harvesting. The
one with the Coyne inside has been earmarked out of use ever
since it was stashed. I put a flag on it to make sure I know if there's
any action—there never has been, it's *never* been opened. It's just
sitting there waiting for the guy who locked it to come back."

"So he just left all that money there for . . . how long?"

"Sixteen years."

"And he doesn't work there now?"

"No."

"So why didn't he take it with him? Even if he couldn't launder
it, wouldn't it have been better to keep it close, hide it under his
bed or something?"

"Coynes are hard to move. If you took it on a flight it'd show up
on a scan and they'd check what was on it. I figure he stole that
money from the company and they were watching him. Even if
he did work out how to launder it, he wouldn't be able to spend
any because that would be *very* conspicuous, so it was a retirement
plan, I think. He intended to go back for it after he left the company, by which time tech would have moved on, and laundering it
would be easier."

Arlo felt himself getting out of his depth with this discussion, so he just nodded. It was strange being talked to as an equal by a nat, and especially one as accomplished as Mia. He'd never had a conversation like it. Even when he'd struck up a rapport with nats while working, the relationship was always soured by him having to try to sell them shit.

"But with the company collapsing," Arlo said, "he's going to go there and get it himself, surely? He's probably on his way there right now, unless—" Oh for fuck's sake. It all fell into place. "It's Joshi Samson, isn't it?"

Mia clapped her hands together twice. "Yes. It's Samson." She turned her head and looked sidelong at Arlo. "You're close to the age he was when I knew him. It's kind of weird meeting you."

Maybe this explained why she treated Arlo more like an equal. "You're probably expecting me to ask you what he was like," he said to her.

She shrugged. "He wasn't the *worst* person I worked with there. Bad at his job, though, *very* bad. Needed to be bailed out all the time. People liked him so he rarely got the blame for anything, but as a colleague he *sucked*."

"I was about to say I'm not interested in him. I don't care."

Mia held up a hand. "Sorry."

"So the eyes you gave me were his, right? Because this locker needs a retina scan?" This was the entire reason eye transplants were routine for mades produced from donor DNA: it meant the donors didn't have to worry about the security implications of there being someone else in the world with the same biometrics as them. Arlo was suddenly very aware of his eyelids sliding across Samson's eyeballs, and felt revolted to have them in his head.

"Yes. When I heard Samson was dying I had to act quickly."

"What happened to him? They told me at the hospital he was in a bad way, but they didn't tell me what was wrong with him—was he ill, or in an accident, or—"

"Oh—*massive* drug overdose. Presumably a reaction to the news about Oakseed going down. A lot of scared people out there. They think he didn't mean it to be fatal, but who knows?"

Arlo couldn't help feeling aggrieved at the idea Samson might have attempted suicide, that Arlo came close to being reaped to save someone who possibly wanted to be dead anyway. He knew that wasn't a fair way to think about suicide, but how he was treated was rarely fair either.

"Personally," said Mia, "I feel sure he wouldn't have killed himself before trying to get that money."

"That does make sense. But wait—just because I've got his eyes, that won't be enough."

"I know."

"I'm sure you do know, you seem very clever, but how—"

"That's why I need more than just you. I'm working on the rest."

SOME SENSE
OF OWNERSHIP

Drienne returned to her bedroll with rations consisting of meat cubes (porkstyle?), potato sauce, and apple, and found Andrée there, glaring sourly at her. Drienne knew she'd spoken to Andrée at some point in the last hour or so, but couldn't remember what she'd said and didn't know exactly what she needed to apologize for.

"Hey," Drienne said, unconvincingly.

"Oh, so you're talking to me now?" said Andrée.

Drienne wanted to ask what she'd said, and disassociate herself from it by making clear that was, in effect, a different person and she wasn't about to say anything like that again. But there was no way of doing this without disclosing her *issues*, and she did not want her *issues* to become known among the temporary population of the gutted Oakseed offices in Lancaster, Pennsylvania. Very soon she would be sold, and if word of her duplisychosis reached the people doing the selling, her destination was likely to become a lot less appealing.

"Sorry about that," Drienne said. "I'm finding this all very stressful."

"So am *I*, but I'm not going around telling people to fuck off."

Oh, was that all it was? That wasn't too bad. She could sort of remember having said it. Memories of her episodes were always like someone showing her a context-free clip of it happening to someone else.

"Sorry," Drienne said again, and was about to attempt an explanation, keeping it vague, alluding to an anxiety problem without actually saying that was what it was. But then she realized it wasn't worth the risk. Even a mild neurological issue would make her less appealing to potential buyers, and ultimately it did not matter if Andrée thought well of her or not. This notion didn't sit well with Drienne but it was undeniable: she and Andrée were unlikely to be in each other's lives for much longer, and in time they would barely remember what passed between them today.

Drienne ate her food, and Andrée did not speak to her.

After she'd eaten, Drienne queued for a shower. The office had staff wetrooms, which was useful, but they were designed to cope with only a handful of people per day, because most employees showered at home. Hundreds and hundreds of people were living here now. Drienne joined a queue that was several dozen long, and when she finally reached the front she was permitted to use the shower for only forty-five seconds—it had been programmed to switch off when her time was up, at which point a securit opened the door and ordered her to vacate the cubicle, affording no respect for the fact she was naked. She got back into the clothes she'd been wearing since her last night of work in Shanghai, which were starting to itch; to her disgust she recalled they still had sweat in them from her attempt to escape the Officials.

When Drienne returned to the open-plan office where her bedroll lay, she became aware the RookDivest reps were moving through the mass of workers, checking identities and leading people away. Which meant it had started. She wasn't surprised: the cost of keeping them all here, where their productivity was zero, must be considerable, and it wasn't clear who was paying the bill. It would ultimately all go on the mades' personal debt ledgers, no doubt, but in the meantime those funds had to come from somewhere. The mades would be off-loaded quickly and any checks on fitness for ownership would be minimal. Drienne felt it pointless trying to resist the onset of another bout of duplisychosis. She might as well surrender herself to the delusions now.

But she managed to hold it together, and they came for her before lunch. One of the RookDivest guys took her metrics, checked them against his records, then told her to follow him. Drienne turned to Andrée and said goodbye.

Andrée nodded and said, "Good luck," which was pretty nice of her, considering.

As Drienne walked alongside the guy from RookDivest she asked, "Have my clothes arrived from Shanghai yet?"

"Nothing's arrived from Shanghai," came the reply.

"Can I have some clean clothes then, please?"

"They're printing some for you now. Have you showered recently?"

"Yes."

They wanted her to look presentable for her new holder. Refurbished goods.

Drienne emerged from the office that was being used as a changing room and was sent to wait at Bay C in the delivery point, where she found only one other person. She'd been expecting to be sold as part of a larger batch—the style of the operation, with remote customers not coming to meet them prior to purchase, seemed geared toward bulk buying. But they were not joined by any others before the car arrived to take them away.

The other person was a small enby, thirtyish years old, stout, and with short light-brown hair, wearing a blank kind of expression. Drienne knew straightaway they were in support, because supports always looked kind of like this. They were supposed to be unobtrusive and self-contained and very patient. They needed to be able to understand tech systems, guide them and adjust them if they went awry, but in practice they spent nearly all their time monitoring those systems and conversing with them to make sure they *weren't* going awry. Drienne once talked to a support who'd told her it was more like being the system's therapist than what IT used to involve. They had to check that the system was clearheaded, its sense of purpose was on track, and it wasn't at risk of becoming a danger to itself or to others.

Drienne introduced herself. The support said their name was Loren Nelsen, and they spelled their first name out, L-O-R-E-N. Drienne wasn't sure if this was because people often got the spelling wrong or if it was some compulsion Loren had. Supports did things like that, they had weird brains. Not that Drienne was disparaging them, she had a weird brain herself.

"Where'd you work?" Drienne asked.

"Wellington," Loren replied. "New Zealand."

Drienne knew Wellington was in New Zealand but she didn't say this. She just nodded and said she'd worked in Shanghai.

"Oh," said Loren. "Big op there. I knew someone who was stationed in Shanghai. Very complicated system apparently, *lot* of overlapping functions."

"Right. I don't know about that stuff."

"No, I know. No one does apart from us. You're a brandie, yeah?"

Drienne laughed.

"What's funny?" said Loren with an entirely straight face. Usually people said that because they were offended by being laughed at, but Loren wasn't: they just didn't know what was funny in this situation, and they wanted to know.

"No one calls us that where I come from," Drienne said.

"Ah."

"I've never heard that before."

"Right. Guess it must sound funny if you've never heard it before."

The car arrived to take them away.

"Did they give you your stuff?" Drienne asked Loren as the car made its way to the port.

"Stuff?"

"Like your personal belongings and stuff. They told me they were going to send mine on after they cleared my apartment."

"Ah, they won't bother doing that."

"I didn't really expect them to," said Drienne, eager not to come across as a naive little baby. She felt sure Loren was much smarter than she was, and didn't want to appear any dumber than necessary. "I had a collection of scented candles I was saving for a special occasion. Wish I'd used them now. I guess you didn't get your stuff either?"

"I didn't have any personal belongings."

"None?"

"No."

"Not even clothes?"

"The farm issued us with clothes, they weren't ours. Any other clothes were, ah, discouraged."

"Wow. I'd hate that."

"Of course you would."

"When I was working I had to wear the new lines, but they still gave me a choice."

"Well, as a brandie you're out there wearing the new stuff and selling it, so you've gotta feel good about wearing the clothes because people respond to that, right?"

"Yeah."

"So the company needs you to feel some sense of ownership about how you look. But it's in your training, isn't it, to feel good about wearing clothes, and to care about it, I bet."

"Oh yeah, that's all true," Drienne said as if it was obvious. But she'd never really thought about it because she assumed everyone felt good about wearing clothes. "I suppose it didn't bother you, wearing whatever clothes you get given."

"Oh, it did bother me. No, didn't like it at all. Dumbest thing is no members of the public ever saw us anyway so we could've worn literally anything. The only people who saw us were each other, could've sat at our stations wearing fucking ball gowns or fetish wear. But of course it wasn't about that, it's just a form of control."

"Huh," said Drienne, feeling chastened even though she didn't think that was Loren's intention.

"I mean this," Loren said, tugging on the lemon-yellow short-sleeved shirt they were wearing, "is the first thing I've worn other than standard-issue hubwear, in, like, literally years; I don't even know when. I don't like the color *at all*, I kind of hate it actually, but it still feels good to be wearing something new."

"So you really didn't have any stuff?"

"Nothing tangible that was *mine*. I had a great box of bits, though."

"Bits?"

"Yeah, you know—little components and fixings, things I'd salvaged from stuff that was broken. I put 'em all in a box that had all these compartments. Some people thought it was daft, when I could just go and print a new one off, but ninety percent of the time I could get my hands on any bit I needed in a couple of seconds and it was more economical, and I found that very satisfying." They nodded to themself. "Not that anyone ever thanked me for it. Anyway, the bits didn't belong to me. I just collected them. And probably they wouldn't be compatible with whatever they've got wherever we're going."

"Where do you think we *are* going?"

"Fuck knows."

It was a fair comment. If they were going to the same place, Drienne couldn't imagine who would buy herself and Loren and *no one* else. What *for*?

8

THE SHOPPING LIST

Arlo was staring at a cluster of windows Mia had brought up, which hovered at different levels over her desk. Each of them displayed some part of the live catalog of Oakseed's retained mades, across various categories. Arlo found it dizzying. He could see the sales being agreed, people blinking out of every window as he watched, being purchased and assigned new lives.

When Mia had opened these windows an hour ago, her top priority was to find a support who'd be able to work with the systems at the cyc plant they were targeting. Arlo's top priority was to find Drienne and convince Mia to acquire her for the team. For all he knew Drienne might already have been sold. If that was the case, he vowed he would track her down when all this was over and use his share of the money to buy her out of wherever she'd ended up. And then lib her, obviously.

"Is it okay if I look up a friend of mine?" Arlo had asked as casually as he could manage. "See if she's still available?"

He'd expected Mia to question why, if she didn't simply refuse. But she asked, "What's her name?"

"Drienne Adams."

"And her work code? If you know it."

Of course Arlo knew it—he could fill in any form that required Drienne's personal details, and she could do the same for him, and they had both done so many times, often committing minor fraud in the process. A window picked up the code as Arlo spoke it, and Mia dragged it over to another window. Drienne's image appeared in this window, dressed in default clothes she would absolutely never wear. There was an option to change the clothes or remove them entirely, if you were interested to know what she looked like naked. Next to the image was a bullet-point biography and a list of her skills. According to the shipping information she was located in Lancaster, Pennsylvania, which seemed bizarre and Arlo wondered if they'd got it wrong somehow.

She might be snapped up at any moment, and Arlo had no idea how to make Mia buy her. How would she fit into the plan?

"Okay," Mia said thoughtfully, reading Drienne's sales info. "Yeah, this could work—trained in brand policing, it says here." She waved a finger at the window.

"Yes," said Arlo. If he was honest they didn't do much of that, because Oakseed fitted their slates with software that automatically checked for brand violations and could usually fix them. But the brand ambassadors did have training to cope with violations beyond the software's capabilities, and Arlo was more than happy to make out Drienne as ideal.

"You know her, you say?" Mia asked him.

"We were partners the whole time we were in Shanghai."

Mia stared at the window and tapped her fingernails on her teeth. "I'll need you to pose as colleagues, so that could be really helpful. And you can vouch for her? She's good?"

"She's great," Arlo said, not entirely sure what he was claiming she was great *at*.

"And would she cause trouble? I know some of you go all in on company loyalty, think of it like family and so on, and would find it hard to go against—"

"*God* no. Honestly, I think a heist would be exactly her vibe."

"Very good." Mia added Drienne to her basket. A window appeared and told her that transport for her purchase would be cheaper if she bought a greater quantity. It recommended a minimum of eight, and made a number of suggestions based on her interest in Drienne. Arlo recognized several of them from Shaw Apartments. One of them, Roman, he'd had a brief, listless affair with shortly after moving in, and they'd hooked up a few other times when they were bored and/or drunk. Roman had a strong dislike for Drienne: The summer before last, she stole a Brand Ambassador of the Week trophy he'd won and never gave it back. It briefly crossed his mind he could try to save Roman, make the case for him being added to the team, but did he care enough?

Mia tutted at the window, said "No," and it closed. "See, it's going to assume I'm buying them for business purposes and therefore I'll need the same type or complementary types and that's exactly what I *don't* need."

Well. Bye, Roman. Hope you land somewhere soft.

"*But* I'm sure I can find a support from the same location, you can always find a support . . ." Mia set up some parameters, quickly found a support she seemed happy with, and added them to the basket. She looked for more workers at the Pennsylvania site, but didn't seem able to find anything that suited. She asked Arlo if he wouldn't mind getting them both a drink from her fridge, and he didn't mind, so he did it. When he returned and handed her the drink she was still listlessly scrolling through mades. He glanced at the basket and noted the workers Mia had chosen, including Drienne, would be released back into the pool in less than three minutes unless she checked out. He pointed this out to her.

"Yes, I *know*," she replied with irritation.

"Sorry." That was the first time she'd spoken to him unkindly since his arrival, and he didn't want it to happen again.

Mia reset her parameters and searched again, twice. Then, as the clock on the basket ticked down to under a minute, she tutted and authorized it to check out, and Arlo could breathe again.

"How many more people do you need?" he asked.

"I don't want the team to be *too* big," said Mia. "Partly for budgetary reasons, but also the more moving parts there are in any machine, the more there is to go wrong, you know?"

"Makes sense."

"So if we can double up on skills anywhere, that would be really helpful."

"Yeah. I mean, mades *are* pretty specialized, though."

"I suppose you are."

"And we don't really develop other skills off our own bat because we've got no control over whether we get to use them. I mean, *some* of us have hobbies, but . . ." He'd never had to explain this to anyone: people either lived like he did and understood, or they didn't care. "We tend to do useless things in our downtime."

"How do you mean?"

"All kinds of things—games and puzzles obviously but also mathematics, hand-coloring images, bird-spotting, cataloging stuff no one cares about. Almost everyone I know does it. We spend so much of our lives being useful—"

"Spending your time uselessly is a sort of act of resistance."

"Yes."

"Do you?"

"I like to bake. Pastries and stuff."

"Are you good at it?"

"I'm okay. I've only ever had cheap ingredients, but I always get edible results."

"Interesting." Mia turned her attention back to the windows. "I can't believe they didn't have any muscle at that location," she grumbled. "Where's all the muscle?"

"Maybe they're still using all the securits to guard the sites they've got left."

"Yes, maybe." Mia shifted to another window and broadened her search to all sites. Arlo wondered what conditions the mades were being kept in at these places. He imagined them all being stored on racks, like a capsule hotel, though he knew it wouldn't be like that.

"There!" said Mia. "They have some securits in Montevideo. Fuck, that's the resort. They're using the xec resort for storage! *Ha!*" Mia quickly found a securit she liked and bagged her before anyone else did, then she actually checked the worker's details. "What do you think?"

Arlo attempted to form an opinion, but the worker looked like any other securit—tall, powerfully built, humorless. "Yeah. I mean, I always think securits are going to be more company-loyal than anyone else. But I might be wrong, probably they'll do whatever you want if it means they get a chance to punch somebody."

"I don't want them to punch anybody if possible, the idea is you get in and out without anyone ever knowing anything was stolen. No one but us knows there's anything to steal. That's what makes this so perfect."

When she talked like this, Arlo felt there was no possibility they could fail. He didn't know if he should be worried by that.

9

THINGS WOULD HAPPEN BECAUSE SHE WAS HERE

Loren always knew they'd miss the routine when it was gone. It was not the same as missing the company. Some of Loren's former colleagues had always insisted it was foolish to resent Oakseed, because without the company, they would never have been created; that they ought to accept the life the company allocated them because it was the entire reason for their existence. And okay, that was true up to a *point*. But it displayed a total ignorance of human affairs and/or a desperate need to make their situation palatable. A parent who produced a child just so they could brutalize it did not deserve love from that child, and would have no defense in the eyes of the law.

Loren didn't view this "abused child" example as a direct analogy with their own situation, just as a means of proving the fallacy of the argument. Oakseed did not treat them as it did for its own gratification, but for profit. It limited their freedom of expression because doing so made them easier to deal with. Loren had always wanted to be free of the routine, but ultimately they had been engineered to *like* the routine, find it reassuring, and enjoy its repetitious nature without ever becoming bored. Their brain had been shaped to be restless and anxious without the routine. It made them reluctant to stop work at the end of a shift, and drove them to log overtime for which they received no extra pay.

Right now, sitting on the flight to Vancouver, Loren wanted—on a gut level—to have their old life back. They experienced their removal from the workplace as a profound wrongness, a distressing absence. But they did not confuse this with liking their old life or the company to which they formerly belonged, because they knew the company had made them like this on purpose. Loren was good at separating how they felt from what they thought, but man, it wasn't *good* for you to feel like this. It made you feel like you were two people: one who did the work and felt good about it, and another one sitting on your shoulder thinking *Fuck, look at that loser who's happy doing this shit.*

Loren's new holder would assign them a new job with its own routine, because that was the kind of worker they were and it would make no sense to obtain them and not give them a routine. They didn't know how they felt about that yet. Hopefully it would be better? But Loren found it unlikely it would liberate their other self, the one they tried to dress up as. The routine was a set of sturdy ropes that bound the other self.

Drienne was telling Loren tales of when she worked in Shanghai and the partner she'd had there. The stories varied in how interesting or funny they were, but the sound of Drienne's voice was a good distraction and helped stop Loren from thinking about the old routine.

"My god," said Drienne as the forest at the edge of the city came into view through the car's windshield.

"You never seen a forest before?" asked Loren.

"Not for a long time. We don't get to travel out to low-density areas. No one to sell shit to in a forest."

Loren had been lucky enough to live in Wellington, where a reasonable amount of woodland survived, and they had sometimes ventured out into it, but usually only when a remote relay needed attention. People who only ever got to see the scorched landscapes that surrounded so many of the world's urban sprawls might have felt jealous of Loren having access to leafy green space, and felt perplexed they made no use of it. Back then Loren had liked the forest well enough, but going too far from the IM farm made them uncomfortable to the point they couldn't enjoy it. But now it was different. Loren didn't have that sense they were meant to be somewhere else. And as the car drove along the avenue leading up to the apartments, the forest filled the view ahead, a surge of rich dark green, and an unfamiliar sense of calm came over Loren. It might be nice, they thought, to be in the middle of the forest. Even though there would be nothing for them to do there, no routine, it might still be nice.

It might—and this thought struggled a little as it pushed its way to the front of their consciousness—be nice *because* there would be nothing for them to do there.

Then the car turned again and all they could see was the inside of the block's parking garage. The car unlocked its doors, Loren and Drienne got out, and a really classy-looking, gorgeous woman was standing there, welcoming them. The woman introduced herself as Mia Ostrander and she knew Loren's and Drienne's names, because she was their new holder. "I'm so glad you're both here," she said. "This is so exciting. I think you'll be excited too when you hear what I want you to do."

Loren already did feel excited. Mia's presence apparently had that effect: you felt like things would happen because she was here. They went up to Mia's apartment, which was not what Loren had expected to happen. They could imagine Drienne being purchased as live-in staff—women like that were often retained as nannies and companions and housemaids, but surely no one would want Loren around their home. And the apartment, though plush and spacious, seemed like it would be crowded if it had more than a couple of people living here.

As Loren looked around the apartment, they became aware Drienne was speaking in a shrill voice, apparently overcome with emotion, and this seemed to be a reaction to the other person in the apartment who wasn't Mia. Loren caught his name, Arlo, and they recalled this was the name of Drienne's partner from Shanghai.

"*What the fuck*, I thought you were *dead*!" Drienne was saying. She hadn't mentioned that part when she'd spoken about him on the flight. "Wait, why are your eyes brown now?"

Arlo explained why he wasn't dead, and at first Loren thought this wasn't something they needed to know about, but they quickly became very interested indeed in his story of how he'd been taken away to be reaped at the very moment the company's collapse was declared, and now he was here drinking good coffee in Vancouver while his xec donor lay dead in Shanghai.

"That's the best story I've ever heard," said Loren, smiling.

"Thanks," said Arlo and went right back to speaking to Drienne. He and Drienne looked so *right* together. They were completely caught up in talking about what had happened to them both in the days since Oakseed collapsed, and Loren and Mia found themselves united in exclusion.

"Can I get you a drink?" asked Mia.

"A beer?" Loren asked. "Is a beer out of the question?"

Mia smiled. "Of course not." And she went and got it herself, as if Loren was a guest and not someone she had full contractual rights to. This all felt deeply odd. It was like this woman wanted to have a party, a small informal gathering of friends, but she didn't have any friends so she'd bought some.

Mia returned with a can of beer, a brand Loren was only aware of because Oakseed sold it and carried advertising for it on its entertainment networks, and Loren had once resolved a context issue with those ads. The ads were never shown in their own feed, as they were not the target market for it. It was absolutely delicious.

"I'm *very* glad we found you," Mia said. "I think you're going to be ideal."

"Okay, thanks," said Loren.

"Yes—I know the profiles in the catalog are probably a little exaggerated, but yours said you actually know how Oakseed's systems *work*. Like, not just what they do and how to use them, but you understand the code."

Loren nodded. They felt surprised this information had made it to the catalog. Everything they did at work was monitored in every detail, but the workplace vibe was always that no one paid much attention to this data unless you fucked up, so it had never occurred to Loren that HR had any sense of who they actually *were*. "Yeah. I mean not *everything*, you must know how complex it is—"

"Mm. Of course."

"But yeah, I like getting stuck into code." Most people in their line of work neither knew nor cared how the code worked—for them, the job was done entirely through explaining to the system what they needed it to do, and refining these processes through observation and feedback. Loren also did this, but they liked making it cleaner and simpler, and that meant going into the code. Systems had a tendency to sprawl as they evolved, adding new code instead of finding ways to make the existing code do new things. The more code there was, the more of it there was to go wrong, and the more you had to plow through in search of the part that had gone wrong—which caused a lot of headaches when the system refused to recognize something was wrong with itself. So Loren would get in there and find out what was changing and how it worked on a nuts-and-bolts level. There was too much code in even the most basic program for anyone to hold more than a fraction of it in their head, but the trick was to find the fraction that mattered.

"Good," Mia said. "I've got some tools you'll really enjoy using for this. I was very lucky to find you. I can't *believe* how cheap you were."

Loren wasn't sure if this was a compliment, or if it was intended to be, so they just nodded and shrugged. "So what's the work? I mean, it's not located here, is it?"

"No, no." Mia turned to Drienne and Arlo, who were still oc-cupied with each other. "I'll let them catch up, but I'm sure you're impatient to know so I'll explain to you now and talk to her when she's done."

And Mia explained.

Loren blinked. "Well that's interesting."

"Is it?"

"It's certainly not boring."

"Because the only one who doesn't have a choice in this is Arlo. He's irreplaceable. I can *force* you to do it, of course, but I don't want anyone on this team who's going to choke or screw it up. Are you going to choke or screw it up?"

Loren considered. "I don't think so, no."

"You're sure?"

"What's the alternative?"

"I send you back for a refund and buy someone else."

"And I get sold to someone else. I mean, the prospects for that aren't great."

"No. The main buyers at the moment are plastic dredgers."

Yeah, that made sense. The people who did that shit kept drowning.

Mia put her hand on Loren's shoulder. The base of Mia's hand rested on Loren's collarbone while her fingertips sat comfortably on the top of their shoulder blade. It felt comforting, reassuring. "You do this job, you get a cut of the money. I very much doubt anyone will offer you that."

"No. But we're taking a big risk, right?"

"I don't think so. Not if you stick to the plan."

"But c'mon. My entire job is plugging holes and fixing bugs, I *know* nothing's infallible. And if we get caught, we're screwed, and I assume *you* will disown us and say we went rogue."

Mia gave a rueful smile. Her hand was off Loren's shoulder by now. "Well, yes. I'm using you because you have the skills I need, but I also want to maintain some distance from the operation."

"And if we try to run off with it, you tell the cops we stole it from *you*? Yeah?"

"I hadn't thought about it that far—"

Loren heard this but did not believe it. "You can tell them anything. 'Course they'd believe your word over ours."

"The thing is," Mia continued, "I don't think you'll steal the money from me. Firstly you'd have to decrypt and launder it—"

"Yeah, I reckon I could work out how to do that. If I wanted to."

Mia smirked and inclined her head slightly. "You probably could. But if you do this job, and you succeed, not only do you get a cut of the money, but I'll cancel your debt."

Loren's eyebrows raised. "Seriously?"

"You have my word."

Loren shook their head and laughed—or at least, it was their version of a laugh. To others it just looked like they were grinning and making a clicking noise with their throat. "Fuck. You know we can't turn that down." No more routine. They could set their *own* routine, if they wanted to.

"Look, I get it," said Mia. "I'm doing all this to buy back the rights to my *soul*, basically. I'd pay anything for it, although"—and here she went sotto voce, speaking out of the side of her mouth— "don't *tell* anyone that, they'll only put the price up."

Loren smiled and nodded. Even if Mia was lying. Even if she was going to take all the money and refuse to lib them and laugh in their faces. They still couldn't turn it down if there was even a chance she was on the level. Otherwise, they'd spend their life wondering if they could've been free, if they'd only had the guts to do this thing.

"So," said Mia, "you're in?"

"Fuck it. Yes."

"Great. So, opinions on the plan? I've been working on it for years, though I had to adapt it to the current situation—"

"You really want my opinion?"

"Of course. Your experience of Oakseed is much more up to date than mine."

"You need another guy."

"For what?"

"You need to fake the brandies' accreditation so they can get in, and you need to monkey around with the workings of the plant, yeah?"

"Yes."

"You need an HR guy. They'll be cheap, they're usually public facers who've been moved inside after getting too old for floor work, and they're mostly valuable for their knowledge of Oakseed operations and specific workplace dynamics, which is all useless now."

Mia smiled. "I'm going to fill Drienne in on the plan, and then you can help me buy one."

10

SECRETLY FRENCH

Education at the Oakseed nurseries had been selective, of course. But outsiders often had mistaken ideas about what the mades were told and what they weren't. For instance, people were often surprised the mades had been taught about slavery. It was important, Arlo had been told at his nursery, that the mades should understand their own situation was very different from the past victims of slavery, especially under the Atlantic slave trade, which had been a racist endeavor, whereas no such consideration entered into how the mades were treated.

The important distinctions were that the mades had been created, rather than having their freedom taken away, and that their legal status was very different because of the debt system. Each made carried with them the debt incurred by their creation and upbringing, and when it was paid off they were free. (Arlo later learned this used to be called indentured servitude, back when it was legal for nats. Oakseed hadn't taught him about that.) Arlo's nursery was sometimes visited by mades who'd paid off their debt, who would talk to the younger ones about how they'd done it. You couldn't even be reaped if your debt was paid—your donor lost their rights. You really were free.

But the debt was *so* high. You needed to regularly pull in high levels of commission and be very frugal with your outgoings to have any hope of paying it off. The accounting system was opaque, and it was common for those making good progress toward settling their debt to find surprisingly high charges added to their account for things like medical treatment or legal costs. Drienne had always told Arlo it was futile trying to pay it off, they weren't meant to ever pay it off, and you'd live a happier life if you gave up on the notion you might. She was adamant the few who'd paid it off had only been allowed to do so to give the rest of them false hope, and to encourage them to work harder. Arlo thought she was probably right.

Even so, Arlo agreed with what the nursery said about slavery: the mades' situation *was* different. But at the same time it seemed revealing how the company took such pains to make this clear, rather than assuming it was obvious.

"There's something she isn't telling us," Drienne said to Arlo as they sat on Mia's balcony and looked out across the forest. It was a warm early evening and the light rain was turning heavy, pattering on the leaves.

Arlo told her to keep her voice down.

Drienne glanced inside, where Mia had several windows open on her desktop and was conversing with Loren about something. "She's not listening. Anyway, so what if she is?"

"She might not appreciate it, dear."

"So what if she doesn't?" Drienne held the margarita she'd made herself in Mia's kitchen, running her finger around the rim of the glass. "She's bought us to do this job, she *needs* us to do it, she doesn't have to *like* us."

"It might help if she *does* like us, I mean she has promised to cancel our—"

"Yeah, I'll believe we're getting libbed when it happens."

"I know we don't have any guarantees—"

"She might just sell us on."

"Yes, I know."

"If she screws us over, who would we complain to? We committed a crime for her and now we go to arbitration to get what we were promised?"

"Yes, I *know*. But that's exactly my point—we don't have any guarantees, so we should stay in her good books. And we can't steal the money and use it to pay off our debt because *she's* the one we'd have to pay it to, and—"

"*Yes*, I know how it works, Arlo."

"I just wanted to make sure—"

"I still think I'm right, though."

"About what?"

Drienne leaned over and said in a stage whisper, "About her not telling us everything."

"I mean, maybe not. But if we do the job there's a chance we get the big prize. If she screws us over, we haven't lost anything."

"There is the third option, where we fuck this up and get caught."

"Yes, I know—"

"She seems very confident in her plan, but we have no experience in this and there's a *lot* that can go wrong."

"Yes—but come on, we could have ended up somewhere a lot worse. I was the one who got you here instead of working clean-up in the scorched zones, or in some zillionaire's sex dungeon pumped full of hormones so you can be his hucow or something—"

"Yes, yes, this is better than either of those options, thank you for saving me from a terrible fate."

"I thought you'd be up for it."

"I am, I am. If you'd given me the choice between this and some other crap, even just going back to being a brand ambassador, I'd have taken it. Sorry if I seem *ungrateful*."

Arlo sniffed and looked out at the forest. "I don't ever want to end up like I was at the hospital. I got away by the skin of my fucking teeth."

"I know."

"I was *this close* and I got out and I'd do anything to stop it happening again."

"Well, if Mia needs spare parts, she's probably going to take them from me rather than you."

"If this job doesn't come off, Mia's not going to keep us. She'll sell us and then we could end up anywhere. We're certainly not getting libbed. So I'm not doing *anything* to risk fucking it up."

Drienne nodded, swallowed, and looked at the floor. "After they took you, all I could think about was how awful it must be. I couldn't even talk too much about it because I was afraid I might disassociate and . . ." Drienne shook her head and sipped at her margarita. "Did you tell her about my—"

"Issues?"

"My duplisychosis, yes."

"No."

"Hmm."

"She doesn't need to know. Anyway, you'll be fine. I'll be with you."

Drienne sighed. "I had an episode this morning, in the place where they put us. Was that today? I lose track. Anyway."

"What happened?"

She shrugged. "Not much. Told a woman to fuck off. All the notes I had on my slate had been wiped, so I started making new ones. I thought my name was Eugénie, apparently."

"Eugénie?"

"Yeah. It's never been Eugénie, before has it?"

"No, it used to be Sandrine."

"Why do I always think I'm secretly French? What's *that* about? At least I didn't try to do the accent this time." She considered for a moment. "Well. If I did, no one mentioned it."

"Anything else?"

"Just the usual fantasies about being from some rich family who live in a big house and have never stopped wondering what really happened to me, hoping I might still be out there somewhere. Nothing in the way of specific details."

"Maybe now you could get some medication for it, finally."

"Maybe." She'd never sought treatment for fear of being removed from floor work. She didn't even dare look up anything about it, in case HR flagged it and sent her for tests and it ended up on her record. So she knew nothing about handling her condition except what she'd learned through living with it. "After all this is done, yeah. It'd be nice not to forget who I am anymore."

Arlo awoke early the next morning (his body clock was all over the place) in one of the apartment's spare rooms, in a bed he was sharing with Drienne. He heard voices, and got up to discover the next member of the crew had arrived: the securit he'd watched Mia purchase. It was hardwired into Arlo to avoid the attention of securits, and ideally prevent them knowing he existed. He did not want to share a space with one, let alone work with one.

Her name was Nadi Kayal, and she conformed to the usual template: tall, heavyset, muscular, unsettling. She was about Arlo's age, he knew that because he'd seen her profile. She spoke fluent English and German but her accent sounded Middle Eastern. She seemed remarkably relaxed about everything, and absorbed Mia's explanation of what she wanted them to do with minimal comment. Perhaps, when you have no imagination, you become used to accepting everything at face value.

Mia said she'd brief them on the plan in more detail after the last guy arrived, and she asked Arlo and Nadi to help her assemble some extra beds they could put in her office and home gym. While the components were printing, he and Nadi moved the gym equipment to one side of the room to create some space.

"So, where you from?" said Nadi brightly as she and Arlo lifted a rowing machine.

"England. But most recently I was in Shanghai."

"Ah! What was that like?"

"Okay, I guess," said Arlo, trying to keep up with Nadi; her feet easily moved across the floor while he needed to rebalance himself with each step. "It's, er, lively. Can you slow down, please?"

"Sorry. Is that better?"

"Yes."

"I worked the Frankfurt site."

"Right." Arlo didn't know what else to say. "Did you like it?"

She shrugged. "It was . . . I didn't like anyone, really? Kind of strange I won't be going there anymore, or seeing any of those people. But I don't care. What do you think of this thing Mia wants us to do?"

"It'll be great if we can pull it off."

"*Right?*" said Nadi, turning to him and grinning broadly. It made her look like a shark. "We might get *libbed*, guy. We lucked out!" She held up a fist for Arlo to bump. He awkwardly returned the gesture.

"Like I said, *if* we pull it off." Arlo felt concerned Nadi hadn't considered the possibility they might fail. Ever since his conversation with Drienne, it was playing on his mind more and more. "I hadn't expected you to be excited about having to do a heist."

"Why not?"

"Just. Y'know. Normally you enforce rules, instead of breaking them."

Nadi shrugged. "The only law that matters for you and me is what our holder wants. What Oakseed wanted wasn't always legal."

This was a good point. "Yeah, but. We won't have Oakseed backing us up. I mean, if we get caught we're fucked."

"Yeah."

"I mean *really* fucked."

"Sure. But it's just one job, that's all we got to do. Which is better than I expected when I got put up for sale."

"I expected your sort would get bought by police, or something."

Nadi shook her head. "Rank-and-file cops *hate* us. We're always getting in their way. No one wants to work with a securit from the megas. Corps got more than they need."

"Military?"

"Not state military, probably a private militia, probably cannon fodder, sent out to the Taymyr Peninsula or somewhere. Or a criminal gang. Dirty deeds done dirt cheap. But *this*—" Nadi whistled.

"Risky, but less risky than I was expecting and *much* more reward-ing. Sorry, probably you were expecting something easier."

Arlo was still trying to come to terms with a securit just shooting the breeze with him. It felt like a trick, her saying everyone com-mits a few crimes from time to time, right? His instinct was she was trying to get him to incriminate himself.

They collected a batch of the parts Mia had printed off, took them to the gym, and started slotting them together. Nadi talked about how insane it was that Oakseed could collapse, and shared with Arlo a theory she'd developed about what was really behind it, that it was all a plot to shrug off the company's debts and unwanted commitments, and the profitable parts would be brought back to-gether under a new banner, apparently under new ownership but not really. "'Course I don't have any evidence for that," she cheer-fully concluded. "But it makes more sense to me than that thing about the company's systems all going to war with each other and destroying it from within."

"What?"

"Oh yeah. That's what everyone's saying."

"That's stupid."

Nadi shrugged. "I don't know anything about systems."

"Why do people find it so hard to believe the company just failed?" said Arlo, sounding more exasperated than he intended, like he hadn't found it hard to believe too. "Anything can fail. Even with fingers in five hundred different pies and systems dynamically adjusting every decision made at every level, someone can still fuck up and commit too much here or there and the whole thing crum-bles out from under you."

"Yeah," said Nadi. "But life goes on."

"Ideally, yes."

The last one arrived midmorning. His name was Kline Farrar. Drienne hadn't encountered a lot of HR guys—mades never had to talk to anyone about contracts or promotions or their rights as employees—and she saw in him a glimpse of the future she and Arlo could have expected at Oakseed. She could tell he'd been a brand ambassador before he'd been moved indoors—he did the walk, the confident one that drew people's eye to you, and he held himself to show off his clothes to their best advantage, even though he was just wearing a cheap brown suit. He didn't hunch or shrink in on himself, he leaned back a little and held his limbs in an open way. This stuff was drilled into you, it never left.

Kline looked to be in his midforties but Drienne knew that was impossible, because Oakseed hadn't been cloning that long. He was probably in his late thirties . . . which would make him part of the original wave. Wow. Drienne hadn't met a lot of originals. She felt impressed.

A lot of the first-wavers looked older than they were, they'd started aging faster in their midthirties. This was thought to be a flaw in the process that had since been ironed out, but someone once told Drienne it was built in deliberately—no one wanted to support them in their old age, so they were engineered not to have one. Drienne didn't know if it would happen to her or not. Kline was still handsome, with a compact, friendly face and swept-back hair, and Drienne would fuck him if she was in the mood and there was no one else available, though he was probably more Arlo's type. It was a shame Kline hadn't been kept out there to sell shit to old ladies. They'd fucking love him. But the company always maintained the older generation didn't respond to brand ambassadors and face-to-face, they'd grown up back in the social media era and you needed to get inside their heads a different way.

Mia took Kline into her kitchen to get him a drink and explain what he was required to do. When he came out of the kitchen he looked nervy and unwell, so Drienne came over and introduced herself. Mia had already introduced the whole group to Kline when he walked into the apartment, but Drienne was sure he wouldn't remember her name. She was mistaken: he did remember.

"I'm an HR guy," he said. "I remember names."

"Oh! I kind of assumed we were all just an anonymous mass to you."

Kline looked at her askance and lowered his voice. "She's brought us all here to steal a hundred million dollars or whatever it is? What the fuck?"

"It's not what I expected either."

"*I* expected to end up doing tedious micronegotiations in local government somewhere—"

"It could be a lot worse."

"They'll have us all *liquidated* if they catch us. She'll say we all went rogue and planned this ourselves. I've dealt with rogue cases. *No one* is buying a made who did that. They will get rid of us."

Drienne knew he was right. But she was committed now, she and Arlo. He needed his debt canned and she was going to make sure they both got that.

"Look," said Drienne, pulling Kline toward the wall, "you can make out to her you've got too much hardwired company loyalty or whatever, or you're just too much of a pussy—I say that without judgment, some of my favorite people are pussies—and she'll send you back for a refund and buy someone else. So you do, in fact, have a choice, right? To an extent."

"Right."

"But what she's offering if we do this? If we pull this off?"

"Yes."

"It's kinda worth it, don't you think?"

Kline breathed in. "I knew it wasn't going to be micronegotiations in local government, not really. Like, I didn't expect *this*, but . . . when I saw my price I knew it wasn't going to be good. Fuck." Then he nodded. "It *is* worth it."

Drienne had been on the verge of pointing out he might not have long left anyway, so may as well go for broke, but it was good she hadn't said that, it might easily have backfired.

ANY QUESTIONS?

Loren had slept for ages, and was still half asleep when they shuffled back into Mia's living room and found a heart-stoppingly beautiful woman standing there. She was tall and powerful and had eyes like dark honey. She introduced herself as Nadi and shook Loren's hand, and Loren wished they'd gone to the bathroom, freshened up, and checked their hair before coming out here.

Loren hadn't interacted much with securits. The IM farm had a cohort of them, but their focus had always been on potential saboteurs and espionage, rather than problems among the workforce. Loren had barely noticed them. They'd have noticed this one.

The two of them exchanged the usual information: where were you sited, what was your role (as if it wasn't obvious), where did they stick you before selling you, where were you when you heard the company had gone down. While they ran through this stuff, Loren tried to think of something else to keep the conversation going, something that wasn't boring.

Nadi finished explaining how she'd been sent via the resort in Montevideo, and the conversation fell dead. Nadi smiled slightly and glanced around the room.

"You been to Vancouver before?" Loren asked. Considering they were so unaccustomed to small talk, coming up with this question seemed a minor triumph.

"No, until a few days ago I'd never gone west of Strasbourg."

"Same. I mean, not with the specific geography, but I never got to go anywhere either."

"It's big, right? Vancouver, I mean."

"I *know*. There's a huge park across the bay, I might go down there if there's time before—"

Mia called their names. She wanted them all to gather around her antique twentieth-c-modern Brazilian rosewood dining table while she detailed the plan in full.

Mia stood at the head of the table and explained it all with such clarity and confidence, it sounded like the operation couldn't possibly fail. But a few aspects of it nagged at Loren. They didn't like how convoluted it was to get the device inside the cyc plant, and when Mia asked if there were any questions, Loren asked if there wasn't an easier way of doing it.

"You can't just walk in with a device like that," Mia said. "You can't just walk in with *anything*. They're very particular about that."

"Can't we target it from outside the building?" said Arlo.

"Nope," said Loren. "Buildings all have shielding against those kinds of attack. Even old ones like that will have it. You have to get inside and as close as you can."

"Exactly," said Mia. "Believe me, I have thought a *lot* about this, and it really is the only way."

Kline raised the question of whether anyone at the plant might recognize Arlo as a clone of someone who formerly worked there.

"That's a good question," Mia said. "But everyone who was there at the same time as Samson has long since moved on. And there certainly won't be any pictures of him on the walls to commemorate what a valued employee he was."

Arlo, Drienne, and Kline laughed at this.

"I still feel," said Loren, "like the process of getting the device in there is kind of tricky?"

"It's as simple as I can make it," said Mia.

"I'm not saying it's trickier than it needs to be, just there are several points where things could go wrong."

"What do you suggest?"

"I dunno, I'm just raising the concern now because . . . it seems like the moment to raise concerns. There's stuff we can't control that depends on the circumstances on the day. And then Arlo's got to reach the locker without being seen—"

"Not necessarily," said Arlo. "Whether I'm seen isn't the main thing, it's whether I'm seen as *suspicious*."

"Which brings me to *another* thing, which is Arlo, Kline, and Nadi have to not get found out and keep their stories and identities straight until we get clear of the place."

"Yes," said Mia. "What's your question?"

"I guess I don't have one, I just wanted to offer them as points for discussion."

"Okay," Mia said. "Let's discuss those points." She looked across the crew. "Anyone want to jump in?"

No one spoke for a moment, and Loren suddenly felt like they'd done something wrong.

Then, Nadi said, "Yeah I . . . I don't know how I'll be at pretending to be someone else, I haven't really had to do that before."

"Yours is the easiest," said Mia. "You just have to lie about your name and where you come from. In all other respects you can just be you—say you're an Oakseed securit who's been transferred to the plant."

"But why would she be transferred to the plant?" asked Loren.

Mia winced and held up a hand. "You're really overestimating how many questions people will ask. They accept company decisions there. It's not worth anyone's while to care."

"Mia does know the plant," said Arlo, "and we don't, so maybe we should trust what she's telling us about what it's like?"

Loren wanted to point out that Mia's experience was outdated, as she'd admitted herself, but instead they looked to Arlo and Drienne. "And you're okay with what you're being asked to do?"

Arlo and Drienne glanced at each other briefly. "Yeah, sure," said Drienne. "We bullshit people every goddamn day, it's like breathing to us." She turned to Mia and winked.

"Good," said Mia. "Anyone else want to comment? Or can we move on?"

Loren decided to stay quiet for the rest of the meeting, in case they found themself returned for a refund. But Mia wouldn't do that now, would she? Not now that Loren had heard the plan.

"I know how Samson set the Coyne up because I saw it," Mia said. "It'll appear to only contain a much smaller amount of money in the local currency. That's what they call a false tray. It's a deflection tactic to stop people looking too closely. The more important contents are encrypted. It's *very* important you leave the tray as it is, because if you're found carrying the Coyne and someone checks what's on it, it'll be much less suspicious. And also, it means we can be sure the real contents are just as Samson left them and no one's skimmed anything off the top. Anyone who lifts the tray will forfeit their share. Okay?"

Everyone murmured in the affirmative.

"I'll be asking each of you to repeat the plan back to me, step by step, at least a couple of times before you leave. No one writes down or records any detail of the plan, yes?"

Everyone assented to this as well.

"I mean," said Loren, breaking their vow not to speak, "if anyone forgets any details, they can always ask me. I remember everything."

"I'm sure that will come in handy," said Mia.

After the briefing was over, Nadi sought Loren out to apologize. She found them sitting on the balcony.

"Apologize for what?" said Loren with a twitch of their head.

"I tried to, I dunno, help you out, I guess."

"When Mia said let's discuss the points I raised?"

"Yeah."

"Why are you apologizing? You're the only one who said anything."

"Yeah, I don't think it helped. It just made me look kind of stupid."

"I don't think it made you look stupid. I also don't think it helped. But that's not your fault. I appreciated it."

"Good."

Loren looked out across the treetops. "She's got a classic tech mentality. See it all the time in xecs in my area. Thinks you just need to get people with different skills together and give them the right leadership and it all happens. Don't like it when you bring them problems, or say you're not sure you can do what they're asking you to do."

"I think I probably can do it."

Loren smiled at Nadi. "I bet you can. I think I can do my bit too. There's just a lot of, you know, variables."

Nadi nodded. "Variables is something I know about."

"'Course, yeah. You want a drink?"

There was something Nadi hadn't said to Arlo when they spoke before, because she was afraid it sounded dumb. A reason she felt glad she'd been bought for this job instead of being part of another muscle squad: She was getting to work with people who weren't securits, and already she was realizing just how deeply unhappy she'd been for years and years, having to fit in with them, not even considering she could be any other way. She felt like she'd surfaced from being deep underwater, and if they pulled off this job, she could spend the rest of her life breathing fresh air.

12

A CROSS BETWEEN A TRASH FIRE AND A TOXIC SWAMP, LITERALLY

"Are you looking forward to seeing England again?" Mia said to Arlo, just after Loren had gone to catch their flight. It was just the three of them now, and Arlo was pulling on his shoes while Drienne lay on Mia's sofa, blowing on her fingernails to make the coat of Naildit dry. They were both dressed in the muted style of house staff, so as to appear less conspicuous as they came and went from Mia's apartment. They'd chuckled when they'd first donned the short-sleeved, high-collared shirts and loose, pocket-heavy pants.

"We won't be going anyplace I ever knew," said Arlo.

"No, but it'll still be familiar," said Mia. "Won't it?"

"When I lived there, I spent all my time at the nursery, which was just like an Oakseed nursery anywhere else except most of the staff had English accents. There was no sense of place. They never even told us where it was exactly, because they didn't want us to be able to make any plans to run away. Practically the only time we went outdoors was to play five-a-side football every morning on the court outside the nursery."

Mia smiled. "What position did you play?"

"Goalkeeper."

She smiled more broadly. "I was a goalkeeper! Were you any good?"

"I wasn't bad. You?"

"I was *great*. I was gonna turn pro, but then Oakseed happened."

"At my nursery in Boston," Drienne said, "when they weren't teaching us they'd use us as test subjects, get us to beta new products, et cetera. All our free time was in controlled environments so they could keep on shaping us psychologically. No outside influences."

"Yes, same at mine," said Arlo. "So I really don't feel any connection to England at all."

"But then you must feel curious about what it's really like," said Mia.

"I hear London is a fucking trash fire," said Drienne. "Like, a cross between a trash fire and a toxic swamp. Literally."

Each member of the crew had an alt-id created for the operation by Loren and Kline. Loren, Kline, and Nadi would all pose as mades with different names and different backgrounds from their own. With so many Oakseed mades changing hands right now, discrepancies in the records would be hard to pick out, and people often changed the names of mades after buying them anyway, so if you had the right credentials, forging a record was simple and unlikely to be noticed. As Mia had explained, Nadi would be operating under a slightly reworked version of her real identity, under the name Pris Hamoudi.

Loren's and Kline's identities were not attached to Mia, as the aim was to avoid any of this being traced back to her, but they had to be held by *someone*. It was possible to create fake holders, but it was easier and more effective to attach the records to random, real people who were wealthy enough to privately hold mades, and who were largely off-grid. Loren found two such people, spoofed their identities, registered Kline to one of them under the name William Clancy, and themself to the other under the name Cas Woodforde. Loren also set up intercepts so that if anyone tried to check any of this, Loren would be able to respond posing as Kline's holder and

Kline would be able to respond posing as Loren's holder, and confirm their made hadn't gone rogue.

Loren's concerns about the job hadn't gone away, but they were really enjoying the tools Mia had sourced for them to use.

The alt-ids for Drienne and Arlo were a different matter. A de-branding op like this involved liaising with xecs in charge of a made-heavy workforce, and RookDivest would send nats to do it. It was riskier for Arlo and Drienne to pose as nats—any crime committed by a made was more serious if carried out while posing as a nat—but Mia insisted they do so. Loren created their ids and Kline established their credentials as RookDivest employees: Drienne would be Annie Clarke, Arlo would be Roland Fernandes. The proximity to their real names was deliberate, to make it easier for them both to remember.

All five of them were supplied with different cover stories about why they were traveling from Vancouver to England, and they traveled in three separate groups. Kline and (to Loren's disappointment) Nadi went first, because they had the most stuff to set up. They flew overnight to Birmingham and shared a car down to London. Loren took a flight into Manchester and traveled down from there. Drienne and Arlo were leaving tonight, going directly to London, and they had a few hours to kill.

Mia had purchased two drone squadrons; standard equipment for the kind of work Arlo and Drienne would be pretending to carry out in London. Each squadron packed neatly into a light carrying case: Mia had acquired two slightly used sets, rightly pointing out that this would look more authentic than brand-new ones. Arlo and Drienne had already spent a day familiarizing themselves with their squadrons and allowing the squadrons to become familiar with them. This kind of equipment became accustomed to your speech patterns and your way of working, so it could respond to you more quickly and accurately, and could anticipate your instructions before you issued them. Mia said another session with them would be time well spent, so Drienne and Arlo traveled out to a hollow urban zone south of Vancouver—nowhere near the same level of decay as London, it had no squatting population to speak of and its commercial district was basically intact, just dirty and a little overgrown with weeds. It looked like it had some hope of regeneration, and most importantly plenty of signage survived for them to practice on.

When Arlo opened his case, his squadron stood to attention, all sixteen of them. They had a retro cartoony design, like old-fashioned avatars of little spacemen, and they were all different colors so you could quickly tell them apart. The dark purple one wished him a good morning and asked him what they were doing today.

Arlo had never been in charge of anyone in his life before he'd been given this squadron. Even his slate had always felt like it was in charge of him: it received his schedule and told him what he was meant to be doing each day, and it dictated the things he was and wasn't allowed to know according to corporate policy.

He explained to the squadron they needed to strip Oakseed branding off everything in the mini-mall. Oakseed had been the dominant brand in this district, having made the usual deal with local government to provide all the typical suburban facilities— food outlets, a gym, vehicle dealership, funeral parlor, et cetera. The squadron acknowledged the instruction and went to work— they didn't ask why this was being done in a district that was clearly not going to be reactivated anytime soon, even though their intelligence was sufficient to register such a question. It wasn't their place to ask.

The drones were adept at seeking out branding and using their tools to scrub it—either by dissolving the top layer of whatever surface it had been applied to, or altering its color, or by destroying the object entirely. Arlo approached the job as if the redevelopment was going to keep the structure in place, telling the squadron how thorough they needed to be and indicating when they could move on. Some properties only needed to be debranded enough to seem clean to prospective buyers who wouldn't ever visit in person; some needed their entire previous existence purged, leaving no trace they had ever been anything else.

When Arlo and Drienne reconvened at the end of this session, he could detect a difference in manner between his squadron and Drienne's. He might have been imagining it, but hers seemed to hover behind her in a looser formation than his did, and they seemed to speak with a lightly mocking tone. He refrained from mentioning this to her, in case she identified ways in which his personality had imprinted on his own squadron, and made fun of him for it.

STALKING IS
LESS SUSPICIOUS

Kline and Nadi had arrived in London via the northwest suburbs yesterday afternoon, then taken the overline to the Oakseed cyc plant, which was located in the north of the city and was called Kentish Cyc (the name was used interchangeably for the plant itself and the corpurbation that now surrounded it). They'd gone to their separate apartments—Kline in the transient block on one side of the street, Nadi in one of the workers' blocks directly opposite. Kline had bought some food from the minivend at the base of the block, entered the apartment he'd booked, and since then had not left these two rooms. He didn't want the neighbors to see him, he didn't want anyone in the area to see him, he wanted to appear on as few cams as possible. He didn't even want to leave traces with his alt-id: if one piece of activity was connected back to him, it could *all* be connected back to him. Besides, the very air in London made him itch, and he wasn't inclined to go walking around in it.

The entire corpurbation around Kentish Cyc extended no more than a couple of hundred meters from the plant; a few of the smarter houses had been renovated for habitation by the xecs, but the workforce lived in simple princrete blocks that lined what had once been the main road. The plant itself was opposite what had once been Kentish Town Station, but was now a cheap coffeehouse called Bizarre?!; the platform for the overline had been constructed just next to it. Kline wasn't missing anything by not getting out and seeing the sights. He'd already seen the entire place. Instead he just stayed in his rooms, did his work, and thought about what he'd do when he got out of here with his freedom.

Kline resisted the urge to look anything up. It was hard to just sit here thinking about, say, moving to Reykjavik, and not check how feasible it was, how much things cost, what immigration was like, et cetera. His wrist turned involuntarily whenever these questions entered his mind and he had to turn it back. This wasn't because he didn't have access to a secure connection—it was piggybacked on Oakseed's network, because outside the corpurbations the entire center of London was a reception blackspot, but Loren had ensured it was secure. Kline's concern was he didn't want the rest of the crew to know anything about his plans for after this job, and all of them would be able to see his activity—Mia had been clear they should all know what the others were doing. If one of the others noticed he'd sent a load of requests for info about Reykjavik—that was just an example, Kline hadn't settled on a destination yet—and then that person got caught and interrogated and told the cops that was where he'd gone, he was screwed. So Kline just lay on the bed and made plans in his head.

Kline then started to worry that doing nothing that left a trace was, in itself, suspicious. His cover story was that he was running errands for his holder, but anyone paying the slightest attention to his movements would see he wasn't. Who sat alone in a transient room doing nothing for hours on end? Criminals, that was who. Criminals who were either waiting to do a job or hiding out after doing one. And there was no reason to come to Kentish Cyc unless you had business related to the plant. It wasn't exactly a prime holiday spot. He could think of no way of being here that didn't look sketchy as hell.

It frustrated Kline that he was required to be in London at all. His role was doable from anywhere. But he could no longer access Oakseed's global systems, because they didn't exist. Everything that was still running was apparently now routed via RookDivest, and Mia was wary of intruding into their systems any more than necessary. Kline suggested Loren could go to London and hook up a terminal he could control from Vancouver, but Mia was unwilling to consider this. She wanted Kline on-site to deal with any problems that came up, and she was his holder so it was pointless to argue.

The plant's system controlled all information flow in the corpurbation, whether for personal or business use, and any of the apartments could be equipped with a terminal for remote working. Before they'd left Vancouver, Loren had given Kline an unbranded terminal preloaded with all the credentials necessary to interface with the plant's HR system. Sure enough, when Kline hooked it up he was presented with the kind of access he'd enjoyed back in Delaware, with a higher level of permissions. The Kentish Cyc workforce was smaller and more homogeneous than the ones he'd usually worked with, and Kline only needed a few hours looking at work patterns and interactions between departments to feel he had the measure of it.

Kentish Cyc was one of the few parts of Oakseed that was still running, post-collapse. All the company's remaining retail outlets and direct services had been closed down as soon as its failure had been confirmed, joining those that had already been closed in the weeks prior, as it desperately attempted to slash costs and save itself from oblivion. And all the backroom infrastructure, like support and HR, had also been halted in anticipation of it being asset-stripped. But the company's cyc plants, even this grubby one in a crumbling city, infallibly generated more value than they cost to run. This would go some small way toward filling the company's black hole of debt, and the plants were considered more appealing to buyers if they were already up and running. So RookDivest had given Kentish Cyc clearance to keep doing what it was doing.

During the briefing, Drienne had noted how frustrating this was: if the place was empty and shut down, they could have just broken in and taken whatever they wanted.

"If it was shut down," Nadi had pointed out, "they'd have it un-der guard, making sure people *didn't* break in and take what they wanted. Especially in London—if anyone heard this place was empty and unguarded, it'd have been looted within hours. And then probably torched."

"Exactly," said Mia. "Business as usual is *good* for us."

Kline's first job upon arrival had been to insert Nadi into the plant. There were no vacancies in harvesting—it was a desirable job for the unqualified and inexperienced, because it came with the opportunity to earn commission, so most employees started off on the underfloor, dissolving salvage. There *were* vacancies on the underfloor, so Kline was able to fake and backdate a request from a xec who'd already left Kentish Cyc for any suitable workers to be sent from the huge pool RookDivest had collected from Oakseed. He also faked and backdated a response from RookDivest, which agreed Nadi—or Pris, as the correspondence referred to her—would be sent to them on the next flight to England. The background checks were minimal, because the HR system believed this person had existed within the company all her life; on top of this, Kline knew exactly what would trigger flags in the process, and had de-signed Nadi's alt-id to ensure a negative response all the way down.

There was a waiting list for promotion to harvesting work, and Kline was able to nudge Nadi to the front of that queue. Mia had as-sured him it would be a formality to get her on harvesting from there, because people were always getting injured on the job and so they always needed temp cover. But either they'd raised their safety stan-dards since Mia worked there or the staff was having a lucky week, because no temp vacancies were opening up. As it stood, the whole plan rested on someone at the plant being unavailable for work.

Kline thought back to how Loren had raised potential problems with Mia's plan and been shut down. Kline hadn't wanted to speak up then, but Loren was right, the plan wasn't as watertight as Mia made it seem. Mia was a considerate and sympathetic holder, provided you didn't challenge her on anything. Kline knew how to handle people like that, but you needed to think for them at times, ideally without them realizing you were doing it.

Kline looked through a few of the harvesters' profiles and had an idea. He wasn't sure if the others would like it, but this type of thing was the whole point of him being on the team. This was what he could do that the others couldn't. It only took him a few minutes to implement it.

Within an hour one of the harvesters, a made called Cody, was taken off his shift and informed a complaint of misconduct had been filed against him, alleging he'd been sneaking up to the support section during late shifts and abusing a printer for his own sexual gratification. He would be suspended while an investigation took place. Kline learned his plan had been successful when a manager at the plant put these notes on Cody's HR record. There were no further details, but Kline knew how these things went: Cody would have protested his innocence and demanded to know who had made this complaint. He'd have been told he wasn't permitted to know, and then ushered off the premises. Kline wasn't a monster, however—he ensured the process would include suspension on full pay, and the investigation ought to clear Cody after assessing the lack of evidence.

The HR system called up Nadi as a replacement before she'd even done a shift on the underfloor. It was possible someone on the underfloor might notice this and wonder how the new hire had jumped the waiting list, but such things happened all the time, and Kline knew too well how opaque the system could be.

After careful consideration, Kline decided that, if challenged about why he'd come to the corpurbation, he would claim he was stalking someone who lived here. He looked out his window at the block on the opposite side of the street and searched for a plausible stalkee. He was frustrated at first—the morning sun was hitting the windows at such an angle he couldn't see a thing. But then there was a commotion in the street below and a few people leaned out their windows to see what was going on, either out of concern or a desire for live entertainment. And then he saw, one floor down and four windows along, standing on the tiny balcony that jutted from her apartment, a tired-looking woman wearing a long skirt and a bikini top, her shoulder-length yellow hair sticking out from under a baseball cap. It was hard to tell from this distance but she seemed to be in her thirties; a little soft-bellied, but her arms looked toned and supple. He guessed she was a manual worker at the plant.

He went over to his terminal and a quick search through the employment records confirmed she was a maintenance mechanic. Her name was Frankie James, she was a nat, thirty-two years old, unmarried, no children.

She was *just* right. Not that Kline would ever stalk anyone, but if he did, she looked like someone he would stalk: younger, a little unconventional, and not entirely unattainable. He could, if it became necessary, claim he was obsessed with her and rented this room so he could watch her from across the street, and was trying to pluck up the courage to talk to her. And it was something people wouldn't readily admit to, so if someone confronted him about why he was here, he could first try a more innocuous explanation, such as he was an artist or poet looking for inspiration in a down-and-out part of the world, and then fall back on the stalker story if they persisted.

Good. He felt better.

To make it convincing he would come to the window and watch for Frankie James from time to time. The commotion was still going on and lots of people were coming to their windows to watch. Two women were arguing about one owing the other money, and the one who'd borrowed the money said she'd spent it on cosmetic surgery to remove scars, and the other didn't believe her and was trying to remove her clothes so she could check. It was unclear if the women were a couple, or an ex-couple, or related to each other, or maybe one of them was seeing the other's ex. Kline wasn't concentrating hard enough to work it out because he was looking at Frankie James across the street. She was leaning on a railing and talking to her neighbor with great amusement, and was too distracted to know Kline was watching her.

14

A PEP TALK
AND SOME POSITIVE
PRODUCTIVITY STATISTICS

Harvesters use the side gate, Nadi reminded herself as she walked up to Kentish Cyc. The building was an imposing light gray box with a ribbed surface, whose only windows were on its top floor. The main entrance vestibule was a steel-and-sapphire affair that looked like it belonged on an entirely different building from the dull, forbidding structure to which it was attached. Atop the entrance was a three-dimensional rendition of Oakseed's acorn logo. To the right of it, set into the wall, was a large metal gate, which stood open. A securit was stationed just inside, and beyond him was a gray, dark passageway broad and tall enough to accommodate a small truck, which ran all the way through the building to the other side. Nadi knew there were two doors inside the passageway that led back into the main building. These doors were used by securits and no one else.

Nadi knew everything about the layout of this building. There were aspects of security work she'd never been good at, but she could effortlessly visualize anywhere she'd familiarized herself with. Loren had asked her about this when they were planning the job, and she'd explained it was like she was looking down on the space from above. If it was a floor of a building, it was like that slice of the building had been removed and she could see into all the rooms, and she could hold that in her head while she also processed what she was seeing with her own eyes.

"That's cool," Loren had said.

"It's pretty normal for securits," Nadi told them.

"It's still cool."

Nadi joined the queue that was forming inside the passageway. Maybe thirty other harvesters stood ahead of her. This was the second shift of the day, which began at 9:00 A.M. The plant didn't send harvesters into the center of the city at night—it was dangerous, and working in the dark was inefficient—but it was July and daylight hours were close to their longest, so they were packing the shifts in while they could. The harvesters shuffled along, single file, passing through a full-body scanner located in the center of the passageway. This registered everything each harvester had on their person, and while it functioned as a check for weapons, drugs, or other offensive equipment, its main purpose was to record everything each worker brought in. At the end of the shift, everyone went back through to ensure they had only what they'd brought in and no more. Walking out with any piece of salvage, however small or valueless, was strictly forbidden. Nadi passed through the scanner, glancing at the securits operating it. They would know she was a former securit, there was no hiding that. They didn't react or treat her differently, and she didn't expect them to. On the other side of the scanner, she was issued a helmet and sent to the platform.

The plant had been built near an old railway line that was sunk down below street level. The tracks had been removed to make nice flat pathways for the trucks that traveled to and from the center. The truck trains had fat, heavy-duty wheels that moved surprisingly fast if they had a stretch of flat ground. Each train was made up of three carriages and a steerage car that pulled the whole thing along. Securits rode in the steerage car. The first carriage contained seats for the harvesters to ride in. The other two were used to store the carts that the harvesters would take out and fill with cycleable material.

Before they all got on the train, a xec came down to the platform. He was middle-aged, with wavy dark hair and a weaving pattern tattooed up one side of his face, and a build of muscle gone to fat. Nadi knew his name was Henrik Paul, because Kline had accessed the records of the plant's xecs and distributed them to the crew. Two of the xecs had already departed to take up other jobs, knowing whoever bought the plant would probably install their own management team; two remained.

Henrik gave them all a pep talk, relating some positive productivity statistics from the previous week and thanking them all for their contribution. Nadi wondered if this happened often. Judging from the bored reaction of his audience, it probably did. When he was done, everyone started boarding the train. As Nadi waited her turn, Henrik approached her and put a hand on her shoulder.

"Could I have a word?" he said.

Nadi nodded guilelessly and followed Henrik through the door that led inside the plant—the door they would all push their carts of salvage through when the time came to unload and deposit everything they'd found that day. Her overwhelming thought was the entire plan was sunk before it had begun: this man knew she wasn't who she claimed to be, he knew she'd used subterfuge to get on the harvesting team, everything was fucked, abort, abort.

"I'm Henrik Paul," the xec said, shaking Nadi's hand. "Pris, yes? Welcome to the team."

Was that all it was? Just a simple hello? "Thanks," Nadi replied, but she still glanced through the glass in the door and considered where she could go if she jumped off the platform and just ran.

"One thing," said Henrik. He seemed anxious, which was strange. She'd had very few encounters with xecs, but they generally didn't seem intimidated by her. "You're a made? Is that right? You came here from another site . . ."

"Yes. Helsinki," she added.

"And that site's been shut down, yes?"

"Yes. In fact, I was up for sale and they took me off the market and sent me here instead."

"So you *do* know about"—he glanced around, lowered his voice—"the *collapse*."

"Yes."

"Have you mentioned it to anyone here?"

"The collapse?"

He winced, smiling tightly. "*Please* keep your voice down."

"No."

"No one in the entire corpurbation?"

"No. I don't know anyone to tell yet."

"Right. Good." Henrik looked relieved. It seemed someone ought to have spoken to Nadi about this before she started work, but everyone had left it up to someone else. "Please keep it to yourself. We're *trying* to keep a lid on it."

"What?"

"Not my idea, you understand—came from higher up. Last order we got, pretty much: don't tell the floor workers until the plant is sold. I did tell them it's not as simple as that, we can control what information people access when they're here, but they do *occasionally* come and go. But no one has any idea what it's like here, they really don't have a clue." He seemed to remember he was speaking to an employee and assumed a more professional countenance. "So, yes."

"*No one* knows?"

"Top floor do. No one else. Our filters are *very* strong, and we've been generating counter-info to make the workers think the company's active and expanding, so if they *did* happen to hear anything about a collapse they'd think it wasn't true. I mean, the idea of Oakseed collapsing is so ludicrous and . . . and *improbable* I can scarcely believe it myself. I'm sure it's going to filter through sooner or later, but it's not going to be for want of trying." Henrik held up crossed fingers.

"Right. Well, you can count on me."

Henrik grinned. "Excellent. Thank you."

He told Nadi she could go, and she boarded the truck train. No one asked her why the boss wanted to speak to her personally. They were too busy amusing each other with impressions of his pep talk. Some of them were pretty funny.

After her shift, Nadi went to meet Loren at the rendezvous spot, where they were all to go after the job was done. This was a court-yard behind the old Underground station whose most notable feature was a statue of Doggy Dogg Jones, the main character in one of Oakseed's most popular media franchises. That would have to go after Kentish Cyc was sold, unless of course it was bought by the same company that acquired the rights to the character.

"They don't know the company's collapsed," Nadi told Loren as they sat on the courtyard's only bench.

"Really?" said Loren, who had been in the corpurbation only a few hours and was still lagged. "Did you ask them?"

"One of the xecs told me not to tell anyone about it."

"Wow. I guess it's a kind of microsocial bubble, here. All their information is controlled centrally; you could put filters up on news and comms and such. People hardly go outside it, or come in from outside. You couldn't keep it from them forever, but until the place is sold—maybe."

"He didn't really explain *why*."

"I guess they haven't told them because they don't need to." Loren brushed their fringe aside—it was sticking to their brow in the heat. It was nice to see Loren again, even if just to talk about the job. Loren was much more interesting than the people Nadi usually got to interact with, and if they had any fear of her they seemed to have gotten over it. "Someone must have figured it would be disruptive and impact production if they knew."

"He seemed very confident no one knows."

"They'll be monitoring chat. Easy enough to flag that kind of thing."

"You didn't mention it to anyone, did you?"

"No. I'm not talking to anyone more than I need to."

"Kline hasn't left his apartment, but I'll make sure he knows too. Does it change anything, though? For us, I mean?"

"I don't think so." Loren thought about this for quite a while, and just when it seemed like they weren't going to say anything else, they added, "I guess it means business as usual. And like Mia said, business as usual is good."

Nadi nodded. That was probably right. They didn't have anything else they needed to discuss, but she didn't want to go back to her apartment just yet.

"Arlo and Drienne should be arriving at the port pretty soon," she said.

"Yep."

"How was your journey?"

"Not great," Loren replied with a short laugh. "There was supposed to be a train, but it didn't run, so I ended up getting a bus, and that didn't go all the way, so I had to get another bus. How about you?"

"Kline and I hired a car. It was okay except the roads got bad farther south. I don't mean busy, they were very quiet, but just *bad*. All broken up."

"I can't imagine what you and Kline talked about for however many hours it took."

"Oakseed stuff. All the way. I don't think he has any other interests. If they need someone to write the definitive history of the company, he's the guy."

Loren smiled and nodded. "That figures. Bet he didn't ask you anything about yourself."

"Actually he did. He was curious about what kind of work they assigned me in Frankfurt. And about my time in nursery."

"Okay."

"And then he said they fucked up when they made me."

"What?"

"Yeah."

"How did he say this? Like was it a joke, or mean, or . . . ?"

"Just like it was a fact that they fucked up. And like it was interesting to him. I asked him what he meant, and he said he'd been watching how I acted and talked and I had a weird mindset for a securit. He said he didn't know how I ended up like I am and they should have seen it and moved me onto other duties. But I'm built for security work, and I have this face, so . . .'"

"Did he say the part about the face?"

"Yes."

"And how do you feel about all that?"

"I don't know. I felt like I should be mad. But I also think he might be right. I keep thinking about it. I wasn't like the other securits and I always felt like that was my fault. But if they fucked up when they made me, then it's not. I think maybe Kline was trying to help, in a way?"

"That's a generous interpretation."

"I like to give people the benefit of the doubt."

"Do you?"

"Yes."

"I guess that proves his point."

A SCENTED CANDLE
SALESMAN HITS TOWN

The port used to be called London Heathrow, but as it was now London's only functioning port, the second part of the name had fallen out of use and it was just referred to as "London." It also used to be the largest and busiest in Europe, but three of its terminals had long since closed and now stood derelict. They were just about visible through the haze as Arlo, Drienne, and the other passengers were bussed from one end of the port to the other. It had very little passenger traffic, and was mostly given over to industrial use, which meant it had minimal facilities and gave little care to the impression it created for visitors. Some of its operation areas were visibly held together by staples and glue.

Arlo had been worried about anxiety giving him away when he presented himself at border control, and mentioned this to Mia and Loren when the identities were being set up. No problem, Mia said, and synthesized a drug he could take that would target that specific source of anxiety and damp it down without impairing his other faculties. She offered one to Drienne too, but she said she'd be fine without it. Arlo had taken the pill ten minutes before the flight landed, as instructed. At first he worried about what he should do if his progress was delayed and the pill wore off before he got through border control. Then the pill kicked in and he stopped worrying about that.

Border control was operated by a mix of humans and systems, and you were randomly assigned to one or the other. Arlo wasn't sure which he'd rather have. Either would be fine. He knew what to say. He was feeling very very relaxed about the whole situation.

He got a human. Cool!

He stepped forward and entered the booth. It was like a confessional, but with an "in" door on one side and an "out" door on the other. Also, it was painted blue.

"Sr. Fernandes," said the immigration officer on the other side of the grille.

"Hi," said Arlo.

"Are you visiting England on business, sir?" the officer asked as Arlo was scanned and recorded from multiple angles, gathering enough information not only to match him with the records they held, but also to create a fully articulated virtual model of him, if they so chose.

"That's right," Arlo said in a very businesslike way.

"What's the nature of your business?"

They'd agreed it was better not to tell border control they were from RookDivest, in case the staff ran a check with the company. It was simpler to claim they were independent businesspeople with a low profile. "I'm setting up a distribution hub here," he said; there were a number of such hubs in the vicinity of the port. "I'm coming in to oversee the renovation of the site." He wanted to add *That's what the drone squadron is for,* but reminded himself not to offer information if he hadn't been asked for it.

"Distribution for what?"

"Candles. Scented candles." This was Drienne's idea, but Arlo liked how he sounded saying it. Maybe when all this was over he'd use his share of the money to start a business selling scented candles.

The officer waved a hand, the door release mechanism activated, and Arlo left the booth as if he'd never harbored any doubt of being allowed to do so. When he got to the other side he pretended to be checking his messages, but in fact he had no messages worth checking because he was using a slate associated with his alt-id and the only messages he received were being generated purely to make it look like his identity was real. They were all about scented candles. In truth he was waiting for Drienne, whose border interview was still going on.

Arlo considered what he might do if Drienne's cover failed and she was barred from entering. Mia's instructions were that if they lost any member of the team for any reason, the others were to carry on without them as best they could. If this was impossible, they were to suspend the operation until Mia could acquire and send a replacement. If suspension was impossible, they were to abandon the operation and attempt to leave England without getting caught. The exception to this was Arlo himself. Until the point they got their hands on the Coyne, he was indispensable and a degree of risk was acceptable if he was in need of rescue. (Naturally, once they had the Coyne, Arlo was as dispensable as any of them.)

This ought to have made Arlo feel more secure. Instead, it just underlined that he was not here on merit but because of who his donor was, and he refused to express gratitude toward his donor, for anything.

If it came to it, Arlo was willing to take a certain amount of risk for Drienne. But, he realized calmly, there was no risk he could take in this situation. If they wanted to deport her back to Vancouver, they would. If they wanted to lock her up for faking her id, they would. Any attempt he made to intervene would only result in suspicion falling on him too. This was why they had separate cover stories for the journey.

That pill was really effective. He didn't feel stressed about the situation at all. It occurred to him that he absolutely could not use these pills during the job itself, as he seemed to have lost any sense of personal danger. He calmly accepted this too.

Arlo passed the time by actually reading his messages, even though they were generated fiction. It proved quite interesting to see the internally consistent world the messages created, the memos from one nonexistent person to another that he'd been copied in on "just FYI." He'd never done anything like this before; it would never have occurred to him to play at having a different job. If he'd tried to get his slate to do something like this back in Shanghai, it would have suggested something profitable to do instead.

Someone walked in front of Arlo, coughing loudly, and he looked up. It was Drienne, and in that cough he could sense her irritation with him for hanging around waiting, looking conspicuous. When they got clear of the port he would explain he'd only done so out of concern for her.

Mia didn't want Arlo and Drienne to stay at Kentish Cyc with the others. She wanted them to arrive in London a couple of days early to acclimatize, and she didn't want anyone to see them in Kentish Cyc and remember them, as this would call into question why they'd hung around for so long before starting the job. There were hotels still operating near the port, but they often exchanged information with border control about their customers, so Arlo and Drienne were to stay in an apartment close to one of the other cyc plants in London, on the other side of the city.

This plant was run by NiZCO and stood on what used to be the Oval cricket ground, hence its name—NiZCOval. The underground rail took Arlo and Drienne from the port to an area called Acton, but the line didn't run any farther than that; apparently the rail network used to run under the center of the city and connect to all kinds of places, but lack of maintenance meant it had long ago been declared unsafe and most of it closed. Arlo and Drienne had to travel back up to ground level and take the overline, which ran on an orbital route around the edge of the city. No one traveled to the center unless they were harvesting, or wanted trouble.

The overline was so sparsely used, only a single carriage ran on each of its two lines, one going clockwise and one counterclockwise. Arlo and Drienne reached the platform and discovered they'd just missed the counterclockwise carriage, and it was quicker to catch the clockwise one even though this meant traveling three times as far.

"Wow," Drienne said, "this place is like the wild fucking west." Even the functional parts of the city seemed shockingly bare, with none of the densely laid surfaces you saw in all urban spaces these days. Every crack and discoloration was painfully visible.

The carriage was like a large cable car that hung from a rail, which was narrow enough and high enough above the ground to discourage people from climbing onto it. Arlo and Drienne were the only passengers. As the carriage skirted the city center, Drienne looked down. You heard stories about London, but it was hard to believe it was all true, especially if you lived in one of the cities that had been protected against the worst effects of climate collapse— like Shanghai, or Vancouver.

London was already in decline when the cyc plants arrived around twenty years ago—in fact, the plants were meant to help turn it around. The idea had been for the megas to regenerate the semi-derelict areas of the city, dismantling the shitty old buildings that had stood for centuries and constructing modern com-res zones in their place. At the time, everyone thought this was a very lucrative project, hence bright young things like Mia and Samson being assigned to the city.

But the decline not only continued, it deepened, faster than anyone thought possible. The city's tallest buildings, the ones that had sprung up eagerly around the turn of the millennium, could not sustain themselves and were abandoned one by one. They needed to be maintained somehow or dismantled, but there was no public money to spend on fixing up huge buildings that used to be the responsibility of private entities. There was no public money at all. That was precisely why regeneration had been farmed out to the megas, who were by this point starting to have doubts over the original project and certainly didn't want to expand its scope. The issue was kicked down the road again and again, and meanwhile the buildings suffered damage from vandalism, theft, and occasional fires. A fad arose for hotwiring lorries, hacking the steering so they wouldn't register buildings as things to avoid, then setting them on a course for the biggest building they could find, preferably one with lots of glass in it.

Eventually one of the buildings fell, crushing large parts of Euston Road. Persistent stories claimed the building had been toppled by factions hoping to provoke the government into doing something about the problem. The government responded by moving the capital, and the House of Commons, to Sheffield. (The old House of Commons was uncomfortably close to the ever-rising river anyway.) The cyc plants had been diverted to clearing the ruins on Euston Road, which took several months. By the time they were done, other areas were in need of similar attention. And so the project morphed from regenerating London to breaking it up for scrap. The megas bought the rest of the land for nominal sums. They employed residents from the suburbs who hadn't been able to afford to move elsewhere, and sent this workforce in to dismantle and recycle the city, building by building.

This had gone on for over a decade and there was still much to be done. What life remained in the city now revolved around the corpurbations that had sprung up around each of the cyc plants, and the orbital overline had been (cheaply) built to connect them. Traditionally, cities evolved out of small towns and villages that grew and merged together, but the reverse seemed to be happening to London: its suburbs were withdrawing into towns, slowly destroying the center that once connected them. People still lived in the center, hundreds of them—maybe thousands, no one cared enough to count—in buildings they didn't own or pay rent for. Many stayed in properties that once cost more money than the average person made in a lifetime.

Maybe when the old city was finally gone, they—or someone else—would build a new London, a greener and more pleasant one. Or maybe the ground would be too wretchedly poisoned for that, and maybe the river would go on rising and swallow it all, and the small vulture towns that had sprung up on the fringes of central London would pack up and leave, and go to break down another failed city. Already this was no longer a place in any meaningful sense. Don't bother going to London: it's not there anymore.

As the carriage passed over what used to be the British Library, Drienne saw a group of teens trying to catch a horse on the plaza. There were five kids and they had the horse surrounded. It must have escaped from a farm to the north—many of the suburban parks were farmland now. Or maybe the kids stole it from a farm and lost control of it because they didn't know how to handle a horse.

Drienne nudged Arlo and pointed out the spectacle taking place beneath them. In a moment they'd be past it. "Look," she said. "Quickly."

"No," was his reply; he was reading something on his slate.

"You'll miss it."

"I don't give a shit."

He didn't want to see it. Drienne looked back down at the scene just in time to see the horse kick one of the teens in the head. The kid flew backward and landed on their back. The carriage sped on, and soon it was impossible to see what was happening, and Drienne would never know whether the kid got up or not.

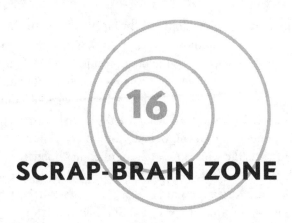

16

SCRAP-BRAIN ZONE

Today, Nadi was on the afternoon shift. Since arriving in England she'd only experienced dry heat, but now the rain was sheeting down as if the clouds had been away on holiday and were catching up on the work that had accumulated in their absence. Every harvester was issued a waterproof jacket with a large hood, which needed to be returned at the end of the shift; other than this, no concessions were made to the weather. They were expected to get on with it and their quotas were unchanged.

Like yesterday, they were harvesting an area formerly known as Bloomsbury. As the regeneration project had failed, the subsequent land-grab had resulted in the city being carved up into salvage zones. Bloomsbury was one of several zones now owned by Oakseed. With a name like that, Nadi thought, it must have had tree-lined streets and flower beds, back when it was flourishing. Now the streets were cracked and overrun with weeds.

The harvesters disembarked from the truck train and donned their helmets. Not only did these protect them from the worst of any falling debris, they were fitted with an analytical camera called a skeye. A clever piece of tech, it directed them toward whatever debris needed to be broken up—it could detect the composition of any given chunk of material; it could highlight the most valuable elements; and it would automatically log everything the harvesters put in their carts. You didn't need to think much about what you were doing. The helmet was the brain, you just had to do the work.

The helmet's cooling system was no match for the sweltering conditions, and the rain did little to take the edge off. On top of that, Nadi had been issued with a helmet that wasn't quite big enough for her head. As she walked from the truck train to today's harvesting site, the white noise of rain filled her hood.

Nadi spent the shift picking through what had once been a quaint-looking Korean restaurant, using a cutter-extractor to glean metal and plastic from its kitchen. She had music on while she worked, which was another thing she liked about the job. Securit work involved a lot of long, boring hours looking at nothing, but you weren't allowed to have anything distract your attention. Here they didn't care as long as you hit your targets. Nadi's love of music had baffled her securit colleagues, none of whom cared about music, nor could they understand why anyone would.

Nadi was about done in the kitchen when she noticed that the three people who'd been stripping it with her had vanished. She paused her music, but could hear little more than the rain. Her first thought was she was due for some hazing ritual, being the new kid. They were probably going to lock her in the building and she'd have to cut her way out before the shift ended and the truck train left. She'd been through several such rituals after joining the securit team in Frankfurt. It only stopped when someone new arrived and they targeted him instead.

One of the other harvesters appeared at the doorway. He was a smallish, wiry guy. Nadi didn't know his name, no one who worked here ever seemed to introduce themselves. He indicated she should follow him. "There's a vague upstairs."

Nadi didn't know what this meant, and she said so.

"Fucking *what?*" the man said incredulously. "Vague. Unhabitant. Squatter. Living here without permission." He seemed exasperated she still didn't understand. But she did understand. She just didn't know what he expected her to do. Maybe people were running out of the building because they were worried the "vague" would attack them. That seemed logical.

"Okay," she said. "So what? I'm not afraid of them."

"Fuck's sake"—and here he adopted a tone as if speaking to a simple child—"come with me and we can *catch* them and get ourselves a *bo-nus.*"

No one had told Nadi about bonuses for getting rid of anyone still living here. She wondered if it was legit. But it was very much within her skill set. She had done exactly that kind of work during events, moving on the homeless to keep the sponsorama clean and clear. So she went with him.

"We work together, yeah?" said the man. "Share the bonus if we get it."

"Okay," said Nadi. She'd be doing most of the work, being taller, stronger, and heavier than him. That was why he'd come back for her instead of tackling this person on his own and claiming the entire bonus for himself. Nadi wanted allies inside the plant, so she'd do this with him. She asked him what his name was.

"Gregg," said the man, evidently irritated she was bringing up such trifles now.

"Pris. Nice to meet you."

They started ascending the stairwell near the entrance of the restaurant. Then Nadi heard a noise coming from the kitchen she had just left. She called up her mental image of the kitchen layout and remembered there was a dumbwaiter for sending food to the upper floor. Someone had been waiting for everyone to leave the kitchen so they could use it to come down that way.

"They're in there," Nadi said, pointing toward the kitchen.

"Shit!" said Gregg and began running back the way they'd come. As he reached the door, it opened quick and hard, pinning him against the wall. His head hit it with a *smack* and he slumped to the floor, a thin line of blood following him down the cinders like a snake.

The young woman who had opened the door glanced up, saw Nadi blocking her way, and ran back inside the kitchen. Opening the door in Gregg's face hadn't been a convenient accident. She'd been waiting.

Nadi dashed after her. There was another door at the end of the kitchen that led to the storerooms, the manager's office, and the staff toilets, but no sign of her quarry. When Nadi got to the rear entrance, she found the back door hanging off its hinges and rushed through it into an alley—

—which was deserted. No footsteps, no sign anything had been disturbed. The rain was still very heavy, lowering visibility, and someone could vanish into it quickly—but not *that* quickly.

Over the sound of the rain, Nadi heard a noise inside the restaurant. The fucker had done it *again*. She must've hidden in one of the other rooms. Smart: she'd calculated that in a straight chase Nadi would catch up with her, so was trying some misdirection to give herself the advantage.

Nadi returned to the kitchen, where she found the door that led through to the restaurant swinging. She heard Gregg cry out in pain. The pattern of events was easy to read: the woman had run back through the kitchen, encountered Gregg again, and assaulted him again.

As Nadi burst onto the restaurant floor, the woman was trying to dodge around piles of debris—she was running in an odd way, as if she'd injured her leg. Nadi raced across the floor, her long strides eating up the distance in a couple of seconds. Nadi was going to reach her before she reached the exit. The woman obviously realized this because she stopped, turned on her heel, and pointed a small, rusted flick knife at Nadi.

Nadi also stopped. The woman was much younger than she'd initially thought—fifteen, sixteen perhaps. She was also pregnant—she looked to be about seven months, but she could be further along and malnourished. Her face was grubby, her eyes were hard. She smelled terrible.

"Drop it," Nadi said. She'd done this a hundred times and always started by giving them fair warning. If they had a weapon and you didn't, they usually thought they had the upper hand and wouldn't want to give it up, but there was a chance you could save yourself the trouble of disarming them. It also gave you a moment to size up the situation, and you could tell a lot from how they reacted: some were scornful, others would assess their chances. This girl seemed angry, either with Nadi for cornering her or, more likely, herself for getting cornered.

The girl glared defiantly and brandished the knife at Nadi. The sequence of moves that would deal with the situation opened up smoothly in Nadi's mind, and then all she had to do was make them. She took a diagonal step to make the angle of attack awkward. The girl tried to plunge the knife sideways, which was predictable. Nadi was ready and punched her hard in the elbow. (Most people aimed for the obvious target of the head or the larger target of the torso, but elbows and kneecaps were excellent weak points if you could land the blow accurately: painful and any injury to them inhibited movement.) The girl cried in pain but didn't drop the knife. Nadi used her other hand to grab the girl's wrist and then brought her fist down on the girl's shoulder. The girl yelled incoherently but *still* didn't drop the knife. Nadi pushed her backward and slammed her hand into the frame of the door.

Finally the knife fell.

Nadi felt satisfied. She'd subdued the target without breaking any bones. More importantly in this case, she had not struck anywhere near her belly.

The girl looked up at Nadi furiously, tears welling in her eyes.

"You shouldn't be living here," Nadi told her. "It's not good for you or the baby. What are you eating?"

The girl spat in Nadi's face.

Nadi wiped it away with her sleeve and pointed to the girl's belly. "If the kid's healthy, you could sell it. Lots of people with money want one, not enough to go around."

The girl gave a bitter laugh. "No one here would *ever* let someone take their kid. Not after what you did to us."

"Me?"

"You're Oakseed."

"Yeah, I know. What did we do?"

Before the girl could answer, the other employees who'd been clearing the restaurant with Nadi appeared. They'd brought a securit, who cuffed the girl.

"You claiming the bonus for this one?" the securit asked Nadi.

Nadi pointed at Gregg, who sat on one of the restaurant's few intact chairs while he dabbed at his bleeding skull with a rag. "He helped. We did it together."

Gregg looked up. "Sorry, what? We did what together?"

"You helped catch this unhabitant?" said the securit.

"Oh yes," said Gregg. "Absolutely, we both—Yes."

FAMOUS BEACH BALL

Kline caught the clockwise overline carriage round the east side of London and down to the NiZCO corpurbation, walked up to the rooms where Arlo and Drienne were staying, and knocked on the door. He could hear their bickering voices coming from inside.

Arlo came to the door, opened it just enough to see out, and didn't invite Kline in.

"Sorry," Arlo said. "Could you come back in half an hour?"

"What?" said Kline. "I told you I was coming—"

"Yeah, I know—"

"It's just taken me almost an hour to get here—"

"I know, I know—"

"How are you not ready? Seriously—"

"Who are you talking to?" said Drienne from somewhere inside the apartment.

"Sorry," Arlo said to Kline, "we're just having a tiny problem."

"Is it someone who knows me?" said Drienne. "Can they help?"

"Please," Arlo continued, ignoring her. "She'll be fine—she just needs a bit of time."

"What's wrong with her?" asked Kline.

"Nothing!" said Arlo brightly.

Drienne's face appeared over Arlo's shoulder, glaring at Kline.

"Oh it's *you*," she said. "You know a *lot* of shit you don't say. I bet you know me."

Arlo put his arm across to stop Drienne walking through the doorway. "I think you should lie down," he told her in a mild voice.

"I *bet* you're involved," Drienne said, still addressing Kline. "You've been involved all along."

Arlo pushed himself in front of Drienne and said to Kline, "Sorry—half an hour, she'll be fine." Then he closed the door.

Kline lingered outside the door for a moment, unsure how to react. He could hear Drienne in there, speaking loudly and sharply, and he wanted to know what was going on. He *needed* to know, it was wired into him, and he wanted to hammer on the door and demand answers. But sometimes the way to get to the bottom of these matters was not to push. If you pushed, they only hid it more. So he went down to a coffeehouse on the ground floor of the block and bought a dish of sweet-and-salted beans and a coffee. He ate and drank these slowly, and then returned to the apartment. The moment thirty minutes were up, he knocked on the door again.

This time Drienne answered. "Hi—sorry about that, I wasn't feeling well. It's a travel thing."

"A travel thing," said Kline.

"Yes."

"But you're all right now?"

"Fine, yes. Come in."

Drienne seemed genial and welcoming, and it was impossible to relate her manner now to the person who'd spoken to him before. Arlo greeted Kline and apologized, and he and Drienne both acted like the whole incident was trivial and embarrassing. Kline had a job to do here, and he would do it, but he would not simply leave this hanging.

Before leaving Vancouver, Loren had made their way into Rook-Divest's system and ensured the debranding of Kentish Cyc was made *super-low priority*. This meant RookDivest wouldn't send their own people in to do the job anytime soon. Now Kline needed to send notice to Kentish Cyc that two debranders from Rook-

Divest would be coming to work on the plant at 18:00 on Friday. The evening shift was likely to have the least xec oversight, especially with the team being two xecs down. For security reasons the plant would require at least twenty-four hours' notice, but Mia had said to give them barely any more than that—the less time passed between Kentish Cyc learning the visit was imminent and the visit actually taking place, the less time there was for something to happen to reveal the subterfuge.

Kline had his terminal with him, which also contained a spoof of RookDivest's portal. When he logged his request with Kentish Cyc, it appeared to the plant's system that it was being routed via RookDivest's offices in Boston. This was the main reason he'd come over to NiZCO to do this: had he done it from his rooms near the plant, the system might have spotted that the connection was being made from within the corpurbation. Arlo and Drienne then connected to the spoof portal with their alt-id slates and told the system they were coming. The plant's security system recorded their physical form, which it would use to identify them on arrival. A notification was sent to the plant's management.

They waited a few minutes, with Kline poised to intervene if there was any pushback from the plant. He was prepared to pose as a RookDivest employee, intercept the contact, and smooth things over. But they duly received an acknowledgment from an actual human, saying they looked forward to welcoming Annie Clarke and Roland Fernandes to the plant, with no follow-up queries. The whole process took no more than ten minutes, and then Kline packed the terminal away.

At Drienne's suggestion, the crew had agreed to convene at her apartment for one last meeting tonight at 8:00 P.M. Kline felt it was a bad and unnecessary idea, but Mia approved, so it was happening. That was a little over three hours away. Drienne declared she was still wiped from yesterday's flight and was going to have a nap, and went to the bedroom.

"Yeah," Arlo said to Kline, "I might actually do the same, so—"

"What was that about before?" said Kline in a lowered voice.

Arlo exhaled heavily. "Don't mention it to her, please—she doesn't remember."

"*That's* reassuring."

"It's fine, she—" Arlo glanced toward the bedroom. "She suffers from duplisychosis."

Kline raised his eyebrows. "Oh, is *that* all? It wasn't on her record."

"We kept it off her record."

"And you didn't tell Mia, or the rest of us, about this because . . ."

"Because it's not a big deal—"

"Because Mia wouldn't have taken her on."

"It'll be fine. I know how to keep her on the level."

"Mm. It looks like it."

"It came out just now because she was tired—look, trust me, it won't be a problem. We've made the plan now, it's too late to change it."

"If it happens while she's inside the plant, you need to know what you're going to do about it."

"Don't worry, I've got it covered. Please don't tell Mia."

Kline thought for a moment, then nodded. "You're right. I've registered you both, we need to go ahead, there's no point changing anything now."

"Thank you," said Arlo, nodding gratefully. And then he said again that he wanted to take a nap before the meeting, and Kline took the hint and left. Kline didn't particularly want to hang around NiZCOval for three hours, but he also didn't want to travel back to his apartment and then back again. He returned to the coffeehouse.

NiZCO had been the frequent butt of jokes back home in Shanghai, not unlike the offensive jokes British people used to make about the Irish. To Oakseed's brand ambassadors NiZCO was a byword for second-rate, cheap, tacky, behind the trends. They used to mock the ambassadors from NiZCO and delighted in stealing their customers.

Arlo recalled this as he shaved in the bathroom of the apartment after a shower. In the window, NiZCO's "beach ball" logo caught his eye flapping on the banners that hung from the lampposts. (It wasn't supposed to represent a beach ball, it was meant to represent NiZCO's expansion in all directions across the globe, but it looked like a beach ball and everyone referred to it as the "beach ball.") He considered the simple truth that NiZCO was still around, and Oakseed was not. So NiZCO must be doing *something* right. Maybe there was no real difference between the two companies. Arlo never thought he took the NiZCO jokes seriously, but now it seemed obvious those jokes had been inserted into the culture deliberately, to give the cynical retained workforce something to bond over, and he'd gone along with it. Oakseed had made a fool of him. As he gained more and more distance from the company, his whole existence increasingly seemed like a sick prank.

Arlo wanted to talk to Drienne about this, because for all she was better than him at resisting this stuff, he was sure she'd made those jokes too. He walked into the living room and started to speak, but quickly realized Drienne wasn't there.

She'd been there when he'd gotten in the shower. They'd napped on the bed for an hour—well, Drienne had napped, Arlo had stared at the ceiling—and then she'd gone to lie on the sofa and play *Goth Opera* on her slate. He'd even heard her singing an aria not ten minutes ago.

He looked in the bedroom and the kitchen. Nothing. None of her stuff had gone.

In a terrified flurry he composed a message to Drienne, demanding to know where she was and telling her not to move. Then he pulled some clothes on and went out looking for her. Hopefully she hadn't gone beyond the boundaries of NiZCOval—the overline carriages were so slow and infrequent, she probably hadn't. But what if she'd had another episode and just wandered away?

She wasn't at the overline platform and the last carriage departed twenty-seven minutes ago, so Arlo found it unlikely she'd gone that way. He walked the perimeter of NiZCOval and ducked inside several shops and eateries, resisting the temptation to ask anyone if they'd seen her—he didn't want anyone in London to remember his face or hers, if he could help it—

Then he saw her. Sitting outside a garish little cocktail bar. With . . . Loren?

Loren caught Arlo's eye and pointed him out to Drienne as he strode over. Drienne looked up and smiled at Arlo. "Ah, you decided to join us."

"What?" he said. "I didn't know you were here. I was looking for you, I was worried."

"I sent you a message," Drienne said, checking the back of her hand and tapping it. "Oh! Didn't send. It wanted me to tone-check it." She laughed. "Sorry, new slate. All the stupid defaults are on. Get yourself a drink."

Arlo went to the bar, relieved to have found Drienne, and also relieved Loren didn't seem curious as to why Arlo had been in such a panic about finding her.

A GOOD TIME
TO GET LOST

Each harvester was responsible for processing their own collection when they returned to the plant. This happened on the workfloor, the largest area of the plant, which was located on the ground floor of the building and contained a series of substance hubs: inverted cones, broad but not too deep, each one large enough for twenty or so workers to stand around its edge. They were all set into the floor and had a large hole at the base, forming a funnel. The slope was steep enough that any materials deposited into the funnel tumbled down and dropped to the level below. Each hub had a barrier around the edge so you couldn't fall in, and atop this barrier was a wide ledge that you could use to sort through what you'd collected. Everyone moved their carts between the different hubs and deposited what they'd found, stripping out as much divergent matter as possible before tossing it in. Everything that went into each hub was subjected to a series of cleansing washes that could dissolve plastic, glass, metal, et cetera, but anything that needed heavy cleaning would clog up the system, meaning you'd have to clean it again *and* you'd be penalized. So it was worth your while to clean everything as thoroughly as you could.

It was always noisy here during working hours: echoing around the high ceiling were the sounds of chattering colleagues, rattling carts, and especially the clatter and clunks of salvage as it was tossed into the hubs and disappeared down the holes. Nadi was at the plastics hub, leaning against the ledge while she used a spudger to scrape a chunk of glue off the casing of a refrigerator. It was coming off in frustratingly tiny pieces. According to her skeye, the glue was an advanced resin, hard to break down and impossible to recycle into anything printable, so it was tough to remove but it also *had* to be removed. No wonder the other harvesters had left it for her to collect. They were probably laughing at her behind her back when she was cheerfully removing it from the kitchen.

Nadi worked at the strip of grimy white plastic, covered in nicks and scratches. To relieve the tedium she thought about what had made all those nicks and scratches. Every surface in the city had its history written on it, from the time when London was still alive. The refrigerator would have been moved around a few times and scraped against walls. And kitchens were busy places. Staff would have bustled past the refrigerator, bumping into it while carrying trays and boxes. In the midst of a hectic shift, someone might lean against it while wearing a pair of jeans with metal rivets, and the rivets would scratch the surface. Maybe late at night, after the place was closed and the staff was done cleaning up, two of them who'd had their eye on each other for weeks would stand by the refrigerator, standing closer than they ever had before, talking tentatively, and then one would lean in against the other and push them up against the refrigerator and they'd kiss, and the kiss would become more urgent, and then, hands fumbling, they'd hastily pull down the lower parts of their clothing and—

"You don't want to put it in there like that," said the woman next to Nadi.

"What?" said Nadi, snapping out of her reverie.

"You got to get all the glue off first," the woman said, pointing at the piece of plastic, which Nadi had put down on the ledge so she could rest her hands for a moment. The woman looked about sixty. Maybe she *was* sixty or maybe it was just a sign of the hard living here, but the woman assumed the authority of one who'd been doing it longer than everyone else, and felt she had a duty to point out to them how they were doing it all wrong.

"I know," said Nadi as neutrally as she could.

"If you put it in like that, you won't get your commission for it."

"I know."

"Because they know who put what in, it's all recorded." The woman tapped her skeye.

"I know. Thank you. They explained it to me." The commission on each individual piece was small, but so were their basic wages, and you needed to top it up by collecting as much as you could. You had to make sure every piece counted, they'd told her at her induction session. Even so, Nadi felt there came a point where you were just throwing your own time away, and she was about ready to give up and toss the plastic into the non-cyc hub. But now this woman had pointed it out she couldn't do that. Nadi was trying to fit in, and that meant when someone told her how things worked around here, she had to go along with what they said.

After Nadi finally got the glue off, she decided now would be a good time to get lost. Her cart still had some compressed hardboard in it, which was just about the lowest value material you could collect. It couldn't be turned into anything printable, no one used it for building materials anymore and it was a notoriously dirty and inefficient fuel source, but it was still incentivized to make sure it didn't get left out there where people might set fire to it.

Nadi saw Gregg and asked him to keep an eye on her cart while she went to the bathroom. It was plain he didn't want to, and only did so because he'd decided she could be useful to him. She knew full well where the nearest bathroom was, due to having studied the floor plan of the plant. The plant had two stairwells, one near the front entrance and another at the back; there was also an elevator by the entrance, which was exclusively for the use of management, and two service elevators by the rear stairwell, which only moved between the workfloor and the underfloor.

Nadi walked toward the bathroom that was located along the back wall. Then she carried on past it and went up the stairs. She counted the steps as she went: they were narrow and steep, and wouldn't be easy to take at pace. The workfloor had a high ceiling—it was the height of two or three floors in a typical office building—and Nadi climbed six separate flights of stairs before reaching the top floor. Each flight had eleven steps. Sixty-six steps.

Nadi hadn't been shown the top floor on her induction. Emerging at the top of the stairwell, she found herself at one end of a corridor. The walls were colored light green and skylights had been set into its ceiling at regular intervals. This corridor had a very different feel from the rest of the building. It was much cleaner, and most of the noise from the operations going on below had been neutralized. There were dwarf trees in pots at regular intervals, and a smell like fresh laundry was in the air.

Nadi remembered how this corridor was bisected by another one, creating a lopsided cross, like the flag of a Scandinavian country. Nadi was looking at it from the back of the building, which meant the support staff's offices were on her right. The smaller admin and HR departments were based in offices on Nadi's left. On the other side of the bisecting corridor were the offices used by the management team: each had their own office, and there was also a kitchen, a synergy zone, a wet room, and a small gym. At the center of the crossed corridors was a cluster of four meeting rooms, one on each corner. It was possible to fold back the walls of these rooms to create one large conference area.

Nadi waited a moment and listened. The support and admin offices would be staffed around the clock. The two remaining xecs would be taking it in shifts, so there would be no more than one of them present.

Nadi walked on down the corridor. She trod as lightly as she could. The carpet helped to muffle her footsteps. When she reached the bisecting corridor, she turned right and walked down it. On her left, directly opposite another door that led to the support department, was the door to the premium store. This door was made of artificial sapphire. It was locked, but its transparency meant Nadi could observe the interior layout without entering. However, it also meant anyone passing couldn't fail to notice any unauthorized persons in the store.

Nadi checked that the corridor was still empty, then took her slate from her pocket, pressed it to the door, and took a capture. Two of the room's walls were lined with lockers: these were plain, once shiny but long since dulled with age, and sturdy enough to survive a fire, a flood, or an explosion. Samson must have been keeping tabs for years on the locker he'd commandeered, checking that no one had queried its being out of action, or that the entire wall of lockers hadn't been ripped out and replaced. Fortunately, no one ever saw much call to refurbish anything at Kentish Cyc, and they had more lockers than they needed anyway.

The store was used for things too valuable to process into basematter—precious metals, jewels, archaeological discoveries and such. The lockers were not permanently assigned to different types of content, but were assigned according to whatever needed to be stored there at that moment. Most items would only be here briefly, until a use had been found for them or a deal had been made to sell them. Then they would be removed and sent elsewhere. When you walked into the store, equipped with a skeye and the correct permissions, you either asked the system to show you where the thing you were looking for was—in which case it would open the locker for you—or told it you needed to deposit something. If you were depositing, the system would either open the locker that contained similar items so you could put it with them, or if there weren't any similar items it would assign a vacant locker to this type and open it for you.

Mia had described to them where Samson's locker was—three from the right, on the second row up from the floor. The bottom two rows were rarely used because they were inconvenient to reach. Nadi leaned down and put her face close to the sapphire door—she just wanted to see the locker door while she was—

"What are you doing?"

Nadi quickly turned to see a diminutive woman in a loose, intricately patterned shirt and colorful shorts stepping into the corridor. Even if Nadi hadn't already seen her record (her name was Zara Astley), she would have known she was a xec. No one else would dress like that for work.

"I couldn't find a supervisor," said Nadi.

"What are you talking about?" said Zara, walking toward her.

Nadi had anticipated being called upon to account for her presence. She fumbled in her pocket and produced a ring with a gem set into it. She had collected this while out harvesting this afternoon: it had been left by Loren for her to find, as a dry run for what they'd need to do tomorrow. "I found this," Nadi said.

The xec took the ring from her. "You're new, aren't you?"

"Yes. They said if I found anything valuable I was to give it to a supervisor and they'd take it up here."

The woman peered at the ring. "This isn't valuable," she remarked. "Your skeye should have told you that. It's just an amethyst."

"The skeye did say it wasn't valuable. But I wasn't sure that was right because it's pretty, isn't it?" Nadi said, playing the dim overgrown child. "Seems a pity to cyc it, someone would like that as it is."

The woman shrugged, shook her head. "Leave it with me. I don't know . . ." She motioned for Nadi to go back to the stairs. "Go and finish your shift."

"Will I still get my commission?"

"If it's sold and you logged it as your find then yes, of course you'll get it."

Nadi thanked her, pretending to be excited, dashed back downstairs and collected her cart from Gregg. She dumped the hardboard, clocked out, and took the overline down to NiZCOval.

THE BIG SERVE

Before they started, Loren swept Arlo and Drienne's apartment for ears. The rooms were sparsely furnished but Loren still found eleven ears—just the standard ones that were in most devices, enabling the user to communicate with the device verbally and allowing the device to harvest data about you on behalf of the manufacturer. Loren expected to find them in the refrigerator and the cabinets, that was standard, but there was one in the *kettle*. What did a kettle need an ear for? You could tell it to switch on, but you still had to stand up and take it to the tap to fill it with water. Instead of disabling the ears, Loren fed them all a stream of indistinct, mundane conversation—if you disabled one, the outlet that controlled them was liable to flag it and send someone to repair it.

"Shall we start, then?" said Arlo once Kline and Nadi arrived.

Loren felt irritation at how Arlo had become the de facto leader of this operation, based seemingly on nothing more than (a) he was the first to be recruited and (b) he was the only irreplaceable member of the team. He wasn't the most qualified. And frankly Loren had come to the conclusion they personally disliked Arlo. During the planning phase, Loren had a sense he was treating them in an offhand, dismissive way, but they tried not to let it bother them. Even gave him the benefit of the doubt when he shut them down at the briefing. But when they were having cocktails together earlier, it was the first time they'd spoken face-to-face since Vancouver, and he'd been *such* a dick. He'd seemed distracted and annoyed they were there, had given terse responses to everything Loren said, and several times he'd asked Drienne if she wanted to go back to the apartment. Loren could tell he just saw them as this sort of gray blob of a person and showed no interest in their views or inner life or whatever. By contrast, Drienne was considerate and engaged, and it seemed weird to Loren she and Arlo were such close friends.

So should Drienne lead the group? She had basically the same skill set as Arlo, and judging from the tales she'd told back in Vancouver, she had a knack for getting away with things and could lie convincingly. But she also seemed like someone who took unnecessary risks. Nadi? She had the most experience of the criminal mindset and she was *super* observant, but she'd followed orders all her life and had no leadership skills. The same was true of Loren, for that matter: they were hands down the most intelligent member of the crew, but their interpersonal skills had been left deliberately undeveloped.

So that left Kline. He didn't seem a natural leader either, because he was the most reluctant of the crew. He visibly resented having to be here and interact with them all, which led to the other point in his disfavor, which was that no one liked him. Even Drienne, who was charismatic and engaging and could get on with anyone, had said to Loren she found him hard work. But Kline understood systems and he understood people. And it might be a good thing that he just wanted the job done so they could all get out of here, and that he appeared not to care if any of the others liked him.

"Okay," said Arlo, "let's go through this step by step—Nadi, you'll be on shift from—"

"I think Kline should go through the plan," said Loren.

"Right. Er, why?"

"Well, maybe he should kind of be the"—Loren searched for another word that wasn't *leader*—"coordinator for this?" They looked around the room. "Like, you three are all gonna be inside the building, I'm gonna be outside and around it—doesn't it make sense for the one guy who's gonna be sitting tight in a room down the street to know everything that's going on, and kind of be the center of planning?"

Kline looked stunned for a moment that one of the others had spoken up for him. Then he said, "Yes."

"Like, I'm not saying you should be in *charge*. But I think if anyone has an overview of this thing, it's you."

"I think that makes a lot of sense," said Kline, nodding. "I'll coordinate."

Arlo looked to Drienne as if expecting her to challenge this.

"It does make sense," Drienne remarked.

"Fine," said Arlo. "I didn't particularly want to do it, this meeting was your idea anyway."

"I know," said Drienne sweetly, "and it's a good one." She sipped the iced tea Arlo had made for them all.

"I actually agree with Arlo that all of us gathering like this is risky," said Kline, "and we shouldn't take any longer than necessary over it, so . . . Nadi, first of all maybe we can take a look at that capture you made of the interior, and we can plot who'll be where when?"

Nadi flipped the capture onto the window on the coffee table so she could open it up and they could all see. Before Arlo cast his gaze down to it he glared briefly at Loren, who gave him an amiable smile in return while feeling a burning need to prove him wrong about something. It didn't particularly matter what.

They'd gone through every step of the plan, but to Kline's chagrin, people kept asking questions. Nadi raised the fact the workforce didn't know the company had collapsed, and whether that might affect things.

"I don't see that it should," said Arlo.

"But you're coming in to debrand it," said Nadi. "People will notice you're doing that and they'll wonder what's going on."

"Will they, though?" said Kline.

"Yes. They're not stupid."

"Look, I've seen plenty of information choke strategies—I've helped implement them. Management have cleared you to come in for the debranding so they must have a plan for this, whether it's to tell the workforce the place is up for sale, or tell them it's not a debranding but something else that looks like a debranding. I can't see it being a problem for us."

Then Drienne wanted to take another look at one of the two devices Loren had built, which they had nicknamed the Lost Weekend, and go through how to operate it again. Drienne also wanted to make sure Nadi and Arlo knew how to operate it in case she was unable to do so, and Nadi wanted to pick it up, to get an idea of its weight and texture as well as its appearance, to ensure she could identify it tomorrow. And because they would be collected by Mia directly after the operation was complete, none of them would get a chance to go back for their suitcases, so all the others had items they wanted to give Kline to put in his luggage—clothes, shoes, a bottle of some soft drink you could only buy in the UK, a couple of books. Kline accepted these items with ill grace.

After that, Kline thought the meeting was finally done. But then Drienne produced a bottle of vodka and told Arlo to get some glasses, ice, and something to mix it with.

"Is it wise to get into a drinking session the night before the operation?" said Arlo.

Drienne looked at him askance. "I'm not proposing a *session*, we just need to toast the plan."

"Do we?"

"I think we should," said Nadi.

"Just have some redjuice if you don't want alcohol," said Drienne.

"No, I'll have *one* drink," said Arlo as he headed for the galley kitchen.

Kline could tell Arlo was anxious, and maybe that was mostly about carrying out the operation, but part of it had to be Drienne. For all Arlo had claimed she'd be fine, that "episode" of Drienne's had rattled him. Drienne had reverted to the gregarious, irreverent person he'd met in Vancouver, with no trace of the angry, paranoid voice he'd heard shouting at Arlo. Which, in a way, made Kline even more concerned.

Arlo returned with glasses, ice, and redjuice. Drienne poured a generous measure of vodka into each one, and topped it up with the redjuice. They took the glasses in their hands and Drienne looked around the group. "So. Uh . . . To wealth and freedom?"

They brought their glasses together and echoed the sentiment. Then the conversation turned to what they'd do with their shares of the money. Arlo and Drienne wanted to open a bar somewhere on the coast, maybe Santiago or somewhere like that, and for once this didn't seem to be a Drienne plan that Arlo had been dragged along with, but a mutual dream. They described their bar in detail: the location, the décor, the music, the vibe, the selection of drinks, the light bites they were planning to offer, the opening hours. They had created this place in their minds over their years together, and could talk about it like they'd been there.

Loren wasn't sure where they wanted to go, but they wanted to design and produce wearables and so a fashion capital like Warsaw would suit them well. They also revealed that on the flight here they had designed outfits for everyone on the team, not for any real reason, just for fun. Loren hadn't kept any images of the other crew members on their slate, for security reasons, so they sent all the designs to everyone else's slates so they could see what they looked like with them on. No one was quite sure what to say, which perhaps gave Loren the impression no one liked their designs—but Kline was impressed by his, a loose cream suit inspired by martial arts gear. He told Loren he would print it when the operation was all over, and he meant it.

Nadi wanted to use her share to open a tennis school in Nova Scotia. Again, this surprised everyone because no one had heard her mention the sport, but she spent a lot of her downtime playing it, apparently, and would have liked to play professionally, had she been able to make any choices for herself.

"Bet you've got a hell of a serve," said Loren, and Nadi reacted modestly while making clear that yes, she did. And then the conversation moved on without ever coming around to Kline and what he intended to do with his share. This annoyed him, but it was also fine, because he didn't want to tell them. It didn't matter where he went, because he had a cast-iron investment plan, he could do it from anywhere, and he didn't want them copying it.

"Is everything okay?" Arlo said to Loren when the others were discussing the current state of their debt.

"Sure," said Loren. "Why d'you ask?"

"There's nothing you want to air? That's really the point of this meeting."

Loren shrugged and said, "Well . . ."

But Drienne was saying she wanted to see Nadi's big serve, and Arlo turned and agreed: he'd never played tennis, but he did watch it. So Nadi swapped her backhand from her left hand to her right and loaded up a tennis sim. She moved to a corner of the apartment by the window, where she wasn't going to knock into any furniture or the light fitting. She loosened her shoulders, tossed an imaginary ball with one hand and *smashed* with the other. The serve was recorded at 218 km/h.

"Fuck," said Arlo. "That's massive."

"I was just warming up," said Nadi. This sounded arrogant, but was true. She served again and again and again, eventually logging eight attempts. The sixth was the best, clocking in at 232 km/h. Arlo wanted to try, so he loaded up the same sim and did what he'd seen Nadi do: his speed was 104 km/h.

"That was shit," Arlo said, but Nadi assured him that was actually good, for someone who didn't play. She gave him some pointers on how he could improve, and after a few more attempts he was serving closer to 130 km/h. The others wanted a go, and coaching from Nadi. Drienne's incompetence caused much hilarity: Far from being embarrassed to fail in front of everyone,

Drienne cheerfully played up to it. Even Kline was convinced to participate.

Drienne poured another round of drinks for everyone, ignoring Arlo's protests, pointing out the vodka was only going to go to waste if they didn't drink it, and Nadi found herself talking to Loren, who had designed an incredible sundress for her. Nadi had never worn any kind of dress in her entire life, and when she saw an avatar of herself wearing it, she felt tearful for reasons she didn't understand.

"It's a shame we'll all have to go our separate ways after all this is over," Nadi remarked. "I feel like we're just getting to know each other."

"Well," said Loren, "we don't *have* to go our separate ways. Nova Scotia sounds nice."

20

BIRMINGHAM
WOULDN'T HAVE HER

Friday.

Nadi was on the afternoon/evening shift because Kline had gone into the rota system and made sure she was. No trace of yesterday's rain, the dry heat was back. Nadi stepped through the security arch, walked out onto the platform, and boarded the truck train. She saw Gregg was there too, and she took the seat next to him.

"Wonder where we're going today," she said, hoping the banality of the remark made it seem innocent. Today, once again, they would be harvesting Bloomsbury—but Nadi didn't know exactly where. Depending on what materials were in demand, or the security situation, the spot they were directed toward might change from day to day—but there was usually gossip between the harvesters about where they were going.

"There's a hospital that's become a big vague hangout lately, our securits have been on it all week," said Gregg. "They'll want it stripped so they can redeploy the staff."

"Makes sense." Nadi looked at the back of her hand, pretending to be checking the weather, but in fact she was sending this information to Loren. The truck train had a relay fitted that bounced the signal back to the plant and Nadi could use this as long as she stayed within range of the truck train, but harvesting would probably take her out of range. "What do you think happened to that girl we found?"

Gregg shrugged with his face rather than his body. "Moved on."

"Moved on where?"

"Somewhere. Somewhere not staked out by the corps."

"You don't think they'll have sent her to prison?"

"What?"

"You don't think so?"

"They'd have to *build* some prisons first. No one in London pays to run any prisons. The only people who *could* put up the money are the megas, and they don't, and they also pay zero tax." He leaned in to Nadi, as if the next part shouldn't be spoken too loudly. "And then they complain when there's crime."

"I suppose she could move north."

"What, to Birmingham?"

"Or somewhere."

Gregg shook his head. "Birmingham wouldn't have her. You can't resettle anywhere from London unless you've got money. And north of Watford they *will* lock you up if you're there illegally."

"Sounds like there's nowhere she *can* go."

"No, but there's nothing *you* can do about it." He nudged her with his elbow. "Look, it's better we found her than the securits. They beat people like her up for giggles."

Nadi knew it would be idiotic to come back to London after the operation was done. It was the last place in the world she should go. But she'd decided last night that she had to find that girl. Maybe she could use her share of the money to hire someone to find her and get her out of wherever she was. Nadi would recognize her again; she was good with faces.

Gregg was right on the money about today's work site: they were breaking down a hospital. As Nadi and the other harvesters disembarked from the truck train, there was a noise from the side of the building: a bunch of unhabitants had heard the trucks coming and opted to vacate the hospital, and a couple of securits accompanying the harvesters briefly gave chase. The harvesters were instructed to wait by the truck train while the securiteam made a quick sweep of the building, to see if any more were inside. The harvesters grumbled about the time they were losing. But this lull allowed Nadi to send Loren a follow-up message confirming they were working on the hospital. Then the securits declared the first two floors safe and the harvesters moved in.

The ground floor was particularly squalid—often the case in larger buildings, ground-floor windows were the first to get broken, and when the panes were gone, all kinds of crap blew in off the street—so the harvesters went up to the first floor, which had already been partly worked over but still offered plenty of untouched rooms. Nadi picked up a positive vibe from the other harvesters, an expectation of rich pickings as they all carried their empty carts up the wide stairwell. Nadi found a room filled with wheeled metal beds, which more importantly had a window that looked out onto the street, and Gregg joined her in the same room. Nadi applied her cutting tool to the beds, breaking each one into pieces small enough to fit into her cart. While doing this she glanced up regularly.

After they'd been working on this room for about twenty minutes, Nadi spotted Loren walking down the opposite side of the street, dressed in their most inconspicuous clothes (dark blue polo shirt and gray shorts) and making minimal noise. They'd walked here from Kentish Cyc, which was less than four kilometers away: they'd set off before the truck train left. Walking through one of the salvage zones in central London wasn't illegal, but entering any of the buildings was, so they needed to be swift and discreet. Securiteam was still occupied with sweeping the upper floors of the building; they must have found something to entertain them up there.

Loren turned, looked up, and briefly caught Nadi's eye. They smiled, then crossed the street. Nadi resisted the temptation to smile back, as she didn't want Gregg to notice, not that he probably would. Nadi looked back down at her work, and when she glanced back a few seconds later, Loren was gone.

Nadi forced herself to focus on harvesting. On her previous shifts the materials she'd collected had been smaller and the cart had filled more slowly, but these chunks of metal bed frame took up a lot of space. Very soon she could take this cart back to the truck and get a fresh one, which would give her an opportunity to collect what Loren was leaving for her. Nadi also wanted to make her quota. It was possible, if this operation went awry, that she might need to stay in London and keep her head down until everything blew over, and if so she'd be grateful to have this job.

Nadi yanked a moldering mattress off another bed; her stomach churned as her senses informed her someone had defecated into a hole in the mattress, the smell turning the air heavy and oppressive. She told Gregg to look out, then she tossed the mattress as far as she could into the corner of the room. She applied her cutter to the bed in swift, decisive strokes. She'd worked out the optimum way of doing it: slice through the side bars first, cutting those into manageable lengths, but let the mesh in the middle hold it together. Then cut around the edges of the mesh and let the whole thing fall apart. Any pieces that were still too large for the cart you could then break up.

She was partway through this process when a message arrived from Loren—they were in close enough proximity to ping slate-to-slate—but Nadi didn't look at her backhand straightaway. She finished filling her cart with metal, straightened up, and left the room, bringing her cart with her.

"You filled that already?" said Gregg.

"Yep," said Nadi brightly.

She stepped into the dingy corridor. It echoed with the sounds of fittings being sliced, equipment being dismantled, and walls being gouged into. She checked the message from Loren, which contained only a dropped pin, no text. The location of the pin was almost directly underneath her.

The cart was too heavy even for Nadi to carry down the stairs, and the hospital's elevators had been removed, being unsafe to use and beyond repair. Instead, the harvesting crews had set up temporary pulleys in the lift shafts. You could attach a cart to a pulley and lower it by using the hand crank. Nadi took the safety brake off, grabbed the cable with her hands, and used her own strength to lower the cart. She was not meant to do this, but it was quicker. When the cart hit the bottom of the shaft, she put the brake back on and slid down the cable instead of taking the stairs. She was not meant to do this either.

On the ground floor, Nadi guided her cart along the path down the center of the rubbish-strewn corridor, where faded tape in different colors had once guided visitors toward different departments. She stopped, left her cart in the corridor, and ducked into the bathroom that Loren's pin had indicated.

The bathroom smelled vile. It had continued to be used by those who entered this building, long after the plumbing had ceased to operate. Loren could have put the thing anywhere, why here? But then Nadi realized the unpleasantness of the hiding place was exactly the point: no one was going to come in for a casual look around. This room was never, ever going to be stripped, it would be left like this until the building was flattened.

At least Loren had concealed it in the cleanest part of the bathroom, behind the door. Nadi took a deep breath of relatively fresh air from the corridor, then reentered. As the door closed behind her, the light on her helmet sensed the darkness and activated. She turned to see the Lost Weekend device in the corner, resting on a small heap of rubble that kept it just clear of the very shallow layer of reeking liquid that covered the entire floor.

Nadi picked it up and allowed her skeye to register it as salvage. The skeye didn't know what it was for, and it didn't need to know—it just assessed what it was made of and confirmed to Nadi it was worth taking.

The Lost Weekend looked like it was broken, because Loren had designed it to look like the kind of junk harvested by Kentish Cyc every day. It was about the size of a dinner plate, but substantially thicker. It was that pale green color that had been standard for technology three decades ago, but looked terribly dated now. Loren had installed it in what looked like the shell of the upper part of a cleaner, the part that housed the guidance system. It was cracked in several places, and through the gaps Nadi could see wires and tubes. It was heavyish, and Loren had explained most of the weight was the battery, as it needed a lot of power but the actual components were simple. They were very clever to have made something so effective with so few parts.

Nadi walked out of the bathroom. The corridor was devoid of people: no one had seen her enter or leave. She returned to her cart, moved some of the broken-up bed frame aside, and stashed the Lost Weekend in the middle of it. Then she pushed her cart out of the hospital, over to the truck train, stowed it on the rear carriage, and took an empty cart from the stack.

If normal operating protocols were observed there would be no problems—no one touched anyone else's carts, because all the salvage in it was logged to its collector and they'd be the one to get the commission. Taking someone else's cart was a waste of time, and could jeopardize your job. But still Nadi didn't like letting the cart out of her sight, and wouldn't feel comfortable until she was back at the plant with it. She checked the time: they were heading back to the plant in four hours and twenty-three minutes.

21
THE MAN WHO FAILED SIDEWAYS

The outfits Arlo and Drienne were putting on were the fruits of a delightful shopping trip back in Vancouver. Mia hadn't given them an unlimited budget for the clothes, but it was far more money than either of them had ever had to spend on clothes before. They looked fucking great: Arlo had a vented collared blazer and a business kilt, Drienne had a formal mesh robe with a simple, stylish tunic dress underneath. It was wild how different they looked wearing quality, *non-Oakseed* clothes, woven not printed. Everything they'd ever been given to wear was accelerated-trend stuff, and much of it seemed sharp and exciting at the time—but that was in comparison with whatever they'd been wearing before, which always seemed passé by then. When you saw *really* great clothes like these, you realized there was something watered down about everything they'd worn before. They looked so *bold*.

Arlo and Drienne took a moment to admire each other. They stroked their fingertips across each other's clothes—this was something they'd done for years whenever either thought the other looked particularly good. Arlo had never thought about why they did this. It was just one of the strange expressions of platonic intimacy they had.

They stepped back from each other and went though their

identities and backstory one more time. *What's your name?* Roland
Fernandes. *What do you do?* I work for RookDivest, I'm a debranding specialist. We're based out of Boston. *You sound like you're from
round here.* That's right, I actually grew up in Cambridge. It's all
changed a lot, though!

The trick was to not say too much. Just because you thought of
a nice detail to use in a certain situation, didn't mean you had to
shoehorn it in. There was a benefit in saying less: often, it meant
the other person would tell *you* something. And if they thought
you were unfriendly and taciturn, so what? Arlo and Drienne were
hardwired to want people to like them, but today they'd have to get
over that; they just needed people to believe them.

It was time to leave. But first . . .

"How are you feeling?" Arlo asked.

"What?" said Drienne, looking up from her case of drones.

"Y'know, with your . . ." Arlo tapped the side of his head.

"Fine."

"Fine?"

"Great. Feeling very, very stable." She smiled and shut her case.

Arlo didn't think Drienne could tell when an episode was coming on. She'd never done anything to mitigate those episodes—for
example, by taking herself out of a social situation, or suspending
access to her own money for a few hours. But stress was often a
trigger for her, and right now she did seem remarkably calm.

Arlo nodded. "Then we've got a job to do."

They picked up their cases and left the room.

Drienne and Arlo took the overline, passing through Acton on
their way up to Kentish Cyc. It struck Drienne that her character—
Annie, she reminded herself, Annie Clarke, repeating it under her
breath—would be even more aghast at the state of London than she
was, and she should lean into that. She felt like she ought to have
some talent for this sort of deep roleplay, due to her tendency to slip

into an alternate persona, but she'd never done it consciously. Her ambassadorial persona was a construct, but there was no authentic self she reverted to when she wasn't working; the construct had long since supplanted it. She was looking forward to finding out if she was good at pretending. It might be a skill she could use in the new life she was going to build after all this.

"Do you think," she said to Arlo, "that if we do this and our debts are canned . . ."

Arlo turned and looked around, in case someone might hear them, but the carriage was empty and even if it hadn't been, they could barely hear each other over the grind of poorly maintained wheels against dusty rails, so anyone not sitting right next to Drienne would have no chance of hearing her.

"Do you think my problems might stop?" she finished. She'd been wanting to say this ever since Mia told her of the reward for success, but she was afraid it sounded foolish.

"I've no idea," said Arlo.

"Neither have I, but what do you think?"

"I suppose it depends whether it's caused by circumstances, or by something, you know . . ."

"In my brain."

"Yeah."

"I just think . . . if the problem is a disconnect between my being a made, and some part of my brain that refuses to accept that's what I am . . ."

"Is that how it works?"

"I don't know." Drienne felt irritated: he should know by now she didn't know how it worked. "But if it *is* that—if my circumstances change, and the fact I'm a made isn't important anymore, will that fix it?"

"Do you think what we are won't be important anymore?"

"It won't, will it? If we're no longer retained . . . it won't matter that we're mades, will it?"

"I don't know. Won't we always be different?"

Drienne didn't know the answer. She looked out the window, and watched some kids taking turns to throw rocks at a rusting double-decker bus.

A man was waiting for them at the platform when they arrived, wearing a shiny dark gray polo and matching baggy trousers—both items Arlo had been pushing a couple of months ago, which spoke volumes. Drienne and Arlo had read the man's personnel file, so they already knew he was very low-status in xec terms. But even if Drienne hadn't known that, she could immediately tell by his clothes. He'd given up.

"Hello, I'm Henrik Paul," he told them. "You must be Roland and Annie."

Drienne and Arlo both remembered to smile in the way you do when someone says your name. Drienne shook Henrik's hand and he asked if they'd had a good journey.

"Very smooth," Drienne said.

"Yes," Arlo agreed. "Much better than I expected."

"Oh god," said Henrik, "have you heard horror stories?"

"Well . . ."

"Nothing specific," said Drienne.

"It's really not that bad," Henrik stressed. "If you're using business routes, the system still basically works. But I don't blame you for the quick turnaround."

Drienne felt sorry for Henrik. His file had not been a long read. He'd been working here eleven years, and there was little of note in that time except a couple of minor disciplinaries. When Mia had been working here, Kentish Cyc was seen as a good, challenging proving ground for young, hungry talent. But its prestige had faded, worn down by the diseased city that housed it, and Henrik was not young, hungry talent. The fact the plant had xecs at all was a relic of a time when it had been an exciting project. Henrik had been sent here in his early thirties, which meant they didn't want him anywhere else. Possibly there'd been an incident that had been kept off his file—maybe he'd fucked up, pissed off someone important, or knew too much and had been pushed to the margins. Or maybe he was just bad at his job. Xecs very rarely got fired for being useless: they could be ruthless with each other if they had something to gain, but it took something major to turn their backs on one of their own. Instead, they just let them fail sideways. Out of the public eye, buried here and in the other Londons of the world no one wanted to acknowledge.

The trio headed down to the street. Before they crossed, Henrik turned to Arlo and Drienne and said, "Crazy, isn't it?"

"Mm," said Drienne, but the question had been directed toward Arlo.

"The company just collapsing out of nowhere, I mean," Henrik went on.

"Yes," said Arlo. "Strange times."

"No one saw it coming, did they? I don't know, maybe you did. Did you?"

"No, we—"

"We had been on alert for it," said Drienne.

"But really only the few weeks before it happened," added Arlo. "It's like they say, you go bankrupt gradually, then very suddenly."

"Who says that?"

"I don't know."

"Ernest Hemingway," said Drienne.

"It's very odd," Henrik said to Arlo without acknowledging Drienne had spoken. "I've no idea what I'm going to do. Most of the workforce will stay when the plant is sold—I mean, half of them are mades anyway, so they'll be sold as part of the package, of course."

"Of *course*," said Drienne, unable to stop herself adding an edge to it that thankfully seemed to go unnoticed.

"But the new owners will want their own top-floor people in, so I'll be out of a job. I'm sure someone's ready to swoop in and buy it the moment you're done and it goes on sale. But that's really why I wanted to meet you off the carriage."

"Because you wanted to ask if there are any jobs going at Rook-Divest?" said Drienne.

Henrik laughed. "Ha! No. I mean, if there *are*—"

"We wouldn't know, sorry," said Arlo, and Drienne could hear him keeping the annoyance out of his voice. He was right, to be fair: the last thing she should do was invite contact between this guy and RookDivest. She would bite her tongue next time.

"Of course. No, it's . . ." Henrik glanced at the plant and lowered his voice slightly. "Er . . . you should know the workforce—everyone below the upper floor, I mean—they don't know the company has collapsed."

"Ah," said Arlo, reacting as if this was new, but not surprising, information.

Taking her cue from this, Drienne added: "We thought that might be the case."

"Is that normal practice in situations like this, then?" Henrik looked from Drienne to Arlo.

"It's not unusual."

"It wasn't my idea. Last instruction I got, so I couldn't query it. It's been hard work keeping it from them, but worth it, I suppose, because productivity has been great. But maybe we can avoid tipping them off?"

"Won't your staff notice when we start removing all the branding?" said Arlo.

"They might notice *something*. But they're not a terribly curious bunch, so just be unobtrusive and they'll figure it's not their business, I think."

So much for Kline's insistence that management would have a plan for this.

"If they do ask," said Drienne, "we could claim to be doing a branding *update*, rather than a debranding."

"If you like," said Henrik, nodding. "Yes, that makes sense." He raised a hand and gestured for them to cross the street. As Arlo and Drienne walked ahead of him, they exchanged a glance they made sure he didn't catch. They always knew when both of them were thinking the same thing, and they both thought this guy was a fucking clown.

The security arch at the main entrance accepted Arlo and Drienne, or rather Roland and Annie, without a hitch. Then they stood in the reception area for several minutes nodding as Henrik droned on about keeping morale high and quotas and his hands-off approach to management. Eventually, Arlo gently suggested they needed to start work.

"I'll accompany you on your way round, of course," Henrik said.

"That isn't necessary," Drienne said in a tone suggesting they didn't want to *inconvenience* him by making him do something as *tedious* as that.

"Oh yes," said Arlo, "we know our way round, we've got a detailed plan of where to go and what to look for."

"I'm sure you do," said Henrik, "but you know what these old places are like—things get moved and modified over the years. I know every inch of this building." He gently punched a support strut, as if joshing with a younger sibling.

"Right." They hadn't prepared for this. Kline had profiled the guy and declared he was much too laissez-faire to have any interest in being involved in a mundane operation in a workplace he would shortly be dismissed from. "That isn't—I mean, I'm sure you've got better things to do."

Henrik smiled and shrugged. "Not really! We're not supposed to change anything until the place is sold, so there's very little for me to do."

"We want to get through it as quickly as possible," said Drienne, "so we were going to split up and—"

"That makes sense," said Henrik, and turned to Arlo. "I'll come with you."

Fuck. Drienne had left the door wide open for that one. And it was dawning on her why Henrik had been giving Arlo more attention—the xec was *attracted* to him. Kline hadn't allowed for that. There wasn't much they could do if he was keen to hang around; well, they could tell him to fuck off, but it was all-important to keep this businesslike and neither of them could think of any good reason why Henrik *shouldn't* help with this process.

"Do you have a bathroom I can use?" Drienne asked.

MORE THAN
SHE'S SAYING

Kline was at the window of his apartment, trying to see if Frankie James was home (she wasn't there this morning, which suggested she'd been on the early shift today, and her window was now open). He'd worn his favorite burgundy suit for the operation—he'd be sitting in here the entire time, and the weather was too warm for it really, but this suit always made him feel sharp, professional, on his game. Drienne messaged him to confirm she and Arlo had got into Kentish Cyc and their cover was proving watertight thus far (of course it was, the credentials he'd created were impeccable, if anything went wrong Arlo and Drienne's performance would be to blame). However, there was a badly worded addendum to this that took Kline a few moments to decipher: xec insisting on accompanying us, tried to shake him off no luck, you said he wouldnt join! need to distract, help.

Kline replied: what do you expect me to do about it?

dont know think of something?? wrote Drienne. thought you could give him something to investigate.

Kline moved away from the window and sat on the apartment's uncomfortable sofa. It wasn't his fault Paul wanted to be involved in the operation: nothing on his record suggested that. He opened up his model of the HR structure of the plant and looked for weak points.

———

After getting back to Kentish Cyc, Nadi had found her four carts of salvage waiting in the collection bay and then lingered there, pretending there was a problem with the couplings. Then she checked no one was looking, delved into the cart that contained the cut-up bed frame pieces, and retrieved the Lost Weekend, relieved to have it in her hands again. The front of Nadi's overalls had a stash pouch on the inside to accommodate the device. This had been Loren's idea. It was uncomfortable, but the overalls were baggy and hung shapelessly over her breasts in such a way that the device, when stashed flat against her stomach, added no noticeable bulk. The securits paid little attention to what you did with salvage while you were still on shift. Their concern was whether you took any of it away with you, and they trusted the exit scanners to take care of that.

Nadi then proceeded to take her carts up to the workfloor, where she dumped all her scrap metal in the appropriate bay. While doing this she received the alert telling her Drienne and Arlo had entered the plant, which meant soon she'd get the word to meet Drienne and pass her the device. They'd agreed to meet in a bathroom near the plastics bay, and to this end Nadi had deliberately sought out more strips of plastic with the same glue that had vexed her yesterday. This meant she would be able to lurk near the plastics bay for several minutes. She stationed herself there and patiently started to scrape away the glue.

While Nadi was doing this, someone tapped her on the shoulder. Probably they were going to give her glue-removal advice like that old woman yesterday. Nadi turned to find a middle-aged woman with sun-weathered skin and very dry hair peering suspiciously at her.

"You came here from one of the other Oakseed sites, yeah?" the woman said.

"Yes," said Nadi, glancing up from the plastic and then returning her attention to it.

"Where was it?"

"Helsinki," Nadi said, this time without looking up. She'd memorized a whole bunch of stuff about Helsinki in case anyone asked her about it and no one had, until the exact moment she really didn't want to talk.

"Listen to me," said the woman.

"I am listening."

"This is important. Don't ignore me."

Nadi guessed the woman was a nat, and had clocked Nadi for a made. Despite them having exactly equivalent status at the plant, the woman had that air of entitlement, like she was a class above. Nadi put the plastic strip down on the ledge and sized the woman up. She was at least twenty centimeters shorter than Nadi and certainly weighed a good deal less. Her hands were slender. She didn't look like she could best Nadi in hand-to-hand combat, so it was interesting she was being so aggressive. Perhaps she didn't expect a confrontation with a made would provoke a violent response. Or maybe she was a skilled fighter, or armed, and fancied her chances if a confrontation kicked off. The arch would have picked up any weapons she'd brought to the plant today but harvesting brought many opportunities to find makeshift weapons: shards of glass, twisted metal, et cetera.

"What was happening in Helsinki when you left?" the woman said.

"I don't know what you mean."

"Is the Helsinki operation still there?"

"Of course it is."

"I think that's bullshit," the woman said with a mirthless smile. "I heard the company's collapsed. Gone. And we're the only bit still running."

"I wouldn't know anything about that," Nadi started to say, but she was interrupted by a middle-aged man with deep scars across the left side of his face, including a diagonal one across his eyebrow that would have given him an angry appearance if he hadn't been angry anyway. It wasn't Nadi he was angry with.

"Sharon," the scarred man said. "Stop this."

"But she knows," said the woman, whose name was apparently Sharon, as she jabbed a finger in the direction of Nadi's face. "She was on a different site less than a week ago. Helsinki. And now they sent her here."

"Okay, so she must know," said the scarred man. He turned to Nadi. "Hi—my name's Mitch, glad to have you on the team."

Mitch put out a hand and Nadi shook it, feeling conscious of the device stashed inside her overalls. She used the handshake as a pretext to lean forward a little just in case the bulge was showing. "Good to meet you," she said.

"Cool. So could you put these rumors to bed for us, at all?" He looked at Nadi hopefully and jerked a thumb in Sharon's direction. "Because she won't shut up about it all of a sudden."

"Everything was normal when I left," Nadi said.

"But did you hear anything?" Sharon glared urgently at her.

"No. I mean, no one ever *tells* us anything."

Mitch nodded, apparently satisfied, and turned to Sharon. "There. Now, can you *please* stop upsetting people with all this talk."

"You're not in charge of *anyone*, Mitch."

"No, but I speak for many of the people here—"

"No, you fucking don't."

"I don't want to have to report you—"

"That's a lie, you shitty little copper, you're *gagging* to report me—"

"Come on—"

Sharon turned and jabbed her finger toward Nadi's face again. "*She* knows more than she's saying."

"I'm sorry," said Nadi, "I really can't tell you any more."

"Hell of a coincidence you got redeployed here now."

"Not really. You needed someone else here and I was available."

"Oh right," Sharon said, taking a step toward Nadi, "you were *available.*"

"Please move away from me and calm down."

Sharon reached out and grabbed Nadi's overalls just below her neck.

What followed was automatic and Nadi would have done it in any situation, but it gained urgency because she didn't want anyone putting a hand on the part of her overalls where the device was stashed, and Sharon's hand was already too close for comfort. Nadi's right hand shot up and grabbed Sharon's wrist, her thumb closing around the heel of Sharon's hand, then she squeezed hard to force Sharon's fingers to lose their grip on the overalls. Before Sharon could react, Nadi turned on the spot, kept her grip on Sharon's wrist, and brought the other woman's arm over her head, twisting it. Sharon yelped in pain and dropped to the ground.

Nadi continued to hold Sharon's wrist for a moment. Then she said, "Leave me alone, please, Sharon," and opened her hand.

Sharon fell to the floor and whimpered. Nadi turned back to the ledge where she'd left the plastic strips she was working on. She needed to check her messages—in the midst of all that she could easily have missed an alert. She turned her wrist to look at her backhand—

And felt a searing pain slash across her forearm.

Nadi turned to see Sharon back on her feet and wielding a shard of glass. Not for the first time, Nadi wondered what the fuck was wrong with this woman. Sharon's next move was predictable—she came at Nadi again with the shard of glass, emboldened by her success with the initial strike. But Nadi had been caught unawares the first time, and she easily dodged the overconfident follow-up. As Sharon's arm arced across empty space Nadi reached out and grabbed it around the elbow. She slammed Sharon's arm down on the ledge and kept pressure on it, trying to make Sharon drop the glass. Sharon stubbornly held on, which was both futile and stupid, because the glass was now cutting into her own hand, blood seeping between her fingers.

Sharon gasped in pain and rage and aimed a kick at Nadi's knee, which connected well, and with her free hand (presumably her nondominant hand) she punched Nadi in the head. This was too weak to cause any real damage but it was enough to make Nadi lose patience with the situation. She reached out and grabbed a belt loop on Sharon's trousers, then made a swift jerking motion and hoisted Sharon off the floor, over the barrier, and into the plastics bay. Sharon tumbled down the funnel and through the hole at the bottom, which turned out to be just large enough to accommodate her.

Nadi turned to see Mitch's startled face.

"I didn't *want* it to go that far, okay?" she assured him.

AN ON-BRAND CARPET

Arlo found it a pleasure to see his squadron of drones again. They radiated such respect and eagerness. They'd been designed this way to make the user feel enthused about working with them, and it was very effective. Henrik leaned against a wall in a storage unit, watching him work, and Arlo reminded himself not to look too delighted by the little drones obeying his commands: this should all appear thoroughly mundane to him.

The aim was for the theft to remain undiscovered until the plant was sold. At that point the new owners would inventory it in full and as long as it matched up with what they thought they'd paid for, they'd be happy. No one knew the Coyne was there, and if you don't know you've got something you're not going to notice if it's stolen—*unless* you see signs of a break-in. It was therefore important that no suspicion should arise during the operation *or* after it. If the staff at Kentish Cyc felt dissatisfied with the work Arlo and Drienne had done, that might lead to a complaint being lodged with RookDivest, who would then look up who had done the work, and discover two people had posed as their employees to gain access to the plant. (Mia had illustrated this on a flowchart that they all called the Flowchart of Fuckups.) Whereas if everything was carried out satisfactorily, then hopefully no one would ever give it another thought. Loren would access RookDivest's systems and log the job as done, and RookDivest's current workload was so enormous, no one would ever think to check who had done it.

Arlo and Drienne had therefore agreed with Mia they should do a good and thorough job of debranding the plant. It might be tempting to cut corners, minimize the time they spent in here, but they would do the thing properly, to the expected standard.

Arlo walked into the staff meal room and one of his squadron immediately alerted him to the carpet. It didn't have any branding on it, but it was a green-and-white design of interlocking leaves that was produced for, and only ever found in, Oakseed properties. When the drone brought this to Arlo's attention he only just managed to stop himself saying "Oh *yeah*" in a tone of amusement. He'd seen carpet like this in some room or other pretty much every single day of his life: the corridors in the nursery had it, so did the strategy hub in his tenement block in Shanghai. It was so familiar, it had never struck him as specifically Oakseed before. But this was exactly the type of thing a debranding specialist would know, and not be remotely surprised by.

"Pull it up?" the drone asked. "Leave as is? Or repattern?"

"Repattern." This was the most labor-intensive option, and involved the squadron using a laser-printing process to change the color of certain strands of carpet. But neither of the other two options were satisfactory: it would look shoddy if there was no carpet and it would look bad if there was a distinctively Oakseed carpet.

"Gosh," said Henrik as the squadron got to work, sweeping methodically across the floor, retoning every white strand, leaving an unpatterned green carpet in their wake. "Will you be doing the same with all the carpet?"

"How much carpet is there?" said Arlo, trying not to let on that his heart was sinking at the potential workload.

"Oh, not much—the workfloor is all tiles and concrete. But there's a carpet like this up on the top floor."

"The top floor?"

"Yes. Just the corridor, not inside the offices. In fact, it's two corridors that cross over in the middle. I think that's the only one, but it's a long one."

"Yes. Yes, we'll be doing that one too." Suddenly it wasn't a problem, it was ideal: a lengthy task that required him to be on the corridor where the lockers were. The only stumbling block was Henrik. Arlo had to get rid of him somehow. Drienne had told Kline, who had said he was working on it. Maybe he could work faster.

"Would you like a drink?" Henrik asked. He was standing by one of the vending machines; even as he spoke and pointed to the machine, one of the drones was removing the M:Pyre logo and the cheerful woodpecker mascot from the viewing window.

"Oh, no thank you," Arlo replied.

"Sure? My treat."

"Mr. Paul?" said a voice from the doorway, and both Arlo and Henrik turned to see a pale young woman step across the carpet and apologize to the two drones she'd just kicked when she hurried in.

"What is it?" said Henrik irritably.

"We've got a situation on the workfloor."

"What sort of situation?"

The pale young woman glanced at Arlo. "I think it's best if you come and see."

Henrik tutted, apologized to Arlo, and strode out of the room, and Arlo inwardly apologized to Kline for having done him a disservice.

Kline hadn't done anything, not yet. At that moment he was logged in to the disciplinary system. His first thought had been to repeat his earlier trick of lodging a complaint of misconduct, but he didn't like using the same method twice—it seemed risky, likely to attract attention. He was sure he could think of something cleverer. And he had, and was very pleased with it. It fitted the circumstances perfectly. He went to close the window for the disciplinary records—and just then, a sub-window flashed up alerting him that Nadi's record (under her assumed name of Pris) had been updated, and Henrik was on his way to deal with the situation.

Kline accessed the report for full details and couldn't believe what he was reading. This was the problem with securits. He'd thought Nadi was different, but like all of them she was too quick to violence. And now the whole job might unravel because of it.

24

NEW TRICKS

Drienne was frantically spamming Arlo with **NOT YET NOT YET** as she tried to establish where Nadi was now. Arlo had told Drienne to meet him on the top-floor corridor, but it wasn't clear from the message whether he was already on his way there. She'd told him she was going to collect the Lost Weekend from Nadi and stash it in her case, in the space where the squadron usually went. But Drienne couldn't find Nadi anywhere on the workfloor.

She didn't get a response from Arlo. **Where are you?** she sent in a follow-up.

Still in the lunchroom, came the reply. **What's happening? I HAVE to move upstairs before Henrik comes back**

Drienne was about to tell him she couldn't find Nadi when Kline sent a message round, explaining Nadi was in the security office on the underfloor, and Henrik was on his way to question her.

Fuck, said Arlo. **We need to pull out**

How are we supposed to get back in? asked Drienne.

We have a plan for that, the backup plan, remember?

And how are we supposed to smuggle the device in without Nadi?

We could pull the same trick again, sent Arlo, **only this time Kline could be the employee on the floor. They don't know him**

I'm not doing that, Kline said—a characteristically irritating response from him, but one Drienne happened to agree with. She didn't like the backup plan—no one liked the backup plan—and they couldn't afford to throw away all the work they'd done at the slightest bit of trouble.

Yeah, said Drienne, **fuck that. We'll find a way.**

A securit ushered Nadi into a small concrete room on the under-floor and told her to sit on one of two benches positioned either side of a small table, the surface of which was scattered with un-washed coffee mugs. The securit tutted at the mugs, hovered by the table as if considering clearing them away, then muttered, "No, why should I?" and sat on the sofa. Nadi had spent a lot of time in security offices, she knew the dynamics. Usually she'd been the one who ended up clearing the mugs away.

The securit had made Nadi hand over her slate and backhand but hadn't searched her. The Lost Weekend was still stowed in her overalls and she was very aware of the pressure of the device against her body. If it was discovered, she intended to say she had found it while harvesting, was unsure what it was, and had put it aside until she could ask someone. This was a stretch—who puts things "aside" in a large overalls pocket?—but she'd just have to play dumb and hope for the best.

Nadi was impatient for someone to show up so she could explain what had happened between her and Sharon. This was not just because she needed to get out there and play her part in the operation. She had done nothing wrong and she wanted to explain herself. It was unfair she was being blamed for the altercation.

The door opened and Henrik entered. He nodded to Nadi in recognition, then told the securit to wait outside. Henrik sat on the other bench, across the table from Nadi, and gave her a tight, but pained, smile. "So what happened?"

"What did they tell you?"

"It doesn't matter what *they* told me, *you* tell me."

"A crazy woman came up to me saying she heard a rumor the company collapsed."

"Where'd she hear that?"

"Not from me," Nadi said quickly.

"But where?"

"I don't know. She just said she'd heard things and thought I knew what was going on."

"And what did you say?"

"That I didn't."

"You told her the company was fine?"

"Yeah. Pretty much. I told her I didn't really know."

"And then what happened?"

"I didn't start the fight. She attacked me."

"And you fought back."

"In self-defense."

"You threw her down the plastics funnel in self-defense."

"I mean, if security had come and helped out a little quicker—"

Henrik sighed. "All right, yes."

"Is she okay?"

"Yes, people take a tumble into those funnels from time to time, we have safety procedures and so on."

"Look," Nadi said earnestly, "I'm really happy to have this position, Mr. Paul. It's good work, I feel like I can do it well—"

Henrik held up his hands. "You're not in trouble. We've had disciplinary issues with Sharon Harris before, I'm sure what you're telling me is true. I just need to know where *she* heard it."

"I don't know that, sorry."

"It's a good thing we got her off the floor before she could spread this any further, I think."

"Right, yeah. So did I do the right thing?" Nadi asked. She knew that, from Henrik's point of view, she absolutely had—but getting him to say it would make him feel like he was in charge of the situation. She was trained to understand basic psychology and how her actions could influence it, but she'd only ever exercised this control on the company's behalf, not her own. This was different, and it gave her a strange feeling: Henrik was a nat, a *xec*, in a position of authority over her, and she was manipulating him.

"Oh yes," said Henrik, nodding vigorously. "Do you think she believed you? Sharon, I mean?"

"I don't know. No, I don't think so. She seemed convinced, I don't think anything I said would have made a difference."

"No." Henrik looked off to one side, thinking. "I suppose this was bound to happen eventually—after all, it's the biggest thing ever to have happened in human history."

It was strange how Henrik was talking to her like a confidante, like they were equals.

"It's a very weird situation," said Nadi. "Which is why I'm so glad to have been reassigned here, with a solid job."

"We're glad to have you, Pris. But for your own safety, we shan't have you up on the workfloor for the rest of this shift."

"Oh."

"Don't worry, I'll have someone else deposit your salvage and you'll still get the commission for it. I just think it might cause consternation and whatnot if you were to return to the floor tonight, and you won't have to deal with any more questions."

And there was also no risk Nadi might let anything slip, no danger she might make some offhand remark. It was easier for *him*. But she'd lucked out so far; she couldn't protest this point.

"In fact," Henrik said, checking her record, "I see you were originally brought here to work on the underfloor . . . on the plastics pipeline, yes. So we'll put you back on there for the rest of the shift. It's quite light duties, it just smells terrible in there. And we'll get you back on harvesting tomorrow."

"That's fine," Nadi said pleasantly. "Can I have my slate back?"

"At the end of the shift, yes. I'll make sure it's on the front desk for you to collect."

Henrik escorted Nadi down to the plastics pipeline. He didn't speak to her as they walked; he seemed distracted. When they arrived, he muttered something about hoping she got on all right, then turned and walked urgently in the other direction.

Drienne watched her squadron remove the faded holographic logos from the housing of a conveyor while she thought about what to do. A plan was coming together in her mind. She would claim to have received a message from her boss saying that, as Nadi was retained by RookDivest, Drienne and Arlo were going to be the ones to deal with her, and they'd been directed to bring her back with them to Boston. If Arlo used all his charm on Henrik, the xec might accept this. It was mad, audacious, but Drienne felt sure it would work—

Then she got a message from Kline. Nadi hadn't been reprimanded, her cover appeared secure, she'd just been placed on other duties on the underfloor. Aw. Drienne wasn't going to get to do her mad, audacious plan. But it all seemed to be going their way.

I'm heading upstairs before Henrik comes back, Arlo said.

I'll be there as quick as I can, Drienne replied. I've got a good feeling about this. It's all going our way.

Don't say that, said Arlo.

"It wasn't my fault," were Nadi's first words when Drienne entered the plastics pipeline room.

"Jesus fucking Christ it *stinks* in here," were Drienne's first words. She was quite right, and what's more it wasn't the smell Nadi had expected. She'd thought it'd be like the smell of burning basematter, like when you left a spoon on the hob by accident. But the smell didn't come from the plastic, it came from the vats of enzymes used to break the plastics down. The enzymes emitted gas as part of the process, and it smelled like decay. All of this was explained on a poster on the wall by the door that was headed *Why Does It Smell?*

The room was large and filled with an industrial hum. They were the only ones in here, but there was a doorway with no door in it that led to metal processing, so it was possible they might be seen or heard. They kept their voices down and focused on their respective tasks while they spoke, as if they were strangers making small talk.

"This woman called Sharon attacked me," Nadi continued while she used a long implement like a spade to turn over the thick, pale yellow slop in the vat, "and I just defended myself—"

"It's fine. It's all good," said Drienne, who was directing her squadron to resurface the health and safety notices—keeping the information intact, but changing the Oakseed-copyright font to opensource. "It's worked out perfectly."

"Has it?"

"You've still got the Lost Weekend, right?"

Nadi turned to the wall and pretended to check a readout that she did not understand and that had not been explained to her. She reached into her overalls, ran a finger down the edge of the stash pouch to open it, and pulled out the device. Then she casually placed it on the nearest convenient surface, as if just setting it down for a moment.

Drienne took her time. Rushing would only draw attention. Drienne left the Lost Weekend there for thirty seconds or so, to give any watching eyes a little time to move on. She instructed her squadron to obliterate two motivational posters, which carried conspicuous branding but more importantly were patronizing. The squadron fired and the posters disintegrated. Drienne smiled and said, "I enjoyed that," then she calmly picked up the device, put it in her case, and left the room.

25

AN INVITATION TO REAPPLY

Loren was sitting in Bizarre?!, the coffeehouse across the street from the plant that was rated as the best place to get something to eat in the corpurbation, which was not saying much. They had eaten a toasted sandwich that, they'd been assured, did contain real bacterial cheese even though its flavor did nothing to support this claim, along with a mug of tomato soup that came from a dispenser next to the cappuccino machine. The place did serve appetizing cakes, but Loren hadn't anticipated there would be time to sample them. They'd expected to be summoned for the next stage of the operation at around 19:30.

It was now 19:55 and they had eaten a slice of red velvet cake. They were starting to feel like it was all fucking up, and they were considering what to do if that was indeed the case. Arlo, Nadi, and Drienne would have to extricate themselves however they could, but there shouldn't be any evidence to connect Loren or Kline to any of this. Might be best for them to split up and avoid all contact until they got back to Vancouver.

Although, should they go back to Vancouver at all? Whatever happened they were still retained by Mia, but did Loren have much to lose by trying to escape and start again somewhere else? Loren suspected Mia had poured most of her money into this operation, gambling on getting back her personality and restarting her career with it. Did she have the resources to search the globe for a couple of rogue mades, perhaps drawing attention to her role in the heist in the process? Or would she just let them disappear?

Loren had reached no conclusions, and was considering ordering a slice of pear-and-custard tart, when Kline told them it was almost time and they ought to get into position. Loren paid the bill, thanked the waitress, picked up their bag, and walked out of Bizarre?!

Kline hadn't achieved what he'd been asked to achieve, and yet it had happened anyway. Most people wouldn't question this stroke of good fortune, but Kline was the kind of person who needed to know what was going on and why. In his former line of work, his superiors wanted and expected him to behave like this, and it was why he'd had access to the internal messages of everyone below a certain pay grade. Even when people's vendettas were petty, Kline enjoyed working out what they were and understanding what was behind them. Even when someone's empire-building was pathetic, he enjoyed tracing it and identifying the extent of its ambitions. Xecs and seeos were always told HR didn't have access to their messages, and that only the lower ranks got spied on that way, but that wasn't true. Xecs and seeos just got spied on by a higher class of HR operative.

A stet had listened to Henrik's interview with Nadi and generated a report, which Kline read. Kline then looked up Henrik's current activity. Henrik was in his office, firing off messages to people who weren't going to answer them because their jobs no longer existed. In fact, the only person reading these messages was Kline. Henrik's messages said information about Oakseed's collapse had leaked through to the workforce, despite his best efforts (he explained what these efforts consisted of), and he wanted to know what he should do about it.

It seemed to Kline a curious coincidence this information had leaked through on the day of the operation.

Kline alerted Arlo that Henrik was in his office and seemed occupied for now, so Arlo and Drienne should work quickly and take
advantage. Arlo sent a reply saying **Thanks**, but Kline barely registered it. He was identifying the employees discussing the rumors
of Oakseed's collapse, accessing their messages, and trying to work
out if they'd all heard it from Sharon Harris, or if there was another
source.

Arlo was debranding the support department: a large, open-plan
L-shaped office that currently had only two staffers present. One
had glanced up at him as he'd walked in, then gone back to her
work. The other didn't even seem to have noticed he was there,
as she was deep in conversation with the system, discussing how
the rewards framework for harvesting could be revised to optimize
production.

The office contained a lot of stuff to be debranded—supports
loved to put up signs and posters and promotional materials, and
often didn't take the old ones down but put new ones on top of
them in layers, so you could dig through them archaeologically
and reveal years of recent history. Arlo instructed his squadron to
resurface any promo into visually similar copyright-free stock images, removing any logos in the process.

Drienne told Arlo she was on her way up with the Lost Weekend, and Arlo told her to take the staircase at the back of the building, as this would enable her to avoid walking past Henrik's office
with its floor-to-ceiling windows that looked out on the corridor.

Duh, Drienne replied. **I did think of that.**

As Drienne entered the support department, she could see Arlo at
the other end of the room, keeping up the debranding facade: the
job was seriously trying her patience now, but Arlo seemed genuinely into it. That was *so* like him.

She signaled for his attention and he said he just had a few things to finish in this office. "You could speed things along by doing that stuff," he added, pointing to a corner kitchen that included a cupboard filled with company mugs.

Drienne felt it would be far more fun to throw all the mugs out a window, but that would attract the wrong sort of attention, and besides none of the windows opened far enough. She duly opened the cupboard and scrubbed all the logos. She also scrubbed a non-branded mug bearing the slogan I'M AN INFERIOR IMITATION OF MYSELF UNTIL I'VE HAD MY COFFEE! out of spite.

When they left the support department, they took the door that came out directly opposite the premium store. Arlo instructed his squadron to get to work on the carpet, and watched over them while Drienne continued along the corridor. She needed to activate the Lost Weekend as close as she could to the on-site servers, which were in the support department; this room was directly adjacent to one of the corner meeting rooms. All the corner rooms were empty. It was an ideal place to activate, apart from one detail: the fold-back walls had large windows in them. Drienne needed to be ready to act innocent if anyone came walking through the corridor.

The meeting room had been used earlier that day, a cake box from a shop called Bizarre?! sat empty on a side table. Drienne picked a bit of stray icing out of the box and licked her finger. Then she took a chair away from the table in the middle of the room, pushed it up to the wall that adjoined the server stacks, and placed the Lost Weekend on the chair. She signaled to Arlo she was in position, and while she waited for the signal back from him, she made her way around the meeting room with her squadron. The walls were decorated with images of Oakseed facilities around the world, placed here to remind employees they were part of something larger. Drienne replaced them all with reproductions of paintings by Paul Gaugin.

Drienne heard a door open down the corridor, and she glanced up. Through the windows she could see Henrik leaving his office.

He spotted her, smiled and waved, and then he started walking toward the door of the room Drienne was in.

Arlo was still standing by the door to the support department, mentally preparing himself to take the final step, making one last check that he hadn't forgotten anything, when he heard Henrik's footsteps coming down the corridor. He breathed *Fuck!* and ducked back inside the support department, holding the door slightly ajar so he could hear what was happening.

"Hello!" Henrik said, sticking his head in the door of the meeting room. "Is your colleague around anywhere?"

The Lost Weekend was still sitting on the chair. If Henrik's attention wasn't drawn to it, he might not notice it. With considerable effort, Drienne forced herself not to glance at the device.

"I'm not sure," she said.

He nodded his head in the direction of the corridor. "Is that his squadron out there, working on the carpet?"

"Er . . ."

"Ah!" said Henrik, pointing to the Gaugin pictures that now decorated the wall behind Drienne's head. "Very nice."

Kline was monitoring the situation and he was already on the case. He felt perversely pleased, because he really liked the earlier solution he'd come up with to keep Henrik occupied, and now he'd get to use it. He had mere moments to execute this idea, but he'd done it literally thousands of times in his former job and it was like breathing to him.

Kline issued Henrik with a standard invitation to reapply for his existing job. This was a preliminary process designed to weed out anyone who was in declining mental or physical health, or anyone who was no longer a good fit for the company's direction, or just anyone they wanted to get rid of but who they legally owed the opportunity to reapply. It was standard practice to give no warning. Henrik would have done this at least a couple of times before in his Oakseed career, and with the plant being sold, it would come as no surprise he was being asked to do it again. He would see it as a lifeline, an indication that maybe the new buyers weren't going to get rid of him after all, and though employees were allowed thirty minutes to start the process or submit their reasons for postponing it, Kline knew from experience that hardly anyone ever waited, and a man as desperate as Henrik certainly wouldn't.

Sure enough, within moments Henrik was back at his desk, placing his Airstrip over his eyes and preparing to begin the interview. Kline had chosen an avatar he thought Henrik would like, a bashful young man who seemed a little self-conscious about the whole procedure.

The process would take about twenty minutes, and Kline shared this info with Arlo and Drienne. He also pointed out, in case they hadn't realized, the next stage of the operation would disrupt the interview, because it would disrupt everything, so this grace period would end the moment Drienne activated the Lost Weekend. Even so, he thought it likely that Henrik's focus would initially be on what had gone wrong with his interview before he realized something had gone wrong with the plant as a whole. **You're welcome,** Kline added.

That done, Kline shrank the window containing Henrik's interview and moved it to the edge of his vision, then he brought back the window containing his own investigation into the workfloor situation. Henrik was no closer to understanding what was going on in his workplace, but Kline had developed a troubling theory, and unfortunately he was confident it was correct.

26

FIFTEEN YEARS, TWO MONTHS, TWENTY-SEVEN DAYS, FIVE HOURS, TEN MINUTES, AND FIFTY-THREE SECONDS

Thank fuck yes he's gone back to his office, read Drienne's message to the group. **Kline you're an evil genius.**

Arlo reemerged from the support department and approached the sapphire door. The only people on this floor right now ought to be himself, Drienne, Henrik, the two supports, and one member of admin staff. All the securits on duty were on the lower floors or posted to the exterior of the building.

Arlo and Drienne's access included the premium store, because they had to debrand *every* part of the plant. No one would consider it a risk to allow them in there: they didn't have permission to open any of the lockers, and they would be scanned on exit to ensure they weren't leaving with anything they didn't bring. So all Arlo had to do was place his hand on the door handle, wait a second for the handle to identify him, hear the lock click open, and then calmly open the door and walk inside. Just another room he had to tick off.

The corridor carpet continued into this room, but that was the only branded item in there. The room had no signage and was plainly decorated—a glorified cupboard, really. While his squadron got to work on the carpet, Arlo located the locker Samson had com-mandeered. He signaled to Drienne it was time.

It should look like a genuine systems failure. Loren had looked up what OS and hardware Kentish Cyc was running on, as well as its stability record, and confirmed that it crashed semi-regularly, so no one would find it surprising or suspicious. Loren had designed the Lost Weekend to be deliberately crude—they could have put to-gether something more targeted that would knock out the essential parts of the system, but then someone might realize the attack *was* targeted. It would be more convincing if the whole thing just fell over for a moment.

Drienne activated the Lost Weekend by flicking the switch just inside the crack at the edge of its casing, then she went to stand on the other side of the meeting room. Rationally, she knew the device wasn't a bomb, it wouldn't explode or affect her in any way, but she couldn't help feeling it was wise to keep her distance.

It didn't explode, or visibly do anything at first. After a few sec-onds it smoked slightly, and then something fizzled and flashed in-side it. Loren had said it would do that, and it was a sign the device had burnt out. But for the brief moments it had been in operation, it had sent out a pulse that overloaded the corpurbation's central server, which was the hub for every system in the immediate area. This forced the server to disconnect and shut down, to protect itself from damage and protect Oakseed's entire network from attacks. Drienne checked her slate and found that it had lost its connection. Loren had said that too would happen, and it meant the device had worked. For the next minute or so they would be out of contact. But they all knew what they were to do.

Loren would have preferred to do this from the comfort of Bi-zarre?!, but given the bulkiness of the signal emitter they'd built for the job, using it in a coffeehouse would have attracted attention. It only just fit in their rucksack. After getting word that Arlo and Drienne were in position, Loren had walked around the side of the main building. This was the area least overseen by securits, whose attention was more focused on the front entrance, the passage that led to the platform, and the platform itself. There was nothing on this side of the plant except the dead-waste outlet, which was fenced off and by definition contained nothing worth stealing. Loren was sitting near the dead-waste yard, leaning against the side wall of the plant. The emitter was in front of them, its mast extended. Like the Lost Weekend, the emitter's interface was brutally simple, because it only needed to do one thing and Loren had programmed it to do that thing already. It had a single switch, off/on, and Loren's finger was poised to flick it.

The moment their slate registered the disruption, they flicked the switch and the emitter sent out a single, powerful signal, one that stated the current time was fifteen years, two months, twenty-seven days, five hours, ten minutes, and fifty-three seconds earlier than it actually was.

The reason for this interval was that fifteen years, two months, twenty-seven days, five hours, ten minutes, and fifty-three seconds was the exact physical age gap between Joshi Samson and Arlo Rahane. It was important to be precise about this. Looking up the difference between their birthdates wouldn't do, because "birth" meant something different for nats and mades, and for nats it wasn't an exact science: biologically, you could be exactly the same age as someone born a month earlier than you, if their mother went into labor two weeks early and yours went into labor two weeks late. You needed to know the moment both people were conceived, and while this information existed for Arlo, Samson's parents had not thought to note this time down on any official records.

This was why Arlo had been dispatched from Shanghai carrying a case that was chained to his wrist. The case contained the toes of

Samson's left foot, preserved moments after his death at a time that had been exactly recorded. Mia had purchased these very cheaply from the hospital, demand for used toes being minimal. She analyzed them and had extrapolated exactly when Samson began, and from there the exact difference in age between him and Arlo, who had been made when Samson was at the academy and had been singled out as someone with xec potential.

All of this was necessary because of the two-step security on the locker. First, a retinal scan identified who you were. This was why all mades were legally required to undergo an eye transplant, which issued them with generic eyes that security systems would immediately identify. But in the event of a made being developed in contravention of international law (possibly without the knowledge of the source donor) and not undergoing a transplant, the lock also required a microscopic genetic sample upon being sealed, from which it would ascertain the age of the owner the same way Mia had done. It could be opened only by someone who matched the owner's genetic profile *and* correct age—which by definition could not be true of a made, who would always be younger than their donor.

Mia had spotted a loophole in this. Age was not a constant: by definition, it changed all the time. So every time the lock wanted to check someone's age was correct, it used a baseline of the time that person's life began, then it referred to the current time and worked out exactly how old they would be now. The current time was maintained with constant reference to a standardized signal, ensuring everything was globally kept in sync and every time stamp was guaranteed to be correct. In most places this signal was impossible to interrupt, as it was received in multiple ways. If the locker couldn't get the signal from multiple verified sources that all agreed on the time, it would presume the signal was being deliberately overridden, and refuse to open. But because Kentish Cyc was isolated and its connection was centralized, all devices got the time from a single satellite signal routed via the IT department.

The Lost Weekend was so called because it knocked out the

systems at Kentish Cyc, and when they came to they didn't know what day it was. They needed to pick up that information again from the satellite. And Loren's emitter was powerful enough to briefly swamp the signal with a false one. Which made the locker think it was fifteen years, two months, twenty-seven days, five hours, ten minutes, and fifty-three seconds ago, and its owner was not lying dead on the other side of the world at the age of forty-one, but was standing right here at the age of twenty-six.

When Arlo crouched down and placed a hand on the locker's handle and attempted to open it, the lock scanned his retinas and collected a scraping of cells from his thumb, and concluded he was the same man who'd set up the lock.

Arlo had a clear image in his mind of what *should* happen next: the door should swing open, revealing the Coyne inside. There was no reason to think it would not. Yet when it actually did swing open before his very eyes, he was overcome with glee and relief and astonishment it had worked. It was like completing a complicated puzzle in a video game, and he felt like doing a little dance. This was *probably* not how proper criminals felt in this situation. He needed to be calm and professional about this.

Arlo reached into the locker, grabbed the dull silver disc from inside, then bent down and shone a light into the interior to make sure there wasn't anything he'd missed. Then he placed the Coyne in his blazer pocket before reaching into his case and removing something that looked exactly like it, except a small dent had been deliberately made in its edge so Arlo could tell them apart. This dummy Coyne had been printed by Loren when they'd arrived in London, and handed to Arlo last night sealed in an airtight bag, meaning when he placed it in his case earlier today, it bore no fingerprints but his—and his fingerprints were the same as Samson's. He placed the dummy inside the locker, checked his pocket again to make sure he had the right Coyne, and finally closed the door.

The primary purpose of bringing the fake Coyne was not to put it in the locker. It was because Arlo's case would be scanned on exit to ensure its mass was the same as when they'd entered, so he needed to bring something of equal size and weight. And if Arlo was going to take a Coyne out, it ought to go unnoticed provided he'd brought one in. As the other Coyne needed to be left behind, it made sense to put it in place of the one they were taking away.

Arlo checked once more he had the correct Coyne on his person, then sent the crew a message saying the objective was secured. Moments later his slate glitched, then the time and date reverted to the actual time and date. He checked just one more time that he had the right Coyne: before leaving the plant he would move it into his case, but until then he was keeping it easily accessible, where he could continue to check it was there every few seconds.

Upon opening the sapphire door and emerging into the corridor, Arlo could hear consternation from the support department regarding the massive glitch. The only person within sight was Drienne, who was standing farther down the corridor, alone, with her back to Arlo. She glanced over her shoulder and he gave her a nod, then she started walking away. Arlo summoned his squadron, stepped out of the premium store, and closed the door behind himself. He returned his attention to debranding the carpet. There was still lots to do. It was a long carpet.

DID I SEE WHAT?

Drienne had placed the Lost Weekend back in her case after its job was done—she would discard it somewhere on the workfloor, where there was plenty of junk scattered around so one more piece wouldn't be conspicuous. She waited in the meeting room for as long as it took for Arlo to confirm he had the Coyne. They'd agreed to complete the debranding job after securing their objective, and Drienne saw the sense in that, but it was her intention to do it as quickly as possible, despite what Arlo had said about leaving no cause for complaint. She was on her way downstairs to hastily debrand every room left on the itinerary when she heard a voice from behind her say, "Did *you* see that just now?"

Drienne turned to see Henrik emerging from his office and striding down the corridor. She resisted the temptation to say *Did I see what?* or some variant thereof. Instead she asked, "Did your system glitch as well?"

"Right in the middle of—I was doing an interview," said Henrik. "Am I meant to start again, or . . . ?" He put both hands on his head and looked around in vexation.

Drienne had to give Kline credit: he'd arranged a very effective distraction. It might not even occur to Henrik this was an attack.

Then a support hurried over and said to Henrik, "I think it was an attack."

"What?" said Henrik.

"What makes you say it was an attack?" said Drienne.

"Who's this?" said the support, who seemingly hadn't noticed Drienne walking through her office fifteen minutes ago.

Drienne regretted having spoken at all, let alone in such a defensive way. She toned down her manner, adopted a genial smile, and put out a hand. "Annie Clarke, I'm with RookDivest."

The support looked wary. She was a made, and probably concerned she was about to be sold off.

"Annie's here to debrand the facility," said Henrik in a low voice. "She's not here to sell anything or anyone, don't worry."

"Oh," said the support. "I'm Rachel, hi."

"If there's been any attempt at sabotage," Drienne said, "I should report it to my boss—that's the sort of thing buyers will want to know." She wanted Henrik to say *Couldn't it just be a systems failure? Just one of those things.* She willed him to say it.

"You're sure it's an attack?" said Henrik urgently.

You motherfucker, thought Drienne.

"That's my best guess," said Rachel. "I was talking to the system and it came out with a rush of gibberish just before it went down. It was an overload and that's weird because there's no reason we should be receiving much of *anything* right now."

Shit. Loren had been so sure that would go unremarked.

"This all makes sense," said Henrik.

Fuck fuck fuck.

"Does it?" said Drienne, trying to appear only mildly curious.

"Before my interview," said Henrik, glancing back at his office, "I was looking into the discourse on the workfloor and the underfloor. People down there know the company's collapsed, they're coming up with wild theories about how all the nat workers are going to be replaced by mades from defunct Oakseed sites, or that all the mades are going to be removed because the new owners won't want them, because there's a compliance issue or something."

"But that's not true?" said Drienne. Then she realized Annie would know whether or not it was true, and so she added, "It's just not true."

"Exactly," Henrik agreed. "And there are people saying the workforce is going to be cut in half, and we're getting rid of the ones with lower productivity records."

"Huh," said Rachel. "I mean, that *is* how we'd do it. If we were going to."

"But we're not going to."

"Yeah, I *know*. But if we were."

"There must be a link to this attack, mustn't there? Someone who works in this building, someone here *right now*, is trying to get revenge."

Drienne tried not to sound too enthusiastic when she agreed Henrik was probably correct about that.

Nadi was aware the crucial part of the operation had taken place, but she'd seen little evidence of it on the underfloor: just a stutter in some of the readouts. Her shift ended in about an hour, and she intended to complete it; if anything went awry, it might be useful for her to be around to help Arlo and Drienne get out. To this end, she would listen out for any messages and keep stirring these stinking vats and—

One of the other workers grasped Nadi's upper arm, seeking her attention. The contact felt rough, unfriendly. Nadi's first instinct was to turn, swipe the hand away, and prepare to put its owner in a choke hold, but she didn't want to cause a scene down here too. She turned to find a stocky, shaven-headed, red-faced man glowering at her. There was a younger, thin-featured man behind him with his arms folded.

"Hey," said the red-faced man. "That woman you were talking to earlier."

"Woman?" said Nadi.

"The classy bint with the drones."

"Oh, her," said Nadi as if the woman had been so inconsequential she'd forgotten her already.

"Who was she?"

"I don't know."

"What did she say to you?"

"Something about the smell. She said do you get used to it. So I was telling her I was new down here and I didn't know yet."

"What was she doing?"

"She didn't say."

"Didn't you ask?" This came from the man with the folded arms.

"No. Didn't you?"

"Did she mess with anything?"

Nadi pointed at a couple of posters on the wall. "She changed those."

The two men peered at the posters, apparently reading every word on them (and muttering the words under their breath) before reacting.

"Fuck, it's true," said the man who'd confronted Nadi.

"I told you," said the other.

And they lost all interest in Nadi, and headed for the door.

Kline read Drienne's gleeful message, the one that said Henrik had got the whole thing wrong, he'd put the attack down to unrest at the plant, no one suspected anything and management would have their hands full with this workforce issue. They were going to get away with it.

Kline sympathized with Henrik to an extent. The man's understanding of his own staff was weak, but his interpretation was understandable: two unusual things had occurred close together, so naturally he'd connected them the only way he could see how. But Kline had worked out how the two things were connected, and he was taking the step of contacting Mia to tell her.

Mia was on her way to London in a helicopter, as per the plan—but what Kline had imagined when he'd heard "helicopter" was not what he saw when a feed of Mia appeared in one of Kline's windows. She sat in a wood-paneled room at a small table, painting her fingernails.

"I told you only to open a line to me if it was urgent," Mia said without looking up from her brushwork.

"Yes," said Kline. "Well, the Coyne is secured and success is very near."

"I know." Mia didn't seem very elated. Perhaps that was just her character, to disengage her emotions until the job was done.

Kline explained about the floor staff not knowing Oakseed had collapsed. It was plain Mia didn't feel this qualified as urgent, but Kline persevered. "A lot of what people are saying about it isn't true," he said. "At first I thought the news about Oakseed had trickled in from somewhere and it got repeated and distorted. But that's not it."

"Isn't it?"

"No. Someone's feeding them this on purpose. I've been looking at how the information spread, and it's *not* distortion of a single source. It's a number of specific scenarios appearing in multiple places, and being disseminated pretty faithfully."

"So where did they start?"

"I traced them to a series of anonymous pins. This information came from outside, it started in the last few hours, and it's spread *very* quickly."

"Right. Sorry, how does this affect the operation?"

It seemed very obvious to Kline, but he tried not to let his irritation show. "None of this is coincidental. If someone's feeding misinformation to the workers just as the place is about to go up for sale . . ."

Mia looked up from her nails. Her eyes widened slightly. "They're trying to drive down the price."

"Exactly."

"A restless workforce, productivity dropping—"

"It looks bad, and how it looks matters."

"Someone must have been watching activity around the plant, noticed the debranding was scheduled for today, and thought the sale was going through faster than they expected. Is it going to affect the operation?"

Kline shrugged. "It's tense in there, people don't know what to believe, and it might turn ugly. And if anyone's going to be a target—"

"It's going to be the people carrying out the debranding."

"Indeed. Just thought you might like to know." Kline felt satisfied as the relevance of his investigation landed like one of those puzzles you have to tilt to make a ball settle in a hole.

"Thank you, Kline. Tell the others to get out of there, now. Without attracting attention."

After Mia cut the call, Kline remained curious about where she got the helicopter. He started trying to find out.

28

LEAVE TO LEAVE

Drienne was doing a barely adequate job of debranding the loading bay in the underfloor when the delightful news came through that they had permission to get the hell out. Arlo queried this, saying they could cover the basics of debranding the remaining areas in about half an hour, but Drienne replied she was leaving regardless of whether Arlo came. Nadi said she would stay until Arlo was ready, but Arlo told her not to worry, he was leaving too, he just wanted everyone to remember he said they should finish the debranding first and if failing to do so proved to be their downfall, it was not his fault.

Drienne was shepherding her squadron back into its case, wondering if Mia would let her keep it after the job was done, when she heard the noise from the workfloor above. She checked the time: a shift changeover was scheduled for about ten minutes from now, so the workfloor ought to be emptying out before the final harvesting party of the day came back. But instead it sounded like people were gathering there. And shouting.

Time to go. Drienne closed the case and hurried from the room—

And was confronted by a securit. Male, pinched features, not the tallest or strongest Drienne had ever seen but tall and strong enough to do her some damage.

"What were you doing in there?" the securit demanded.

"Nothing," said a startled Drienne. "Nothing I'm not meant to be—I'm here to debrand this facility." She held out her backhand and her credentials flashed up on the securit's visor.

"What?" said the securit. "They told us you were just prepping for a rebrand."

"Right," said Drienne. "No, we're—"

"Then they're selling it? It's true?"

Drienne sighed; she didn't have the energy for another artfully constructed untruth. "They're selling everything, man. The company collapsed."

"Yeah, but . . . How?"

"I don't know the details, I'm just doing my job—in fact, I've *done* my job and now I need to leave, so—"

"They say they're getting rid of us, is that true?"

"Who says?"

"People."

"I think the place is getting sold with you in it." She actually did feel sorry for him. She wanted to tell him he'd probably be fine, they'd still need securits in the plant after it was sold so it would make no sense to sell him separately. But then, their holders often failed to act in a way that made sense.

Drienne reminded herself that as far as he knew she wasn't a made, but an important visitor from another company and she could talk to him differently from how she'd talked to securits back in Shanghai. She straightened up and said, "I need to meet my colleague and leave." She started to walk past him.

"You must know *something*," he insisted, grabbing her arm. Instinctively, Drienne wanted to do the whole *how dare you, don't you know who you're talking to* bit. She felt sure she could carry it off, though she worried these thoughts were her duplisychosis pushing through and going with them might be risky. But she prepared to deliver her rebuke regardless.

It turned out there wasn't even time for that, because above them the noise was getting louder and it wasn't just voices now, things were being thrown.

"Stay here," the securit said to Drienne, who pretended she was going to do as she was told.

Arlo was still on the top floor, in an office belonging to one of the departed xecs, absorbing updates from Kline about developments on the workfloor. The workforce had started by noisily demanding answers from management. They had gathered around the stairwell toward the front of the building. Securits had blocked the way to the top floor, telling them Henrik was going to come down and address them, but when ten minutes passed and he didn't materialize, they attempted to force entry. The fire shutters to the stairwell closed. The workforce headed for the stairwell at the back, only to find the fire shutters were down there too.

Henrik's failure to meet the workers and offer them an explanation was the worst thing he could have done. By not denying any of the contradictory rumors about what was going on with Oakseed, he made them all seem true. Arlo was only now realizing how ingrained the company's culture of information control was. Withholding knowledge was a form of power, and if you gave people knowledge, you relinquished that power. So information would be withheld as a matter of course, just in case there was power in it. And Henrik didn't know how to handle a decision like this on his own, and he could no longer refer it up the chain. So he remained on the top floor, paralyzed.

The angry and frustrated workforce were now using whatever salvage was still in their carts to attack the interior of the plant, and the securits had backed off entirely—perhaps they even felt solidarity with the workers. If someone had indeed sowed misinformation with the aim of lowering the price, that person must be delighted with the outcome, assuming they didn't mind paying for the repairs.

At least Arlo could now justify leaving the building. With the fire shutters down on the workfloor, the stairs now only allowed movement between the top floor and the underfloor. They were not designed to be used as a security measure, but to confine fires to one area of the building. There was still one other route to the main entrance: the management elevator, which Arlo had access permissions for. He hurried to the end of the corridor and pressed the call button, feeling guilty for leaving without alerting everyone on this floor that they should leave too. But the best thing for the plan was if he walked out the doors without being witnessed by anybody.

The display by the call button said the elevator was at the entrance, and it remained there. Arlo hit the call button again. Still nothing happened.

Maybe it had been shut down in response to the rioting. Maybe Henrik could override it. Arlo went back down the corridor to Henrik's office and knocked on the door.

There was no response.

He pressed his ear to the door, and heard nothing.

Arlo walked farther down the corridor and peered around the door of the support department. A support was telling the system its proposals for how to proceed weren't acceptable.

"Is Henrik around?" Arlo said.

"In his office," she replied tetchily, without looking up.

"He's not. Could you find him for me?"

The support tutted and asked the system to locate Henrik.

After getting confirmation through that Arlo had the Coyne, Loren had taken the emitter and thrown it over the fence into the dead-waste yard. The fence was high and it took Loren four attempts to yeet the emitter higher, but they got it eventually. Then they'd returned to the street outside the plant and loitered there, wearing their almost-empty rucksack and trying to give off the air of someone waiting for a friend whose shift would finish soon.

Loren had seen images of Henrik on his staff record, but even if they hadn't, they would have guessed who he was the moment they spotted him descending the ladder that ran down the side of the building from an emergency exit on the top floor. He scrambled down and hurried away from the plant—not running, but walking hastily.

Henrik looked up and saw Loren. He wasn't interested in Loren or why they were there, but he was visibly concerned someone had seen him leave. Loren had been following events inside the plant and felt pretty sure whatever Henrik was supposed to be doing, skipping out through an emergency exit was not it. There was such panic on his face that Loren suspected the man would have shot them if he'd had a gun, just to eliminate any witnesses.

After a moment Henrik collected himself, straightened up, nodded to Loren as if in casual greeting, and walked on at what was obviously supposed to be a relaxed pace. He was visibly jumpy, his feet jerking forward with each step, but nevertheless trying to give the impression he left work every day by a ladder down the side of the building.

Loren messaged the others to tell them what they'd just seen.

Arlo quickly replied, And you just let him leave??

What did you want me to do, Loren replied, fucking rugby-tackle him?

Kline added, I doubt Loren, a person he had never previously met, would have been able to find a means to make him go back inside a building full of his angry subordinates.

Loren smirked at that.

Arlo tried to calm down, telling himself all this actually made things easier. No really, it did. From Loren's description, Henrik had left via the emergency exit on the right-hand side of the building. There were two such exits on the top floor, at either end of the horizontal crisscross corridor. At the planning stage Drienne had suggested using one of these exits the moment they got their hands on the Coyne—but even if they'd wanted to do this they couldn't, because the emergency exits wouldn't open until there was an emergency.

Designing a building this way was strictly illegal in many countries, but in dereg zones like England it was acceptable to prioritize employee monitoring over employee safety, so it was not possible to bypass the security arches by slipping out through an emergency exit. The system would release the doors if it identified fire, for example, or atmospheric toxicity inside the plant, but otherwise the exits would open only if management authorized it. It seemed Henrik had done so, which meant they would all be able to use the exits, and the remaining top-floor staff agreed to take advantage. Arlo followed them to the emergency exit, pretending he didn't know where it was. He messaged the crew, telling Drienne and Nadi to find their nearest exit and head for the rendezvous point.

But the emergency exit on the top floor refused to open. Henrik had left this way, but had not declared an emergency situation. He'd used xec privilege to open the exit and let it close behind him, and no one left inside had the credentials to open it again. They tried the exit at the opposite end of the corridor, but it was useless. Rachel tried to convince the system this *was* an emergency and they didn't need to wait for it to be declared as such. The system's response was skeptical.

Loren paced in agitated loops on the ground outside, considering what they knew about the plant's system and how it might be convinced to release the exits. The systems must be aware there was a riot underway inside, and that this was causing damage to the interior, so Loren felt it should be possible to convince the systems of the logic of evacuating the building without permission from a xec. Kline was working on it too, trying to use HR protocols to give himself clearance to open the exits, but the system wasn't playing ball.

Loren was explaining their suggested tactics to Arlo when they heard a vehicle approaching. They turned to see a police deployment transport approaching from the north, large enough to accommodate about twenty officers. Loren stood well back on the pavement as it passed them and stopped outside the entrance to Kentish Cyc. A second transport followed and parked behind it, and the officers got out and streamed toward the doors of the plant.

IT'S FUN TO
BE CREATIVE

Arlo suggested Loren's argument to Rachel, but she insisted she'd already tried it. "The system has decided its priority is to avoid spreading damage across the corpurbation. It doesn't seem like it wants *any* of us to leave, and its other priority is to deal with the rioters."

"Henrik didn't want anyone to follow him," said the other support. "What a *prick.*"

"To be fair, I think the workforce might actually have killed him if they'd caught up with him. We need to stay up here and not get drawn into what's going on down there."

Arlo received Loren's message, confirming police were entering the building. *Actual cops.* None of them had anticipated this. The Metropolitan Police only operated out in the suburban ring these days. The megas had their own security forces and had signed up to all the treaties necessary to handle law enforcement on their own land, lightening the policing burden and getting away with many corporate illegalities in return. The operation had therefore factored in having to deal with only Oakseed securits. But Henrik evidently didn't trust his own workforce anymore, and had called in the actual cops.

Kline did his best to work out what was happening by interpreting the employee activity patterns. There'd been a rush toward the main entrance, which coincided exactly with the moment Loren had seen the doors open to let the police in. The police had driven the employees back toward the workfloor and closed the front doors behind themselves.

The activity patterns allowed Kline to see who'd got involved in the riot and who'd kept out of it. The police could have used the same information to target those who were actively involved; they had the technology to do so. They were not. They were attacking everyone indiscriminately. They were so rarely given any jurisdiction over this area, and they were going to enjoy it. No doubt a multitude of grudges had built up over the years, cases they hadn't been allowed to pursue because Oakseed had taken ownership of them, and this was their chance for some ill-targeted but cathartic revenge.

A couple of minutes later, the front doors opened and Loren saw two cops drag two workers out in cuffs. The cops pushed the workers up against the wagon and searched them, confiscating their slates—standard practice, to prevent communication and recording. Loren told the others this was happening.

They're going to arrest us too, Drienne said. She and Nadi were still on the underfloor, having checked the emergency exits and found them all closed. There was still no way to get from there to the workfloor, not that anyone wanted to right now.

They might not, said Nadi.

At the very least they're going to search us, said Drienne.

Arlo agreed. The Coyne wasn't a weapon but it would make the cops *very* suspicious. They'd want to know what was on it, they'd have ways of getting past the false tray, and when they found the money they'd wonder why a debranding operative was carrying such a vast sum. The most basic background check on Arlo and Drienne would reveal they weren't legit RookDivest employees. There was no way of spinning this to make it look innocent.

So what do we do? said Arlo.

Nadi said she had an idea.

Arlo took the stairs straight down to the underfloor, ignoring the sound of violent clashes behind the fire doors. He emerged into a corridor on the underfloor that, in contrast to the open space of the workfloor and the simple orderliness of the top floor, was an awkwardly laid out warren of passages that connected rooms of different sizes, many adapted from their original purpose.

He found Drienne and Nadi waiting in an otherwise unoccupied room; most of the workforce seemed to have joined the protests upstairs. Drienne quickly embraced Arlo, then they listened while Nadi explained her idea.

The plant broke down every single thing that could be reused, and what was left went down a disposal chute that came out in the dead-waste yard at the back corner of the building, next to the passage that led to the platform. The chute dumped it into a cart, and the cart took it to a compactor, after which it was sent to a landfill. The access point for the chute was on the underfloor.

"You're suggesting we go down the chute?" asked Drienne.

"No," said Nadi, "it's too small for a person. But if we drop the Coyne into it—"

"No," said Arlo.

"—it'll come out into one of the carts—"

"No."

"There won't be anyone there, the carts are all auto. So if someone can go down there and collect it—"

"Yes," said Drienne abruptly. "This is a great idea."

"No, it isn't," said Arlo. "You're talking about putting it into a *compactor chain*. It's too risky."

"It's really not. Loren can pick it up, the cops won't catch you carrying it, and we can focus on getting out of here without getting the living shit beaten out of us." Drienne had seized on this idea, and when she seized on an idea they always ended up doing it.

"Show me," Arlo said to Nadi, determined not to promise anything just yet.

Nadi took them to a short, wide, grimy corridor that ended at a pipe set into the wall at an angle. In front of the pipe there was a jack on the floor that raised harvesting carts up to the level of the pipe and tipped their contents into it, and also an industrial saw with which you could cut up anything that was too large for the pipe. The pipe was indeed too small to accommodate any of them.

Arlo still disliked the idea of letting the Coyne out of his sight. "Can't we force the emergency exits to open?"

"How?" said Nadi.

"We could start a fire."

"What?" said Drienne. "That sounds like one of *my* dumb ideas."

"I'm surprised you didn't suggest it yourself, dear."

"Well, *I* was going to say we should release some toxic gas."

"Why, have you seen some?"

"No! I was fucking joking."

"We haven't got time for jokes—look, it could just be a *small* fire, enough to set off the alarms and release the exits."

"I don't know if you're aware, but small fires have a habit of turning into *bigger* fires."

"There isn't anything to set fire to down here anyway," said Nadi. "Everything wood-based is sealed in a silo and waiting for—"

Noises came from down the corridor, around the corner from where they were standing. Two sets of footsteps. A voice shouted, "Against the wall!"

Nadi, Arlo, and Drienne looked at each other, wondering if this had been directed at them. But then another voice spoke, at a normal volume, hard to make out; it did not sound aggressive or confrontational. This was who the first speaker had been addressing. The next sounds were a rapid set of footsteps and something striking the second speaker, causing them to cry out in pain.

Before Drienne or Arlo could stop her, Nadi strode over to the corner and peered around it.

Farther along the corridor, one of the cops was standing half in, half out of a doorway. On the floor beneath him were a pair of feet. The rest of the person connected to the feet was on the other side of the doorway. From the angle of the feet it was clear he was lying on his stomach, wriggling while the cop tried to cuff him.

"I haven't done anything," the person was saying.

The cop ignored this and, gripping a wrist in each hand, heavily planted a foot in the small of his back, provoking a howl of pain.

"Hey!" said Nadi. "You don't need to do that."

The cop looked up sharply and saw Nadi approaching. He swiftly wrapped the cuffs around his victim's wrists and let the bound hands fall. Then he straightened up and readied himself as Nadi reached him.

"Look, some of us are just trying to get out of here," said Nadi. "We're not part of this, we don't want—"

The cop reached out for her shoulder. But Nadi knew these moves only too well: he was aiming to pin her to the wall, face-first. The instant she saw his hand move, she dipped her shoulder and his hand failed to find any purchase. Nadi took a step back and put her hand out to him, a placatory gesture designed to keep him at a distance. "Hey . . ."

The cop reached down to his side and removed his nightstick from its catch. There was a sleek metal noise as it automatically extended in his hand. He brought it round in an arc and landed a blow on the side of Nadi's head.

Nadi's training told her to remain calm when faced with provocative situations. But since getting away from Oakseed, she'd become more and more frustrated with the person her training had made her into, and how others had used it to manipulate her. The impact of the nightstick rang through her head and she staggered back, and it was as if the blow rebounded back off the core of her being and surged into her chest. She drew back a fist and flung it squarely into the cop's nose with a cry of rage, which turned to a yelp of exhilaration as she saw blood force its way through his nostrils and the ruptures she'd made in his skin. At that moment, he was every colleague she'd ever hated and she thrilled to see him hurt.

The cop tried to come back at Nadi, but she had already grasped the other end of his nightstick. He wasn't about to let go of it but, in a maneuver she came up with on the spot, she used it to take control of his right hand and, with a quick jabbing motion that took him by surprise, she made him punch himself in the balls. Using your training was all very well, but it was fun to be creative sometimes.

The cop lost his grip on the nightstick and Nadi was able to use it on him in just the way he'd used it on her, and after that he couldn't recover. As he fell to the floor, he grabbed her around the waist and tried to push her over, but when you go for a move like that you *have* to execute it, otherwise you're left staggering around like you're in a drunken hug. Nadi was presented with an easy shot: she brought the tip of the stick down sharply on the top of his neck, and he reeled away.

Nadi figured he was too dazed and in pain to follow her, so she headed for the stairwell—if one cop had got down there, the fire shutters must be up and there must be a way out. But as she approached the stairwell, she heard boots stomping down it. The cavalry was coming. There was nowhere to run and very soon they'd find Arlo and Drienne down here. All Nadi could do now was buy them some time.

Four more officers emerged from the stairwell and onto the corridor. Nadi gripped the nightstick and charged at them.

Arlo and Drienne peered around the corner, saw what was going on, and withdrew out of sight.

"We need to fucking do something before they find us," Drienne said in a low, urgent voice. "We need to do like Nadi said and put the thing down the pipe."

"What if Loren can't get it and it gets crushed and sent to land-fill?"

"It won't get crushed and sent to fucking landfill. The system has stopped and I've already told Kline to grant Loren access and they're heading down there now."

"When did you do that?"

"Just now, while Nadi was beating up that cop. We've got to do this, there'll be more of them coming. Give me the Coyne." Dri-enne put her hand out.

"Drienne, I don't think—"

"Fucking *give me it.*"

Arlo put his hand in his pocket and gave her the Coyne.

"Have we got anything to put it in?" she asked.

Arlo checked his pockets and happened upon his sunglasses inside their case. He removed the sunglasses and gave Drienne the case: the Coyne just about fit inside it, at a slight angle. She snapped the case closed and, with only the barest hesitation, tossed it down the pipe.

Eleven seconds later, a cop marched around the corner. Arlo and Drienne took an involuntary step back. Arlo was still holding his sunglasses; he dropped them as he thrust his hands in the air. He was wondering whether to say *We surrender!* or something of the sort when Drienne cried, "Thank *god* you're here!"

Kline felt annoyed at being given another job to do; he already had a lot to think about and he was trying to prepare to leave the apart-ment. He'd packed his suitcase earlier this afternoon, including some of the items the others had given him (but only some—he had disposed of a number of items he considered too heavy or too frivolous). And now he had to do something that wasn't even his skill set: logistics, not human resources. He could do it, sure, but the thing was, he shouldn't *have* to.

Grudgingly, Kline identified the process that governed the dead-waste outlet, located the hierarchy of responsibility for managing that process, and inserted Loren's alt-id into that hierarchy as casual labor, which meant Loren could use their slate to log a maintenance ticket on the outlet. He had one last check of the apartment, then one last glance at the apartment across the street (no sign of Frankie James), before returning to his windows to see if Loren had reported back. But he found he was receiving no information at all. At first he assumed a fault, and tried to get it back online—but when this failed to produce any results, it became clear the plant's connection had been taken down. The cops must have gone to the top floor and forced it offline to prevent anyone from streaming what was going on in there. This meant no devices could communicate in the vicinity of the plant, and the crew was entirely out of contact.

For a couple of minutes Kline stood in the middle of the apartment and considered this development. It aligned with some other thoughts he'd been having. He made some decisions and then he left.

THE DEAD-WASTE YARD

This was working out unexpectedly well, Loren thought as they listened at the gate to the dead-waste yard, checking no one was in there already. Not the riot and the cops and stuff, that was all really bad, but this particular aspect of things was better than they could have hoped for. There didn't seem to be anyone at the yard— anyone who wasn't trapped inside the plant had already left its immediate vicinity—so Loren entered.

The dead-waste yard was a small, untidy, slightly sunken area surrounded by a high fence, with a protruding corner of the main building overhanging it. It contained a loop of track with three tall carts that passed under the outlet pipe that stuck out from the building: when a cart was full it moved along the track and tipped into the compactor. A cart stood under the outlet. It had a ladder built into one side. Loren climbed up and peered into the cart.

Drienne had told them the Coyne would be inside Arlo's sunglasses case, and Loren had a moment of panic when it wasn't on top of the pile of junk inside the cart—but they quickly spotted it had bounced to one side and lodged inside a web of larger chunks of uncyclable crap. They levered their body against the side of the cart and tipped themselves toward the case, reaching out with their fingers—

Loren heard a noise from outside the yard. Someone was walking around the fence—maybe someone who'd seen them enter? Could be cops checking if anyone was hanging around outside. At any moment they might enter the yard. Loren's best chance of not being found was to hop inside the cart, and they did so as noiselessly as possible—but should they grab the Coyne as well, and stuff it in their rucksack? If it was the cops, they'd search Loren and find it and that was the entire operation sunk. They could leave the Coyne in the cart for now, in the sunglasses case—no one would look twice at it in among all this stuff. But Loren hated the thought of being so close to their objective and not claiming it—

The gate to the yard opened. Loren was unsure if any part of themself was visible above the top of the cart. Their right foot, perhaps, but to an onlooker it would hopefully appear someone had simply thrown a shoe out with the waste. They kept as still as they could and listened as whoever it was moved around the yard. Was it one person, or more? It sounded like one set of footsteps.

The footsteps came closer, then stopped next to the cart. Then the ladder creaked as someone stepped on it.

Drienne was doing very well, Arlo thought. Her opening gambit had stopped the cops from giving them an immediate kicking, though Arlo wasn't yet confident the kicking hadn't simply been deferred: kicked down the road, as it were. The cops visibly sized them up, trying to work out if they might get into trouble for committing violence against these people.

"We're visitors on important business," Drienne had told them in her most xeccy voice. Certainly Arlo and Drienne's upmarket clothing gave them a different look from everyone else currently inside the plant, unlike poor Nadi, who'd dressed to blend in and had been immediately identified by the cops as fair game.

"What business?" said one of the cops as Drienne held up her backhand so they could id her. Arlo did the same, though he wasn't confident their alt-ids would check out on a police database.

"We're debranding this facility," said Drienne. "We flew in from Boston a few days ago."

Don't tell them that, Arlo wanted to shout. *There's no need to tell them that, they didn't ask and we didn't actually fly in from Boston at all.* He saw one of the other cops tap his backhand—was he running a check on their flight?

"What are you doing in here?" said the cop who was questioning Drienne.

"Debranding it, of course. Then that woman came in and started *haranguing* us."

"The tall woman who just—"

"*Yes*, the tall woman. Have you arrested her?"

"She's in custody now."

"Good."

"I mean," Arlo put in, "she didn't *do* anything to us."

"It was *quite* alarming, though."

"Yes, yes. But I don't think she committed a crime."

"She has now," said the cop. "Assault on a police officer."

"On *several* police officers," added the one checking his backhand.

Arlo heard this with dismay. There was no getting Nadi back from that. Drienne's instinct to distance them from Nadi didn't sit well with him, but it was correct: there was no sense in them both going down with her.

"Please, can we leave now?" said Drienne. "We've been stuck down here for some time and it's pretty scary, actually."

"Yes," Arlo added.

"We had no *idea* London was like this now."

The cop did not say they could leave, nor did he say they couldn't. He nodded to a colleague and together they searched Arlo and Drienne, who submitted with weary sighs, as if it was of no consequence to them but all rather tiresome. Arlo's mind was frantically going over everything he was carrying on his person, assessing whether any of it was suspicious. Would they find it weird he had sunglasses with no case? And he *had* given Drienne the Coyne, hadn't he? And she *had* put it into the pipe? He hadn't just imagined it all in the panic?

The cops also took the cases that contained the drone squadrons, but didn't find anything worth remarking on.

"So can we go?" Arlo asked.

"Not yet," the main cop told him.

Arlo was willing to accept this response, for the time being at least, but Drienne remained fully in character. "When?" she demanded. "What are you waiting for?"

"For your own safety," the cop said. "It's chaos up there, you're better off down here." He directed them to an empty storage bay, then stayed by the door to guard them while his colleagues swept the rest of the underfloor. He did not give their cases back.

Arlo checked his backhand, and the cop on the door gave him a warning glare.

"I'm just checking my messages," said Arlo.

"We cut the whole place off," the cop told him. "You won't get a signal."

"Oh," said Arlo lightly and let his hand fall to his side. When the cop wasn't looking, he glanced at Drienne, looking for her reaction. She gave a slight shrug, and he got her meaning: *It is what it is.* They just had to hope Loren had the Coyne, and they'd head for the rendezvous and meet them and Kline there, and Nadi if she somehow got free of the cops.

The cops found several employees who'd been cowering on the underfloor, hoping to sit out the riot. Some of them were ushered to join Arlo and Drienne in the storage bay. Some of them, the cops beat up. Arlo didn't speak out against what the cops were doing and he knew this made him a bad person, but he had to act like the only thing he was unhappy about was being kept here. Nadi had tried to intervene, and look how that had turned out. Maybe there was something they could do for her, further down the line: lodge a legal challenge perhaps, or at least keep her share of the loot safe until she got out of prison. Whatever it took, he'd make sure she wasn't forgotten.

Nadi only realized they were dragging her out of the building when she felt the cool evening breeze on her face. A third wagon had joined the first two, this one a prisoner transport. It was already filling up. The cops carrying her opened up the rear doors and pushed her inside. She struggled to stay on her feet. The other prisoners were sitting on the bare floor in the back, and she landed on a couple of them when she fell. Some of the prisoners shouted at her for being careless, some of them shouted at the cops, some of them helped her up into a sitting position against the wall.

"You okay?" said a voice close to Nadi's face.

Nadi managed to open her eyes a little, though it was difficult with all the cuts around them and the blood on the lids that was becoming sticky. She saw a face and recognized it.

"Gregg," she said, her jaw moving painfully.

The guy who'd "helped" her catch that poor girl they'd found at the Korean restaurant. Nadi should have told Arlo or Loren or someone about that girl, because she wasn't sure she was going to get out of here and no one else would save the girl now. She turned her hand to send a message—

But of course, she didn't have her slate.

"She doesn't look good," said Gregg to the others. "She needs medical help."

A couple of the others went to the back doors of the wagon and banged on it, trying to attract someone's attention, saying they needed a medic. When there was no response, several more joined them. It was nice to know people cared, Nadi thought as she slid into unconsciousness.

LARGE GREEN ARROWS

The cop watching Arlo and Drienne and the others on the under-floor had stepped out of the storage bay for a moment to speak to a colleague. Arlo noticed Drienne was looking down at the floor and shaking her head.

"Everything okay?" Arlo said.

She looked up at him with resentment, and her expression worried him. This was just the kind of situation in which she was prone to disassociate. He went to put a hand on her shoulder, but she swatted it away.

"Look—I know," he said.

"Fucking outrageous," she muttered.

"We're getting out of here soon."

"Bullshit." She was getting loud. Was she still acting up for the cops' benefit? Or was this something else?

"Okay," said the cop, returning to the room. "Let's move, guys. Quickly. Single file."

All the employees walked out of the storage bay under the cop's watchful eye. Arlo and Drienne tried to pick up their cases, but the cop said he'd be taking those. Together they proceeded down the corridor to where the other cops waited impatiently for them, making clear it was a huge imposition to have to escort these idiots out of the building. The cops headed for the stairs first and the rest of them followed—

And then something up on the workfloor exploded, with enough force to make the walls shake down on the underfloor. Up ahead a door swung violently open, hitting two cops and sending both fly-ing to the floor. One of them wasn't moving, and his head seemed to be burned and bleeding. The other one, the one who'd guarded them in the room and still had their cases, was trapped under the door, which had blown off its hinges. Wild flickering light came from the open doorway, and the cop at the front of the line, who had just missed being hit by the door, shielded her face as a draft of hot air poured into the corridor. She dashed away toward the stairs and quickly became invisible behind a combination of heat haze and light from the fire. An alarm went off and didn't stop.

Arlo knew the door led to one of the silos that the workfloor fun-nels fed directly into. Whatever material it contained was inflam-mable, and whether by accident or design, something had inflamed it. And the walls between the silo room and the corridor he stood in were not thick: in fact, they appeared to be fiber dividers inserted between concrete support posts. Flames were curling around the doorframe and spreading out from there. The remaining cops yelled at everyone to stay back, but it wasn't as if anyone was likely to rush toward the source of the fire.

Flat black panels were fixed to the corridor walls at regular inter-vals, and these now lit up with a chunky green arrow pointing away from the fire, and the word EXIT in large letters above.

"The exits are open!" shouted one of the employees.

"Fucking *finally*," shouted another.

Everyone turned and obeyed the arrows, which led them to a door halfway along the next corridor. One of the employees in their group pulled it aside, revealing a short narrow windowless corridor with dim red-orange lighting and another door at the end. They all dashed for this outer door, and the employee who'd opened the inner door complained the others were crushing her and needed to give her some space so she could open it. But when she had the space, it wouldn't open. Someone else told her she was doing it wrong, barged her out of the way and tried to open it themselves, with no success. Perhaps something was blocking it on the outside, or its release systems had failed. A third person made their own desperate attempt before the group accepted the door was not going to open and jostled each other back down the corridor in search of another exit. But with the fire blocking their way, it seemed they were out of options on the underfloor. They headed up the rear stairwell to the workfloor, but the fire shutters blocked them from passing through the workfloor to the building's rear exit. They could only go up.

"I say we go to the top floor," Arlo said. "There are two exits there."

"Fires *spread* upward," said Drienne, "you do know that."

"Yes, that's why we have to go *now* before the fire reaches it."

Arlo was right, the top floor wasn't on fire—yet. But smoke was starting to rise through the carpet in the central corridor. The group arrived at the crossroads to find the exit that lay past the premium store was already open: they rushed toward it and one of the cops barked at them all to slow down and stop pushing. To be fair, it would be dumb for them to get this close to safety and then die by falling from the emergency exit due to excessive haste. The jittery group managed to file through the exit one by one. Drienne was second through the door: she'd ended up ahead of Arlo and was getting into increasingly tetchy exchanges with the cops. Arlo needed to get her somewhere quiet so she could cool off and stabilize.

Arlo ended up the penultimate member of the party to descend, followed by the cop who'd guarded them on the underfloor. The ladder was basic—rungs affixed to the side of the building, with a series of larger loops to catch you if you fell—and triggered lurching anxiety in Arlo. He could descend only by forcing himself to stare directly at the pale, sun-weathered wall, watching it scroll from the bottom of his vision to the top, from bottom to top, from bottom to top. Eventually one of his feet, expecting to find another rung, instead struck the ground (*ouch*) and he stumbled away. Once he'd checked his ankle wasn't sprained, he turned to look for Drienne.

She wasn't there.

They had come out in the alley that ran down the left-hand side of the plant, which also served as the emergency exit from the truck train platform. Arlo's fellow escapees were dashing toward the street, and Arlo supposed Drienne had done the same—but when he reached the street he still couldn't see her. He asked one of the other escapees where she went, but got no response. Surely Drienne couldn't have got out of sight so quickly, if she was heading for the rendezvous? Did she go the other way, toward the platform? Why would she do that?

He heard a truck train pulling out from the platform.

Arlo ran back down the alley, but when he reached the steps leading down to the platform the truck train was vanishing from view. One of the cops lay on the ground, moaning in pain. Had Drienne taken the train? Surely she couldn't have operated it herself—and why hadn't she waited for him?

Arlo wanted to believe Drienne was still okay and sticking to the plan, because if she wasn't, there was absolutely nothing he could do about it. All he could do was head for the rendezvous and hope she was there.

LEAVE A LABEL
OF AN OWL
ON THE BENCH

Kline sat alone on a bench at the rendezvous point, reclining his feet on his suitcase, sipping from a bottle of M:Pyre. If M:Pyre didn't get bought (and it might not, as the brand was so closely associated with Oakseed) these remaining bottles might become collector's items, and Kline was struck by the thought he should have left it unopened, kept it and auctioned it in a couple of years. But then, how much would he make from that? A few thousand? With the money he was about to net from this job, and the plans he had for that money, in a couple of years he hoped to be the kind of person who *spent* thousands on frivolous shit at auctions, not the one trying to *make* thousands from it.

Anyway, he was thirsty right now.

Kline was wondering if he would be the only one to make it to the rendezvous. They hadn't agreed how long they should wait for each other once they got here, because such things were contingent on the situation, and Kline intended to wait for the shortest possible time while making it appear he'd given the others a fair chance to turn up. He had no idea where the others were, but he had a sense of what was unfolding inside Kentish Cyc, and reasoned that since the others weren't already at the rendezvous, they must have been caught in the chaos.

Kline checked his slate. He couldn't update Mia on the situation either. It was unsettling being so thoroughly out of contact. They'd agreed that if any of them failed to make it to the rendezvous, the ones who did make it should leave a mark on the bench before leaving, so any latecomers would know they'd been and gone and there was no need to wait for them. It had been Kline's idea they should carry labels for this purpose, with a different design for each member of the team: meaningless to anyone else but immediately recognizable to the others. Kline's labels bore an image of an owl, and he was just searching through his pockets for them when Arlo turned up, frantic, his clothes drenched in sweat. He barely acknowledged Kline, and instead he walked all around the Doggy Dogg Jones statue to check if anyone, or anything, was behind it.

"Have you seen Drienne?" he asked.

"I haven't seen anyone," Kline said.

"Loren?"

"No."

Arlo stared in panic. "Loren should've got here first. So where's the Coyne?"

Kline reached into a pocket and produced the Coyne with quiet, smug triumph.

"How'd you get it?" Arlo said.

"I went to the dead-waste outlet in case Loren needed help. They weren't there but this was."

"But what happened to Loren? Did the police get them?"

"Probably—cops were everywhere. I had to bluff my way past some; I said I'd come to visit my niece. They told me to get the hell out."

"It's on fire," Arlo said, shaking his head. "The whole place is going up, and I don't know where Drienne or Loren are . . ."

"Nadi?"

"Cops got her. Probably dragged her out and put her in a wagon. Which is, y'know, bad, but better than being caught in the fire."

"If the plant's burning down, the comms aren't coming back on."

"So we've got no way of getting in touch with any of them."

"At least we got the Coyne," Kline said, smiling. "I mean, we *did* it. We just need to get out of here, and—"

"I just can't understand what's happened to Drienne. She was with me, and then . . ."

Just then they became aware of an approaching noise, and turned to see a drone descending toward them, about the size and shape of a tin can. Kline stood up: he and Arlo both assumed it was a police drone. It was matte black with no markings, and it settled on the bench.

Arlo and Kline glanced at each other. Then both of them simultaneously received a message from the drone, a short bounce. The message dropped a pin onto their maps, due south-southwest, with an instruction for them to go there immediately. This wasn't the plan. They were meant to catch the overline back to NiZCOval and wait for Mia to arrive. If they'd succeeded, she would split the money, give them their freedom, and they could go their separate ways. If they'd failed, Mia would take them back to Vancouver to be sold. But the message said the overline had been suspended due to events in Kentish Cyc, so Mia would pick them up at the pin instead.

"So what, are we just supposed to walk there?" said Arlo.

"It's only a little over two kilometers," Kline replied.

"What about the others?"

"They'll have to make their own way."

"But how will they know to go there?"

"If they come here they'll get the same message from the drone." The drone looked conspicuous on the bench, so Kline moved it underneath, just behind one of the legs. Arlo still seemed unhappy about it, but they both left their label on the bench (Arlo's had an image of a lily) and started walking.

As Arlo and Kline returned to the main road, Kline towing his suitcase, they saw firefighters trying to dampen the blaze, but there was no saving the plant. They could only prevent the fire from spreading further. The structure was starting to collapse in on itself.

"Well," said Kline in a low voice, "we could hardly have hoped for a better cover."

Arlo had to admit this was true, but he also pointed out people had certainly died in there.

"No one *made* them burn the place down," said Kline. "We certainly didn't."

"Those workers were manipulated," Arlo said. "Just like we were. At every stage. If they hadn't been kept in the dark about the collapse of the company, there wouldn't have been this whole wave of paranoia—"

"So what, they were justified in burning the place down?"

Arlo shrugged. "Yeah. Maybe." Despite his concern for those caught in the fire, his own terrifying experience of escaping from it, and his distaste for Kline hailing its convenience, it didn't feel entirely *wrong* that it had happened. The plant passing into new ownership would change nothing. All Oakseed facilities would be run along the same exploitative lines as before. The only meaningful thing you could do was destroy the asset completely, even if it wasn't in your best interests.

But Arlo could tell Kline had no patience for this line of thought, and they didn't want to have this argument within earshot of anyone who might report them for seditious activity, so they started walking down the road that led to Camden Town.

Once they hit the edge of the corpurbation, Arlo was struck by how abruptly it ended. He'd seen this from the carriage on the way here, but it was even starker on the ground. Although this was not the most lucrative patch of the city, it was the closest to the plant and so, whenever circumstances made travel into the center difficult, these areas had been harvested instead. Practically everything had gone. Between the dry weeds you could see the footprints of what had once been buildings, and sunken areas that were formerly basements. You could trace outlines of roads and curbs in the cracked tarmac, concrete, and stone. But Oakseed had taken everything else and fed it into their machine, leaving a hard, flat plain behind. Kentish Cyc might be dead but the other plants would continue its work until this barren vista had rolled over the whole city.

Arlo and Kline barely spoke. They didn't want to attract attention, but they had nothing to say to each other anyway. Arlo regularly looked behind himself, pretending to be keeping an eye out for cops or vagues, but really he was hoping to see Drienne catching up, castigating them for not waiting for her. They took turns wheeling Kline's suitcase over the uneven ground.

As they neared the pin Mia had sent them, they started to encounter buildings that hadn't been harvested yet. The sun was sinking behind the battered skyline. And then Kline noticed a copter crossing the sky, getting lower and moving closer. It was black and had no markings, just like the drone that had told them to come here.

"Is that Mia?" said Arlo.

"I assume so," said Kline.

They walked toward the copter as it landed on the exact spot indicated by the pin. It was a vehicle of substantial size, probably a military-political model. The cockpit was blacked out, and while there was room for a human pilot it probably didn't have one. It was transport for someone very wealthy and important; as the door on the side slid back, they could see its interior décor was understated but luxurious. And there was only one person inside it, and that was Mia.

Mia stood on the threshold, looking from Kline to Arlo. "You do have it?" she asked them urgently.

Kline reached into his pocket and brought out the Coyne.

"Excellent." She smiled broadly and clapped her hands together. "Come aboard."

Arlo went first, and Mia put out a hand to help him up. "We should fly back over there and look for the others," he said.

"No."

"But we may be able to help—"

"Arlo," Mia said, putting a hand on Arlo's shoulder. "I'd love to go looking for them, I would. But I didn't make you both walk down here for fun, I did it so no one sees me or this copter anywhere near that plant."

"She's right," Kline said. (He still hadn't boarded the copter, Arlo noted.)

Mia turned to Kline and said, "Thank you," in a tone that made clear his support was absolutely meaningless.

"The others could be arrested or dead or, at best, they got taken to hospital where their identities will probably be blown. If they haven't they have to contact us so we can pick them up. If they can't contact us they have to make it to the port and out of the country under their own steam."

"But I think Drienne might have escaped from there on a truck train," said Arlo. "She's probably gone back to NiZCOval, we could go looking—"

"Why would she escape on a truck train?" said Mia. "Why not go to the rendezvous as agreed?"

"It was a chaotic situation—"

"She suffers from duplisychosis," said Kline, who still hadn't boarded.

Mia's eyes flicked up and fixed on Kline. "Duplisychosis."

"Yes, it's a condition some mades suffer from where—"

"I know what it is." She turned to Arlo. "You didn't think to mention this earlier?"

"Well. I thought you might not want her on the operation," Arlo said.

"Possibly not, no, but we could've mitigated it if I'd known. But you didn't tell me and now *this* has happened."

"Sorry. But with that in mind, can we go and look—"

"No. Hopefully she'll come to her senses and find a way to contact us or make her own way back." She motioned for Kline to come aboard.

Kline didn't move. "When you said you were coming in a copter, I didn't expect *this*. How'd you afford a vehicle this fancy?"

Mia laughed. "This isn't *mine*."

"Oh."

"I called in a favor from a client. He doesn't know what I'm doing with it."

"Ah, right. Yeah, that makes sense." Kline still didn't step aboard. He put the Coyne back into his pocket.

"Kline, what the fuck are you doing?" said Arlo.

"I'd like to renegotiate the terms," said Kline.

JUST LIKE
FLOATING AWAY

Kline really wanted to step aboard the copter. From where he stood he could catch the wood-and-leather scent of the interior, he could see its finely upholstered chairs and compact, elegant fittings. He particularly liked the drinks cabinet. Looking at the copter, and imagining being in it and rising above the desolate landscape, he felt a fundamental shift at the core of his being. He didn't belong down here, he belonged in *there*, soaring above it all. When he got his share of the money, and after he'd made his first few investments and they'd paid out, he was definitely going to buy a copter of his own. He could happily live in one of these, and maybe he would. But all of this confirmed to him the necessity of what he was about to do.

"I want to talk about our share," said Kline. "There's only three of us here—"

"I was clear about that," said Mia, glaring furiously at him. "We still don't know what happened to the others; I'll be holding their shares for now. And you each get ten percent, whatever happens."

"And I understand why you said that, because you didn't want us disposing of each other to get a better share—"

"This is nonnegotiable, Kline."

"Is it, though? Because I've got the money, and as it stands you've a lot more to lose than I have."

Mia's eyes narrowed. "I *own* you."

"So what, you're going to report me to the police?"

"Come on, you prick," said Arlo, "we had a deal, it's a great deal, just give her the Coyne—we still need her to get out of here."

"Do we? With the money on there we can do anything we like."

"It hasn't been laundered. And the security—"

"We can get around that, the encryption on this thing must be ancient." Kline imagined it crumbling like a rusty padlock, because that was effectively what it was.

Mia made an exasperated noise. "It's not as simple as you think. This is your last chance. Hand it over now."

Kline had been building up to this part. He still had his trump card to play, he just wanted to see how she reacted when he didn't do as he was told. "See, there's something else I found out about—"

Mia pulled a small pistol from her pocket and shot Kline through the head.

Arlo was so dazed, it took several seconds for him to realize Mia might very well shoot him too. He was the only witness to what had just happened. It was much simpler all round to just kill them both—the law wouldn't touch her for it, and it would also mean she didn't have to pay them. Arlo was still on the copter and wondered if he should hop off and run for his life. But he didn't, and Mia paid Arlo no attention at all as she crouched next to Kline and took the Coyne from his pocket. Then she climbed back into the copter. Arlo watched as the door slid closed on the sight of Kline's maroon-suited body and his suitcase lying next to each other on the ground. Arlo abstractly remembered the suitcase contained a nice golf shirt he'd asked Kline to pack for him, but he did nothing to claim it.

The copter's suspension cancellation was so effective, you could barely feel any movement inside as it took off. It was just like floating away, as if the physical forces of the world outside had no effect.

Arlo sat in one of the chairs while Mia poured him a drink, and he absorbed what he'd just witnessed. He recalled Mia had raised her gun high and held her arm very straight, clearly conscious of the risk she might damage the Coyne if she tried to shoot Kline anywhere other than his head. She'd made a clean shot to exposed skin in a fatal area. She'd done the whole thing so calmly.

Mia handed Arlo a highball, saying, "Sorry you had to see that." He didn't remember her asking him what he wanted to drink— had she remembered from Vancouver what his drink was? How thoughtful.

"Was that necessary?" he asked.

Mia thought for a moment. "On balance, yes, I think it was. He was the one member of the party I was never sure about, and I decided before you left Vancouver that if he made trouble I wasn't going to fuck around. I did give him a chance, didn't I? You saw me."

"Right." Pause. "I mean—"

"What?"

"Nothing." He'd been about to point out she hadn't warned Kline she was going to kill him, but then thought better of it. When Arlo met Mia he hadn't thought her capable of murder. But then he hadn't spent a lot of time around murderers. Of course, legally she *wasn't* a murderer, she'd probably never consider killing a nat—but that was exactly it, until now he'd felt like she treated him and the rest of the crew as real people. She'd even offered them the chance to legally *become* real people.

Mia sat at a desk with the Coyne. There was a compartment by the side of her seat: she reached into it and retrieved a facer plugged into a slate. The tech looked clunky, like something Arlo would have used at nursery—it was probably vintage, as old as the Coyne itself. "I would *like* to know what's happened to the others."

"Can you check arrest records for their alt-ids?" said Arlo.

Mia smiled as she brought the Coyne within range of the facer. "Obviously. But this is the priority."

Arlo kept seeing the foolish expression on Kline's face as he'd been shot. Yeah, he was annoying, aloof, and he'd been greedy, but he hadn't asked to be involved in this. None of them had. And they'd just left his body out there in the rubble, where no one would care what had happened to him, just another fool who went wandering in the badlands—

"*What?*" said Mia, eyes still fixed on the Coyne, her forehead creasing in irritation and puzzlement.

"Is something wrong?"

"It's a fake."

"What do you mean?"

"I mean what I said, it's a fucking fake. It's printed." Mia tapped it against the table.

Arlo couldn't have felt more panicked if a trapdoor had just opened directly underneath him in the floor of the copter. "It can't be. That's the one that came from the locker."

"You're sure you didn't screw up and leave the real one in the locker and take the copy away with you?"

"No—absolutely not. I was so worried about doing that—"

"Why would you worry about that? Why would that even be a *possibility*?"

"Because I worry about things. But no—there was a dent . . ." He took the Coyne from Mia. "Yes. This one has no dent. This has to be the one I took from the locker."

"Then why's it fake, Arlo?"

"Well . . . I mean, the Coyne was out of my sight for—"

"How long?"

"I had to throw it down a trash pipe, and—"

"A *trash pipe*?"

"To make sure the police didn't catch us carrying it. That's how come Kline had it instead of me. Loren was meant to pick it up, but they—"

"Didn't?"

"Doesn't seem like it, Kline got there and found it and there was no one around."

"That's what *he* told you. *You* weren't there."

"Well . . . yes."

"Jesus Christ . . ."

"I didn't have a choice."

"But a *trash pipe*? So Kline could have picked up the wrong thing by mistake at the other end?"

"No—look, there's no way this would've been put down the trash pipe. It's basematter, you can cycle this easily. No way would someone forego the commission by chucking it in the trash, which is more effort than cycling it."

Mia glared at him, and he thought she was going to tell him what an idiot he'd been. But instead, eventually, she said, "You're right. It's not impossible, but it's *so* unlikely it's not worth considering."

"Plus, it was in my sunglasses case. I told Loren it was in my sunglasses case."

"But Loren didn't pick it up. Kline did. Did he know it was in your sunglasses case?"

"I don't know. It was just before the network went down so he might not have seen the message. I mean, you could ask him if you hadn't—"

"*Please*, let's not get into whether or not I should have killed Kline."

"But if *this*"—he held up the Coyne—"is the one I took from the locker, it must have been a fake all along."

"No. It was real, Samson got me to work on it, remember?"

"Samson switched it out for a fake, then. After you worked on it. That must be it." Arlo took this in. "So there's no money. It was all for nothing—"

"Shut up," said Mia. She thought for a moment. "Why put a fake in a locker only you can open? Who are you fooling? Doesn't make sense." She jabbed the air with her finger. "No. This is easy. We can figure this out." She located a device that looked like a thick pen with a jelly tip, plugged it into her slate, and ran the tip over the surface of the fake Coyne. She looked at the window her slate brought up, then put pen and slate down and pointed at the fake. "It's new. Printed in the last day or so."

"You're sure?"

"The structure is consistent with a new model, not one from years and years ago. And you can just tell, it's fresh."

"Then Kline must have made it. He was going to keep the real one and give you that one."

"But why demand a share of the money and then give me a fake that has nothing on it? Why do that if he was going to steal it all?"

"I don't know, but—"

"If I took the fake from his pocket, that means the real one is—"

"Still with him. It must be."

They returned to Kline's body, which still lay where it fell, with no sign it had been disturbed; if someone had ransacked the body you could guarantee they would also have rifled through his suitcase, but the case was also exactly as it had been when they left. The light was failing, so Mia told Arlo to hold a flashlight while she searched all Kline's pockets and then his case. But she found nothing.

"It doesn't make sense," Mia said eventually, sitting in the doorway of the grounded copter. "From the way he acted, he was negotiating with a full hand. Or what he thought was a full hand. But he never had the money."

"Maybe he hid it somewhere?" said Arlo, who was looking through the case and discovering Kline had *not* packed Arlo's golf shirt, the bastard.

"But why try to bargain for a larger share of the money if he secretly had it all? No, I know what makes sense"—and here Mia stood, pulled out her pistol and pointed it at Arlo—"is you and Drienne decided to take all the money for yourselves and set up Kline as the fall guy for it."

"No!" Arlo yelled, standing up and stepping back.

"Yes, this makes *lots* of sense. You put this fake Coyne down the trash pipe, Drienne holds on to the real one, Kline gets the fake, you come here telling me Drienne's disappeared and make sure Kline takes the blame."

"No, that's not . . ." Arlo was about to say he didn't know what she was talking about, but that was what guilty people in dramas said and it always sounded *so guilty*. But he *didn't* know what she was talking about. Instead he said, "If I was going to do that, wouldn't I have disappeared along with Drienne? Why would I risk confronting you instead of letting Kline come alone?"

Mia's arm—the one that held the gun—relaxed a little. "Huh."

"All I ever wanted was my cut and my debt canceled. Mostly the latter, I'm the one who's been telling everyone to focus on that all along. You said the debt only got canned if we completed the job, but this isn't completing the job, is it? So why would I do that?"

Mia considered this and let the gun fall slightly to one side. "That's true. I don't think you're screwing me."

Arlo exhaled with relief.

"Your friend *is*," said Mia. "So we're going looking for her after all."

34

EASY TO SAY
IN RETROSPECT

As Drienne steered the truck train she and Loren had stolen straight through the center of London, she wondered if she'd done the right thing by leaving Arlo behind. Rationally she knew it was better he remained unaware of what she was doing. If he'd known it would have freaked him out, and made him anxious, and then he'd never have been able to lie convincingly to Mia about it. And this way he might get what he wanted even if Drienne didn't.

Anyway, there'd have been no need to leave Arlo behind if not for Kline. Kline had really fucked this whole thing, and Drienne was going to fucking kill him when she saw him again.

When Loren had lain inside the cart at the dead-waste yard, listening to someone climbing the ladder, they'd been ready to leap up, surprise them, punch them in the face, and knock them to the ground. After they'd done that they intended to grab Arlo's sunglasses case and jump out of the cart (ideally landing *on* the person and injuring them further) before running away. They were winding up to deliver this blow when they rolled over and realized the person leaning over the side of the cart was Kline, just in time to pull their punch.

In retrospect, Loren should have done as they originally intended. Instead they said, "Kline, thank fuck it's you. Help me out of here."

Kline didn't help them out of the cart. "Have you got the Coyne?" he asked.

Loren said, "Yes, it's—"

Kline cut off this sentence by whipping Loren hard across the head with a small cosh he'd taken from his pocket. Then he delivered a second blow, knocking them unconscious.

When Loren awoke, they saw Arlo's sunglasses case still lodged in the junk, right in front of their eyes. *Ah, I should grab that,* they thought. *It's important.* They also realized the cart was moving. It took them a moment to process what this meant, but when they did, they grabbed the case and leapt out of the cart in a panic before it tipped them into the compactor. It was just starting to activate, its mechanisms warming up, as Loren picked themself up off the ground.

It wasn't hard to fill in what had happened in the interim. Loren looked inside their rucksack and yes, the dummy Coyne they'd printed off earlier that day had gone. Kline had searched the bag, found what he thought was the real Coyne, and taken it. He'd also taken Loren's slate and used the access privileges he'd granted them to set the cart in motion, then left the scene. The fact he had not stayed to watch them die suggested a degree of squeamishness, or maybe just overconfidence. He'd probably overestimated how long they'd remain unconscious for—you had to hit someone seriously hard to knock them out for more than a few minutes.

Loren made their way to a corner of the yard to get cleaned up. The cosh had struck them on the temple and on the cheekbone, drawing blood, and the wounds were swelling. This was irritating as there were cops everywhere looking for people who had taken part in a riot, and Loren now looked exactly like someone who had taken part in a riot.

The upside was Loren was now free to examine the Coyne, which was what they'd wanted all along. Kline's betrayal gave them the perfect excuse to disappear for a bit: probably he'd go to the rendezvous, maybe he'd tell the others Loren was dead or he didn't know what had happened to them, and they'd all catch the overline to NiZCOval. Presumably Kline also had something else planned, probably a play for more money with Loren out of the picture. As he was now carrying a dummy, that might not go too well—but that wasn't Loren's problem.

Loren felt confident they could crack the archaic security on the Coyne's false tray in ten minutes, tops, but they didn't want to do it while hanging around with stolen goods in a facility swarming with police. They left the yard through the gate and headed round to the platform, where a truck train was waiting. They stepped inside the steerage truck, turned the power on, and within a few minutes had assumed control of the train. They would head out, stop somewhere quiet, take a look at the Coyne and then maybe take the train all the way down—

Fuck. Kline took their slate. Maybe there was something on the train they could adapt to use as an interface . . .

They looked up and saw Drienne descending the fire escape at the side of the building. There were cops with her, and Loren wondered if she was under arrest. Loren stepped out of the truck to get a better view.

Drienne looked in Loren's direction, saw them, and sped up her descent. Moments later, she was hurrying down the steps that led to the platform.

Loren quickly formed a plan. They would tell Drienne what had happened with Kline; reassure her they had the real Coyne and Kline had a dummy; borrow Drienne's slate so they could get to work on lifting the tray; Drienne would then meet the others and travel down with them to NiZCOval. Loren would take the train straight there and be like *Surprise, motherfucker* when they saw Kline again.

As Drienne approached, Loren saw one of the cops descend the steps, shouting for Drienne to stop and come back. Drienne wasn't prepared to wait and find out why. Loren stepped back inside the steerage truck, Drienne dashed the last few steps and dived in, and Loren told the truck train to start moving. Its acceleration was slow at first, and the cop had time to reach it and grab a doorframe. As he tried to climb inside, the train jolted into a higher gear, causing him to lose his grip. Loren peered from the window and saw him tumble to the platform.

When Loren put their head back inside, Drienne said, "Thank *fuck*," and pulled Loren into an embrace. This surprised Loren, as they weren't a tactile person and Drienne hadn't shown much sign of regarding them with fondness. But recent days had bonded them, in an odd way.

Drienne had her suspicions from the start. It was easy to say that in retrospect, but she really had. She'd been wary of checking out those suspicions while staying at Mia's apartment in Vancouver, because Mia had access to their activity records. Drienne needed an unregistered terminal and a connection outside of Mia's range, which was why she'd confided in Loren. At the time Loren was ordering lots of equipment for the job, including slates they were going to register with the crew's alt-ids, so they bought an extra one and claimed it was an emergency spare. Loren had no issue with Drienne doing this background research, regarding it as due diligence.

Drienne took the spare slate with her on the first day she and Arlo went out to practice with the drone squadrons, and used it to look up the backstory Mia had told them. If it was as significant as Mia claimed, there should be something about it online—and there was. It had indeed been a landmark case, famous in legal circles. As well as academic articles there were documentaries, gameplays, and a twenty-six-part animated series telling the story. The case and its aftermath dominated Mia's public profile, and you had to dig deep to find anything else about her at all. It must be odd to be famous for something shitty that happened to you so long ago, as if nothing else you did could ever possibly matter.

But the important thing was: every account Drienne found matched Mia's.

Drienne had to talk to someone about it, but Arlo was so earnest about not rocking the boat with Mia, fully invested in their holder being the real deal. So the following morning, when Loren went out for a run, Drienne casually said she would go too, hoping no one else spontaneously opted to join them. (Nadi was still asleep.) They ran around the park, which was so much farther than Drienne would ever usually try to run, and when she stopped for a rest, this wasn't just because she wanted to talk to Loren, she needed to stop before she collapsed and died.

"Everything Mia told us seems true," Drienne said.

"Well, that's good, isn't it?" said Loren.

"Suppose so."

"Good idea to check it out, though. We should know the whole story. No nasty surprises later."

Drienne nodded. "I still think something's not right."

"What's that?"

"I said I still think something's not right."

"I heard you, I meant what d'you think's not right?"

"I don't know. The money . . . I don't quite buy this thing about Samson not being able to find anyone who could launder it."

"Probably didn't want to tell anyone else about the money. He'd already told Mia and didn't want more people to know."

"But would he really leave it there all these years, halfway across the world?"

"Mia did say it was a retirement plan, and that it was difficult to move a Coyne."

"Yeah, but if I had retirement savings . . ."

Loren laughed shortly.

"I know, man," Drienne continued, "good joke. But if I did, I'd find a way to move them somewhere I could see them. There *must* be a way. I wouldn't trust it to still be there all those years later."

"You would, I would. But nats think differently about this stuff. Xecs especially. And there could be all kinds of"—Loren shrugged—"factors here we don't know about."

"Exactly, yeah, that's what I'm saying."

"But it doesn't mean there's something Mia isn't telling us. Maybe she doesn't know either."

"But if she's so smart—like, she's smarter than me, right? So if I'm asking these questions, why isn't she?"

"She probably has and she couldn't find the answers, so didn't want to confuse us with a bunch of extra information."

This seemed fair, and Drienne was tired of looking for holes in the story, so she dropped it and they finished their run at a pace Loren clearly found frustrating.

It was later, in London, that Loren came to Drienne at the NiZCOval apartment and said they needed to talk. Drienne considered bringing Arlo into it at this point, mostly because she found it hard to exclude him. She'd never kept anything from him before and their habitual closeness made it difficult to do so now. But she still felt it was in his best interest not to involve him just yet: if Mia found out they were poking into her background, Drienne didn't want to get Arlo in trouble and risk him not getting his freedom and his share of the loot. He could stay clean. He was literally getting clean in the shower when Loren arrived, so it was easy for Drienne to slip out of the apartment and not tell him where she'd gone.

Drienne and Loren bought chilled soup and ate it sitting in the plaza that had been built next to the old pavilion, and Loren explained. In the course of learning about Kentish Cyc and infiltrating its systems, Loren had come across huge chunks of leaked Oakseed data. Usually, Oakseed's bots would have tracked and scrubbed stuff like this, but the bots had been shut down so all this data was just swimming around online, being replicated and chewed through.

There was an insane amount of it, more than a human brain could process in a thousand lifetimes, but Loren was skilled at fishing and the conversation with Drienne back in Vancouver had stuck with them. The support spent much of their downtime in London fishing for data about Mia, figuring there was bound to be stuff Oakseed knew about her that had never been made public.

"And what did you find out?" Drienne asked.

"A lot," said Loren. "Well, too much and not enough—I couldn't track down her personnel file, maybe she's got her own bots scrubbing that stuff. What I found was mostly activity tracking, correspondence and so on, and I filtered it and, well, headline: Mia never worked at Kentish Cyc."

"What?"

"Yep."

"But the articles about the court case mentioned it. That was, like, her humble beginnings."

"I reckon those were inserts."

"You mean she changed the story—"

"In case we looked it up, yeah."

"Is that hard to do? Insert details into reports? It seems like that should be hard to do."

"They're designed to update with fresh data, so if you could change a couple of key sources that are considered reliable, and then trigger an update, you could change a lot of stuff. Especially if you made it seem like a detail in the original story was wrong, and tricked the system into accepting your new info as the correction."

"But how did you work this out without her employee record?"

"Oh simple—I crunched all her activity patterns into a timeline, and there's just no gaps, no time when she could have worked there. I can account for every day until she quit."

Drienne absorbed this. "Could be she got the information about the Coyne from someone else and now she's cutting them out of the operation and doesn't want us to know. So she's making out this is personal experience when it's actually secondhand."

"But if someone else knows about this, why aren't *they* trying to get the money?"

"Maybe they *will* try to get it. Could mean trouble for us."

"Mia's planned this in detail, it's obviously important to her we succeed, yeah?" said Loren, gesturing with the bread roll they'd bought to go with the soup. (It was stale, and gesturing was the best use for it.) "So if there's a possibility some other prick might swoop in and snatch it, she'd tell us so we could be prepared. So I don't think it's that."

"Okay. What if Mia got this info from someone else, and they're dead?"

"Why not just tell us that? And *you* were the one who thought something was off about Mia."

"I know, I'm just trying to cover all the possibilities instead of jumping to conclusions."

"Well, same. But do you think Mia would go to the effort of inserting this detail into a bunch of records because it was simpler than telling us the truth?"

Drienne considered this. "No. I don't. But I don't know what *is* going on." She sighed. "Look, maybe it'll be fine. If we bring back the Coyne like she told us to . . . I mean, just because she lied to us doesn't automatically mean she won't give us our cut or can our debts."

"No. No, that's true."

"I just wish I could work out *why* she lied."

"Me too."

After this uneasy, inconclusive discussion they cheered themselves up by going to the bar in the old pavilion and ordering cocktails, and it was there that Arlo found them.

While the operation ramped up, Loren continued to spend their downtime trawling Oakseed's data on Mia, looking into the details of the case between them and what had happened with Mia's creations after it was over. Loren made prompts that targeted inconsistencies and oddities, and searched for colleagues Mia had a lot of contact with, in case that told them anything.

Around lunchtime on the day of the operation, while Loren was killing time waiting to take the Lost Weekend down to Blooms-bury, they found it.

Oakseed had made a number of offers to Mia after the case was finally settled, hoping to lure her back to the company—not so much because they wanted her, but because they wanted the publicity such a climbdown would provide. It would create a powerful sense the company couldn't be beaten, and also make them look generous, to an extent. Mia had refused them all. A brief internal exchange took place six years after Mia lost the case, noting she had suffered severe brain damage. She'd tried to erase areas of her memory with an experimental technique, hoping to remove those parts of herself Oakseed had laid claim to. Had this worked, she planned to reopen the case and establish ownership of her personality, but it had gone badly wrong, rendering her barely capable of dressing and feeding herself.

When Loren read this they had to take a break for a few minutes, because they had some sense of what Mia had been through for her to resort to such extreme measures, and it hit them surprisingly hard.

There was no reversing what Mia had done to herself. The internal communications that had closed Oakseed's file on Mia stated she would be housed at one of their discreet assisted living facilities under an assumed name, and her family had been paid off to ensure no details of this emerged publicly, because they figured the story would play badly. But it meant the person Loren had met in Vancouver wasn't Mia.

Loren had no opportunity to discuss this with Drienne before the operation commenced, but Loren had decided not to give the Coyne to Mia until they'd examined it themselves and found out what was actually on it. To this end they printed off another fake Coyne using the same template for the one they'd given Arlo, only without the dent he'd asked them to include. Loren knew Arlo wouldn't let them have the Coyne, but Drienne could get Arlo to do anything, so if she could convince Arlo to let her carry it, she could then covertly pass it to Loren—probably the journey on the overline would be the best time. Loren could stash it in their rucksack and scan it through the canvas and the others would have no clue what they were doing. The fake might turn out to be unnecessary, but Loren felt it could come in handy: Drienne could keep it in everyone's view and no one would suspect Loren had it—classic misdirection.

"If it turned out Mia was straight with us about what was on it," Loren told Drienne as the truck train rumbled south, "I was gonna just restore it to the state it was in when we found it, and get you to hand it back to Arlo."

"And risk Mia finding out you looked, and risk her cutting you out of your share."

"I could've covered my tracks, I reckon. She was bluffing when she said she'd know if any of us looked, I think."

"But you don't think it's legit?"

"I think you were spot-on about Samson and the laundering business. Doesn't feel right. I'm convinced it's not money on there, and the only thing I can think is it's information."

"Something compromising, you mean?"

"Presumably. I just can't see what else would be worth all the effort. Now, if it's not money, Mia lied to us and we're not getting rich from this and I don't trust her to lib us either. But if it's compromising information—"

"That could be worth something."

"*Must* be worth something. And if there's no money, the only way we're getting anything out of this situation is if we use it as leverage with Mia."

On the surface, the Coyne appeared to contain a mere r95,000 in cash: more money than Drienne or Loren had ever seen, but some way short of what they'd been promised. Loren had already started the process of poking around to find where the false tray could be lifted, and they assured Drienne this wouldn't take long. Drienne focused on steering the truck train and telling herself they weren't making a terrible mistake.

35

STUPID ENOUGH TO WALK THE DERELICT STREETS SHOUTING HER NAME

Mia sat at her table in the copter with several windows open in front of her, trying to locate Drienne and Loren. Arlo wasn't sure if he should help or not. If Drienne was having an episode, she needed to be found as soon as possible, and she *must* be having an episode, because he couldn't imagine she'd be so stupid as to steal the money, and even if she did she'd never cut him out of it. But Arlo wasn't sure Mia would take such a charitable view. (Arlo didn't know Loren well enough to say whether it was in character for them to steal the money. They seemed smarter than that. But then, they'd been off with him at the final meeting. Maybe they'd been plotting this all along?)

"Doesn't look like security footage from the plant got uploaded before the cops took the network down," Mia said. "But neither Loren nor Drienne have been arrested or listed dead . . . They *must* have taken that truck train, there's no way they'd just hang around with all that shit going down . . ." She stared at her windows for a while. Then she smiled and pointed at one of them. "Yes. We have it. Ha!"

———

The stolen truck train was still feeding its location back to the plant using its relay. There was no plant to receive this signal, but the truck kept feeding it back regardless, because if the plant wasn't there anymore then it made no sense for the truck to be in operation. The plant hadn't received this information, but Mia had.

The train registered two people had been inside it on its journey. It identified one of them as Annie Clarke, the visiting debrander from RookDivest, and the other as casual laborer Cas Woodforde, who'd been logged minutes before the system had gone down. It had stopped just across the river from NiZCOval, and Mia felt sure Drienne and Loren were either still inside or had not gone far. The copter was on its way there now.

"I'd like you to go and talk to them first," she told Arlo.

Arlo also wanted this, but felt unsure why Mia did, and said so.

"If they *are* trying to steal the money, they'll freak out if I walk in there. You'll get a calmer response. *Don't* tell them I'm here."

"Okay."

"I'm serious," she said, fixing him with a hard glare. "Don't tell them."

"How do I explain how I got here? They'll hear the copter."

"I'll land a reasonable distance away and you can walk. Tell them you managed to get a ride part of the way somehow, I don't know."

Arlo nodded; it didn't matter, he'd think of something. He wanted to go in alone too, talk to them before Mia did. But before he went, there was something he needed to hear. "You'll keep your word, won't you? If we deliver the money?"

Mia looked up, surprised. "What?"

"You really will free us? Like you promised?"

"Of course. I do business on the level, I always have." She made a rueful face. "That's how Oakseed screwed me."

In the light of this it made sense she'd shot Kline dead as soon as he refused to do business with her on the level. Perhaps that was, after all, a reasonable thing to do. And if Arlo continued to deal with her on the level, she was no threat to him.

Drienne wished she had a better weapon. All she'd been able to find was a metal bar that looked like it had once been a support for a rack of shelving, which had been twisted apart and had an awkward sharp point at one end. The building they were in had been an office, but had likely been cleared out prior to London's collapse; it contained very little in the way of furniture. The only light in the room came from Loren's windows.

Loren had been so confident that lifting the tray would take less time than driving the truck train from Kentish Cyc to NiZCOval, but this had not been the case and they needed to lift it before they arrived at NiZCOval, in case Mia was waiting for them. So Drienne parked up near an old art gallery and asked how much longer it was going to take.

"I don't *know*," said Loren.

Despite the darkness, they were very conspicuous parked in the street, and Drienne was concerned about being preyed on by vagues. She found the whole environment unsettling, and suggested they go inside the office while Loren finished the job. If anyone did come, they'd check out the truck train first, so Drienne wanted to keep it in sight, so they'd have some warning and could sneak away.

Drienne was wondering how Loren could have been so badly wrong about their ability to lift the tray, but hassling them would only be counterproductive, so Drienne occupied herself by working out the explanation she'd provide to Mia of what had happened and why they'd taken the truck train instead of going to the rendezvous. It didn't need to be too far from the truth, but there were certain details that needed to be—

Then, through the broken office window, Drienne heard someone shouting her name. Her *real* name. Only four people currently in London knew her real name, and one of them was inside this room. She heard it again, and it was the voice she knew best in all the world. Which made sense, because only Arlo would be stupid enough to walk the derelict London streets shouting her name. She edged over to the window, peered through the grimy pane—and there he was, standing by the truck train, looking around.

Loren had heard it too and identified the voice. "What the fuck is he doing?" they asked.

"Keep working," said Drienne, and headed downstairs.

From the doorway (there was no door) Drienne managed to attract Arlo's attention by hissing his name and waving a hand. He hurried over to her, she pulled him inside the building, embraced him quickly, told him she was glad to see him, then asked if he had gone completely insane, shouting her name like that.

"I didn't know how else to find you," he replied. "Where did you *go*?"

"I . . ." She'd been all set to spin him a yarn, but now they were face-to-face, she couldn't. She'd confided everything to him when they'd lived together; she seldom had private thoughts of any significance. She'd confessed some dreadful things to him, and here they were, still together, because *he'd* told Mia to buy her for this operation. And now she was the one fucking it up for everyone because she didn't trust Mia. But she couldn't lie to Arlo about it.

And so Drienne led Arlo up to the office where Loren was still trying to lift the tray. Loren barely looked up to greet him, and Arlo's first words to them were, "You *do* have the real Coyne. What . . . ? I don't understand."

"Okay, Loren found out Mia never really worked in London," said Drienne. "And the person we're working for isn't the real Mia."

"How do you know this?" asked Arlo skeptically.

"I dredged some data," said Loren, "and—"

"Have *you* seen evidence of this?" Arlo said to Drienne, then he pointed at Loren. "Because *they've* been acting weird since—"

"*I've* been acting weird?" said Loren.

"Yes, since last night."

"*You're* the one who's got a problem with *me*."

"What?"

"Loren—just focus on the Coyne," Drienne said. Then she explained to Arlo the suspicions she and Loren had developed.

Arlo thought for a moment, and Drienne could see it made sense to him. "So . . . you think our Mia's a made, like us?" he said.

"If Oakseed had someone supersmart on staff they'd make a backup, right?"

"But she'd be younger . . . she must have made herself look older with cosmetics." Arlo gave a sudden laugh. "When she first brought me to her apartment my eyes were bandaged, and she spoke to me and I had a mental picture of someone younger. I remember being surprised when the bandages came off."

"So she's impersonating her donor," said Loren. "Just like you did to open the locker. But seems like her goal is to do it full-time— she wants to buy the rights to the *real* Mia's personality and IP, and then she'll take over."

"She could have just told us all this," said Arlo. "We'd have understood."

"Well, there's another possibility—"

"But wait." Arlo put his fingers to his eyes. "If she's a made, she can't be our legal holder. Someone else is. So she can't cancel our debts either."

"No," said Drienne. "If she's falsified the deeds, the deals she made are null and void and our holding reverts to RookDivest."

"Or maybe the deals are in someone else's name." Arlo grasped at this possibility. "Maybe that person will free us—if Mia tells them to."

"Do you think that's likely, though? She's already lied to us about a bunch of stuff, we can't trust anything she says."

"So what's your plan? You've run off with her money, what now?"

"That's just it," said Loren. "I don't think this is about money." They kept their attention on the windows running the programs that were trying to lift the false tray, but spoke in the most fluent and confident manner Drienne had heard from them in the short time they'd known each other. "Drienne wasn't convinced by that stuff about Samson stashing money as a nest egg, and I agree. I think there's something else going on here and when we find out what it is, then we'll have some bargaining power with—" And their face fell.

"What is it?" said Drienne.

"Can't be right . . ." said Loren, looking from one window to another.

"What?" said Arlo.

"There's nothing." Loren looked up. "There *is* no false tray."

"You said it'd be easy to crack," said Drienne, striding across the room to look over Loren's shoulder.

"That's why it was so hard to crack, there *isn't* one. I've checked the whole thing, there's nothing on here but the ninety-five grand. There's no other money, no eighty million dollars."

"So you were wrong," said Arlo. "Fuck!"

"I wasn't wrong about there being no more money."

"But you said there'd be something else," said Drienne, "something we could use as leverage. You haven't, like, wiped the data by accident—"

"*No,* I know what I'm doing. Jesus."

"But if there's no eighty million, and *nothing* else, why—"

"Drienne," said Arlo abruptly, "there's something you should know. Mia's already here, in London, and she's looking for you."

"What?"

"Yes, look—there's no time, we need to work out how we're going to play this because she's going to be here, like *right* here, any minute."

"Wait—why didn't you tell us this at—" Drienne said, stepping forward, intending to cross the room to Arlo. But she didn't get there, or complete the sentence, because a bullet whizzed through the open window, missing her by centimeters. She dodged back.

"What the fuck was that?" said Loren.

Arlo swallowed. "Mia had a gun. She killed Kline—"

"Arlo," Drienne said, "why the *fuck* didn't you tell us—"

"She told me not to tell you. Look, she killed Kline—I thought she was going to kill me . . ."

Through the window they could hear heavy footfalls heading their way and Arlo's first thought was the police must have caught up with them. But did that make sense? Why send a *sniper* after them for stealing a truck train?

"This way," Loren said and pointed toward a door that led into another office that overlooked the back of the building. This room had windows big enough to climb out of, and one was already open. Arlo and Drienne helped Loren climb onto the frame—they were only one floor up, but in the darkness it was impossible to see what they were jumping into. They could hear footsteps inside the building, coming up the stairs, so Loren jumped.

Drienne could hear them land painfully and cry out.

"I'm okay," Loren said in a stage whisper.

"You next," Drienne said to Arlo, and he didn't waste time protesting—he clambered up and jumped out, stumbling as he landed.

Drienne pulled herself up to the window ledge—

And a gunshot sounded from outside the room. The pane in the open window shattered, glass exploding past her face. A man entered through the door they'd just used, wearing black combat clothes with no identifying markings, and carrying a handgun. He wasn't police. Drienne raised her hands.

"Go!" Drienne yelled down to Arlo and Loren.

"They're getting away out the back!" shouted the black-clad soldier to others in the building.

Drienne heard footsteps running away into the night. It sounded like only one set of footsteps, and she knew exactly what her dumbass partner was doing right now.

"You too, Arlo," she shouted.

The soldier marched over to her, brandishing his gun. "Out of the way."

"Oh, you want me to get down from here?"

"Yes."

"I'm in your way? Is that the problem?"

The soldier reached out, grabbed Drienne's hand, and went to pull her down from the window—but as he leaned in, she kicked down on the hand with the gun, forcing him to drop it. Then she threw herself off the ledge and onto him, knocking him to the floor. She kicked him in the head, grabbed the gun, hauled herself back onto the ledge—

And Mia walked in, with two more soldiers behind her, wearing the same dark clothes. All three of them were armed. Mia directed a weary look at Drienne.

"Do you have it?" Mia asked.

Drienne hesitated before saying, "Yeah."

"Liar."

Mia nodded, and one of the soldiers shot Drienne in the throat.

Arlo was still waiting for Drienne in the alley behind the office. He heard the shot and saw her fall from the window ledge, out of the building. He should have run away at that point. He should have run when Drienne told him to. He should have run the moment his feet hit the ground. But you didn't leave your partner, it wasn't done.

She landed horribly, heavily. He ran to her side.

She was still conscious, but weakening, and if she moved her mouth it just brought up more blood. She could hear someone at her side, asking if she was okay. It was Arlo, and he called her Drienne. She couldn't speak to tell him not to use that name.

All she could think was, how *dare* they do this to her. They probably thought she was a common made and they could kill her with impunity. Well, now that she was dying it would all finally come out. There'd be an autopsy and they'd realize the truth and *then* there'd be trouble. They would all realize how wrong they'd been.

She didn't deserve this. It had all been wrong, from the start.

They'd stolen the life she should have had, and now they'd killed her for trying to get it back. She comforted herself with the thought this had all been deeply unfair and she had done her best in the circumstances. Everything that had ever gone wrong in her life was someone else's fault, and her final thoughts were that her death was someone else's fault too.

In her dimming vision she saw Arlo looking down at her, stroking her hair, telling her she'd be fine, it wasn't that bad, she just had to hang on. He'd always been there, and he'd always been so patient.

36

A HOT MORNING
AT SUNGLOW

It was very difficult to locate anyone in this city at night, Loren knew that. Once they'd got out of sight, their chances of avoiding the people chasing them were pretty good. They just had to be rational and calm about the situation. But this was not easy, when so much about the situation was so unclear. Who was chasing them? What did Mia really want?

Running to the next street, they found a hotel and dashed inside, treading as lightly as possible so their footsteps wouldn't carry. They had an idea: every room in the place was vacant, so if you were going to hide here, you'd hide in one of the guest rooms, right? And if their pursuers came looking in here, they'd focus on searching those. So Loren went past the front desk, down the corridor, and found the room used to store people's luggage when they weren't ready to check in yet. They went inside the oddly shaped little room, hid round the corner, and slumped to the floor. They stayed there until morning, and were disturbed only by their own thoughts and worries. If they slept, it was light and brief.

Loren couldn't hide in the ruins forever. They weren't cut out to live like a vague. Eventually they would have to resurface, and when they did it would be hard to avoid detection. They appeared to be on their own now. Drienne hadn't got out of the building, and Arlo had stayed to help her. Kline was dead. And Nadi had been arrested. However Loren got out of this, they'd have to work it out for themself.

When the sun was up, Loren left the little room and slowly, carefully made their way out of the hotel. They needed something to eat, so they headed south.

NiZCOval was only a short walk away, but Mia would probably be looking for them there. The next nearest corpurbation was the one operated by Sunglow, and it was across the river, on the site of a rail interchange formerly known as Clapham Junction. It took Loren over an hour to walk there, at which point they had a choice: they could try to launder the currency on the Coyne and use that to pay for some breakfast, or they could use Drienne's alt-id slate, which they still possessed. The slate would be easily traceable, but probably the Coyne would be too. There was no way they could pay for anything without risking being located.

They lurked around a food court, where morning shift workers and overnight cleaning staff were eating. When a group stood up to leave and didn't clear their table, Loren went over and cleared it for them, as if they might be intending to occupy the table themself, or as if they were a member of staff employed to do this (though a member of staff would probably not be in such a disheveled state as Loren was). When they reached the waste disposal, they furtively ate the remaining scraps of food. After repeating this a few times, they felt satisfied and started to plan their next move.

Loren didn't think the people who'd shot at them were the police or Oakseed security, so either they'd been hired by Mia or by someone else. Out in the salvage zones you could get away with sending in a small militia at night, but you couldn't just march into a corpurbation and drag someone away, you'd have to make an application to the security division of the governing corp; it was complicated and political. This meant Loren was relatively safe here, but just because the militia hadn't swarmed on Loren yet didn't mean they didn't know where they were. Someone could well be watching and waiting for them to leave the food court.

Loren wondered if they might be able to set up another alt-id and live here. Get a job as a support at the Sunglow plant. Maybe by some miracle everyone would give up and leave them alone. But even if they did, ultimately someone here would realize Loren was a made and want to know who held them and it would all unravel. Living an independent life as a made was impossible if someone didn't want you to.

Of course, this raised the question of who actually held Loren. They hoped they found that out at least, before all this was over. They'd hate to die not knowing.

Arlo was having a conversation in his head with Drienne. This wasn't unusual for Arlo, but before it had been like a rehearsal for a conversation they might have later, when they came back together. This one would remain painfully unresolved.

I need to explain, he imagined saying. About Mia.

What about Mia?

I needed to know you weren't stealing the money before I told you she was here. That's why I didn't tell you straightaway.

Why? I'd have told you the truth.

But Mia might have thought you were lying to me. Anyway, you didn't tell me the truth about all this stuff you were doing with Loren.

I was protecting you. I knew something was wrong but I didn't want to spoil your chance of getting free.

I know that now, but when I walked into that room, all I knew was you hadn't told me the truth.

I took all the risk for you.

Variations on this had gone around Arlo's head for hours and hours. He couldn't stop his mind replaying their final minutes to-gether, trying to do things differently. Sometimes it replayed the moment when she'd told him to go through the window first and he hadn't argued. He kept telling himself there hadn't been time to argue, and he never won arguments with Drienne anyway. But he kept seeing other versions of that moment, versions where he told her to go first and she just did it, and some of those versions ended with him being shot instead and some of them didn't. But none of them became real, and he'd be bounced back to the start again, or have that conversation with Drienne again, the one where he explained he hadn't betrayed her, he'd just been doing the best he could, trying not to get them all killed.

But he had got her killed. This was all his fault. He'd thought he was being so clever, bringing her onto the crew. He should have left her to whatever life she'd have otherwise had: a shit life, but a life nevertheless.

The grief was too big, he could tell. He could only feel a little of it. His brain was looping in this nonsense way, lying to him that if he just went through the steps of what he could have done differently one more time, he could fix this, because otherwise it might have to deal with what had happened and could not be changed. Because she couldn't possibly be gone, it didn't make sense that the world didn't have her in it anymore. Somehow it felt worse than when he'd thought he was going to be reaped, because at least that wasn't his fault. Now he was going to live, maybe—but all his life he'd hate himself for getting her killed.

He wondered what they'd done with her body. They'd dragged him away from her, but whether they'd just left her body in the alley like they did Kline, he didn't know.

Arlo had spent the night aboard Mia's copter, guarded by a member of the small militia she'd acquired from somewhere. There seemed to be five soldiers in total: from time to time one of them would come back to Mia's copter to take over watching Arlo, and the one who'd been watching him would go out to search. He wasn't sure which of them had actually shot Drienne. He didn't really care, he wanted to kill them all. Several times he had to screw his eyes shut tight and dig his thumbnails into his skin until the urge to leap up and attack the guard passed. He had to listen to Drienne's voice telling him that would be stupid, because the guard would kill him. He wasn't even sure that's what she'd have said. She might have told him to go for it. Avenge her. He really wanted to. It was like a cliff he couldn't wait to throw himself over.

But no, he'd keep himself alive for now. Maybe a better opportunity would present itself.

There was a second copter parked near Mia's, a more utilitarian affair without the plush xec interior. Arlo surmised this was the one the soldiers had arrived in. It had stood empty for most of the night while the militia searched. They'd used heat-sensitive equipment, but this had only led them to vagues and wild animals. Mia remained at her desk in the copter, quiet and calm as she coordinated the search using a detailed model of the area to locate potential hiding places. When the soldiers reported back, she didn't shout at them about their failure to locate Loren, just treated it as a problem to be solved.

Arlo spoke abruptly, for the first time in several hours. Mia looked startled, but listened.

"If you had all these guys," Arlo said, indicating the man guarding him, "why didn't you use them to carry out the operation?"

Mia leaned back in her chair and directed her eyes at the ceiling. "I couldn't just send a team of soldiers to march in and grab it. It had to be an infiltration operation. Plus I needed you to open the locker. And I needed to use people who couldn't be linked back to me."

"We know you're not the real Mia."

"I know you know. Look—it's complicated, and I don't need to explain to you, so I'm not going to." Mia went back to her windows, as if Arlo was a needy child distracting Mummy from her work.

Shortly after sunrise, Mia received a call from someone who was being far less calm about all this. She went into the copter's bedroom and closed the door, and though Arlo couldn't make out her words, he could detect the distinctive tones of a person trying to placate someone who was screaming at them. Mia came out and returned to her desk. Arlo caught her eye and forced a smile, letting her know he knew she was in trouble, even if he didn't know who with.

Half an hour later, Mia straightened up in her chair, looked closely at one of her open windows, then smiled and sat back. The relief on her face told Arlo everything.

Loren was sitting on a bench opposite a coffeehouse, dreaming of iced tea. Not too sweet, plenty of lemon. It was just after ten o'clock and the temperature was creeping up: it would be the hottest day of the year so far, the report on the window above Loren's head said. Loren was in the shade and felt like if they stood and crossed the sunlit space between themself and the coffeehouse they'd pass out. The food they'd scavenged had kept them going, but there'd been little in the way of liquid and they were getting a headache, which was making it difficult to think.

At present they had no ideas better than to head for the port, take their chances, and try to catch a flight somewhere. But getting to the port unnoticed would depend on someone, somewhere fucking up, or some other bit of dumb luck. They had to think of something better, but meanwhile they were just getting hungrier and thirstier and increasing the chance of someone finding them.

They had their eyes closed, trying to use a meditation technique that focused on the headache in a way that was supposed to make it go away. But it wasn't working, probably because they couldn't stop thinking about the Coyne, which was inside a zip pocket on their tunic. Trying to meditate when your mind was very much on material concerns like that was pointless.

They'd just decided to make their way to the port—on foot perhaps, was that feasible?—when a man sat down next to them on the bench.

"Loren, yes?" said the man. "Thank heavens I got to you before they did."

THIS PLAN
WAS MY PLAN

The man Loren found themself sitting next to was probably in his midfifties, but you had to pay attention to notice because at first glance he looked younger. He was very healthy and lean, and had probably been to the gym five times a week for the last three or four decades. His hair was thick and dark brown. His skin was in great condition, neither pallid nor sun-damaged, suggesting regular facials and expensive daily creams. His face was rather narrow and his features strangely delicate, contrasting with his voice, which was low and warm. Loren liked his outfit a lot—a gray sleeveless shirt and matching vented trousers, and an orange tie. He smiled at Loren, and seemed very relaxed around them—not like a friend, but like an old colleague you'd had a good rapport with.

Loren was unsure whether to admit their name was Loren. But it seemed futile to deny it: if this guy knew their name and had managed to track them down, he wasn't just fishing. He knew.

He introduced himself as Ackland. "You're in quite a situation, aren't you, Loren?"

"Maybe," said Loren, because that *did* sound like fishing, trying to get the details.

"You stole a Coyne from a locker at Kentish Cyc yesterday evening," he said. "Three members of your operation are dead, a fourth has been captured alive, leaving you the only one at liberty."

"Three? Which ones?"

"The survivor is called Arlo."

Fuck. They'd killed Drienne, and Nadi . . . she must have died in custody. Christ. Both hit Loren hard, for different reasons. But they had to shut that out and focus on what this guy was telling them.

"You still have the Coyne, you've made your way here, so: what's your next move?" He turned to face them with a sympathetic smile. This wasn't a trap; he knew they had no next move.

Loren shrugged.

"Yep," said Ackland. "It's tough. But I can help you."

"You can?"

"I knew Joshi Samson. We used to work together. Nice guy, not too bright, but . . . Anyway, he told me about this nest egg of his years ago. This plan you were bought to carry out was *my* plan, I came up with it—Arlo, the eyes, tricking the time stamp, all of it. But after the company collapsed I was busy trying to secure my own future, you know, and I didn't realize Samson was dead until about a day later, by which time someone stole my plan and bought Arlo, and I didn't know who'd bought him or where he'd gone. They covered their tracks too well. So all I could do was watch for what happened at the plant." He smiled again. "Didn't go *entirely* smoothly for you, did it?"

Loren bobbed their head from side to side. "I mean *I* did *my* bit."

"And making off with the money? Was that part of the plan?"

"I figured Mia was lying to us and I wanted to know what was really—" Loren stopped, realizing they were saying more than they needed to.

Ackland splayed his fingers into a claw shape and tapped them on his knee. "Look—I don't care what you did. *You* didn't steal my plan, someone bought you to execute it—and if I'd carried it out myself I'd have needed a team, and I'd have paid them. So what I'm proposing is you give the money to me, I launder it, and we split it fifty-fifty."

"What about Mia and those soldier guys?"

"I make all that go away, don't you worry. You just give it to me and all this stops."

"I want my freedom too."

Ackland smiled. "I'll buy out your debt and cancel it."

Loren considered whether it was to their advantage to say the next part. But they didn't want Ackland to go back on his promises if he felt they'd been dishonest with him, so they said it. "It's not as much money as Mia told us."

"You've seen what's on it?"

"Yeah. Nowhere near as much money, in fact. She told us there'd be a big chunk of cash hidden on it, but I've checked. It's only ninety-five thousand reps."

"Oh dear." Ackland shook his head. "Samson was prone to exaggeration. But I stand by what I said, we'll share the money and I'll take care of Mia."

"Okay."

"I mean, it's only money. It isn't worth dying over, is it?"

Loren thought about this for a while. Then they swallowed uncomfortably. "I've got a headache. I could do with a drink."

Ackland nodded. "Of course. I'll get you something."

"Iced tea."

"Sounds good."

Together they stood and walked into the coffeehouse.

"I can't force you to give me the money," Ackland said. "I wouldn't—that's not the kind of person I am, my intention was to do this clean. But I think it's a compelling offer considering the position you're in."

"I don't disagree—Sorry, I can't think with this headache."

"Sure." Ackland turned to the young man behind the counter and ordered an iced tea for Loren and a complicated coffee for himself. The young man told him it came to r33.70 and Ackland was about to tap his finger on the terminal, but Loren quickly said, "Oh no, let me," and waved the Coyne over the terminal, which deducted a tiny percentage of its currency and flashed up a cheerful message saying *Thank you!*

Ackland turned to Loren slowly with a cold stare. "What . . . did you just do?"

"I paid. My treat. No need to thank me."

"But it had to—" Ackland lowered his voice to a hiss. "It had to be laundered first—I told you I was going to—"

"Yeah, and I think I know why. See, I always thought there was more to this than just money, because surely it wouldn't be that hard to launder it? People do it every day."

Ackland looked around. The coffeehouse wasn't busy, but the guy behind the counter was taking notice of this conversation and so were some of the customers.

"I wouldn't worry about who's listening right now," said Loren. "So anyway, *I* thought there was something else on here other than money, like something you'd blackmail someone with. But it *is* just money, and a lot less than we thought."

"Of course it's just money—"

"Ah, but it *isn't* just money. See, not only is this not as much as Mia told us, it also wouldn't be that difficult to launder."

The bewildered barista had placed their drinks on the counter. Loren thanked him and took their iced tea.

"Maybe Mia told Joshi it was impossible to launder because she wanted to steal it from him later?" said Ackland, following Loren as they walked over to a table. The barista hurried over with the coffee, which Ackland grabbed indelicately, causing some of the liquid to bubble over the side and scald his hand. He grunted with irritation.

"What, construct an elaborate heist years later to get it, instead of taking the easy money for just doing the job?" Loren said as they sat down. "Nah, that money wasn't ever laundered because it was more valuable as blackmail material than money. This money's got someone's fingerprints on it, I reckon, and the cops have been looking for it. When someone spends it, a flag goes up saying this money is connected to a crime. Maybe the cops even put this particular bundle of cash out themselves to trap someone. I reckon Samson was meant to launder it for someone else, but he kept it instead, or some of it. I think he put it on the Coyne for safekeeping. He left it in London because maybe it was too difficult to take across borders—if someone checked what was on it, the flag would go up and there's no more black-mail." Then Loren's face lit up. "Oh, *or* Samson split the money. He had another device he took with him, he had some of the money on that, and left this one behind as insurance. He might even have kept several hidden in different places."

"Very clever," said Ackland flatly.

"Ah, good," said Loren, pleased to have worked that out. "Anyway, when the plant gets sold, all the contents pass to the new owners, all the lockers get reset, anyone can open them, they get inventoried, new owners find the money and bank it and"—Loren made a noise like a siren—"big red light flashes at the cop shop. So the person Samson was blackmailing needed to steal it before that happened. Samson was dead, so they could do the trick with Arlo and the eye transplant. They'd let their newly assembled heist crew believe it was just a big old chunk of money, enough to make it worth the effort. Then when it was delivered they'd launder it or even just destroy it; if they have enough money that ninety-five thousand doesn't mean much to them."

"You're saying Mia was being blackmailed."

"No, c'mon, mate. *You* were being blackmailed. I bet Samson got plenty of promotions and perks out of you. I wasn't totally sure until I saw how you reacted when I spent the money. Mia—or whatever her name is, because she's not Mia—belongs to you, and you did this whole thing through her so no one could connect it to you. Also because you knew we'd respond to her tragic backstory more than whatever the fuck yours is."

"You've been very stupid about all of this, Loren."

"You must've got desperate, though, eh? To come to me your-self, show your face. I guess you figured I'd stopped trusting Mia so maybe I'd trust you. So I guess you're my *actual* holder, and now I've disobeyed you, you can report me, can't you."

Ackland said nothing.

"Ah—you *don't* hold us. Yeah that makes sense, you registered us to someone else so we couldn't get connected back to you. Who's our holder, then?"

"Fuck you."

"I'll find out."

"You think you can just walk away with that money?"

"That's the plan."

"I'll tell the police you stole it."

"We stole it because *you* told us to, y'dingus. I know you made sure to keep your hands clean, but that's not gonna wash now, is it? Because that money leads back to *you*, which means you're the *only* one who'd go to all this effort to steal it. Do you want a theft charge on top of everything else that's coming your way? Make it even *more* obvious how guilty you are? But look—no one knows where this money's been all this time, so I'm okay with leaving it all a big mystery how it turned up suddenly after all these years if you are." Loren drained the rest of their iced tea and placed the glass on the table. "Thanks for that. Oh no, wait—I paid, didn't I?" Loren stood up from the table.

"I'm going to kill you," said Ackland quietly.

Loren gestured around the coffeehouse. "What, in front of all these people?"

Ackland reached inside his jacket, and Loren realized they'd pushed this too far. He wasn't going to act rationally, he *was* going to kill them in front of all these people and who knows, he might get away with it—

Then someone arrived at Loren's side, reached across the table, and grabbed Ackland's arm, the one that was going for his weapon. She held it firmly as she punched him cleanly and confidently between his eyes. She punched him twice more, then while he was dazed she moved around to the other side of the table, put one hand on his chest and the other underneath the chair seat and tipped the chair backward, ensuring his head hit the tile floor. She reached into his pocket and took out the small pistol he was carrying, then kicked him hard in the ribs.

As Nadi straightened up, everyone in the café applauded, and Loren joined in, feeling like they might cry.

The overfilled police wagon parked outside Kentish Cyc had already been at the boiling point when Nadi had been thrown into it. The cops' failure to get medical attention for her had lit the spark, and the next time the doors were opened to put someone in, the prisoners rushed them.

This happened around the same time the fire started inside the plant—Nadi wasn't sure if it had happened before or after, but it meant the cops' attention was not fully on their escaping prisoners, and few of them were recaptured. Gregg helped Nadi out of the wagon and took her to his apartment to recover. He'd wanted to get out of the corpurbation altogether, away from the burning building and the cops who might be looking to rearrest him—but the overline was down and he had nowhere else to go but home. Nadi's own memories of this were patchy and she inferred much of it from talking to Gregg as she sat on his sofa, taking breaths that were made painful by the bruising on her ribs.

Gregg thought she had a concussion. Nadi knew she had a concussion. But as soon as she was lucid enough to walk in a straight line, she had to go back to the plant. He tried to stop her, but couldn't, let's be real.

Nadi stepped unsteadily onto the street and saw straightaway the plant was burning to the ground. She thought about this for a moment, trying to force her brutalized brain into giving her a course of action.

Then she saw a copter flying overhead. It wasn't part of any emergency services operation: it had no markings. Mia was meant to be coming to get them in a copter—not here, that wasn't the plan. But the overline wasn't running, Gregg had said. So maybe the plan had changed.

Nadi headed in the direction of the copter, trying to keep sight of it. By then it was dark and Nadi hadn't seen exactly where it had landed, but she just kept going and hoped for the best.

Then Nadi saw the copter take off, and felt despair: they'd left her behind.

Then it came back down again.

Maybe they'd seen her, knew she was on her way, they just had to give her more time. She moved faster, as fast as her battered limbs would allow. She had a better sense of where the copter was now—she could just about see the moonlight reflecting off it—

Then it took off again.

Nadi kept moving because she couldn't think what else to do. The copter had come back once, perhaps it would again. At last she reached the spot from which it had taken off, and there she found Kline's body.

Nadi buried Kline, after a fashion—she didn't have anything to dig with, so she carried his body into the exposed cellar of a demolished building and covered it over with a broken door. She'd already searched him, in case he had anything important in his pockets. She took his slate and backhand, even though she couldn't use them to communicate with the others. Then she returned to the spot where the copter had landed. Kline's suitcase still lay there.

Nadi didn't know why Kline was dead. But waiting for the copter to come back no longer appealed. All she could do now, it seemed, was head to one of the two places they'd agreed to meet. She couldn't possibly go back to Kentish Cyc, so it would have to be NiZCOval. She picked up Kline's suitcase and started walking.

It took Nadi some hours to reach NiZCOval on foot; had it not been for the genetic tweaks that had improved her stamina and rate of healing, she would never have made it. When she got there she checked if Kline's slate had received any messages from the others. It hadn't, so she lay on the dry grass and rested.

When she awoke, the sun was up. She'd only slept for a few hours, and she still felt terrible, but markedly less terrible. She checked Kline's slate again: nothing on the crew's network.

However, Nadi realized the slate had access to another network. She wasn't sure what she was looking at when she initially accessed it—the messages were from Mia, but they weren't directed toward the crew. After looking at a few of these she realized Kline had got into Mia's own messages, and there was activity on there. How long he'd had access to this, she didn't know. But the messages said where Loren was at that moment, and what was going to happen to them.

Nadi stood up, leaving Kline's suitcase behind, and hurried in the direction of Sunglow. She ran as much of the way as she could manage.

When she arrived, she looked through the window of a coffeehouse and saw Loren, and her chest surged. They looked grimy and bruised, but they were smiling as they spoke to some xeccy guy. He looked familiar. Maybe he was the guy she'd seen on that balcony in Montevideo, maybe he wasn't.

Nadi waited. Whatever Loren was doing, Nadi felt she should let it play out. If they seemed to be in danger, she'd step in . . .

Loren embraced Nadi, and Nadi returned the gesture, trying not to squeeze too hard. She had never done this affectionately before. She leaned down, and Loren stretched up, and they kissed—quickly, lightly, shyly, but happily.

"Are we good to go?" said Nadi.

Loren looked down at Ackland on the floor, and so did Nadi. "D'you think he's defeated? He looks defeated." They nodded to themself, picked up their empty glass, and returned it to the barista. They were about to walk away, then turned and said, "Sorry, I didn't leave a tip, did I? How rude of me." They told the tip jar they wanted to leave r10, then waved the Coyne over it. And Loren and Nadi walked out of the door, hand in hand.

LUCKY DIP BOX

The militia kicked Arlo out of the copter without explanation. Before this happened, Mia told Arlo a name: Karyn Shaw. "Your real holder," Mia had said. Arlo didn't know why she told him that, and didn't get a chance to ask: the copter flew away.

Arlo walked across to NiZCOval, where he was able to get a signal. To his surprise he also found Kline's suitcase on the grass. Loren told Arlo to stay by the suitcase: they would come and find him.

When Loren and Nadi filled him in on what had happened, Arlo thought maybe he should feel a little sorry for Mia. She'd been a pawn in this like the rest of them, and when it had all fallen apart, she'd tried to make amends by giving him the only thing of any value she had to offer. But he didn't feel sorry for her at all. He physically couldn't.

The world was bored of the ongoing collapse of Oakseed and endless analysis of what it meant, which had descended into corporate technical speak and mind-numbing human-interest stories, and there was nothing to fill the gap but witless conspiracy theories—and yet it was so huge, it seemed the only thing worth talking about. So when it emerged that Ackland Miles, a *very* senior xec at the company, had been deeply involved in a scandal that dated back many years, it was exactly what people wanted to hear. Not only was it a fresh angle, it created a strong sense the company had been rotten anyway and its collapse was a good thing, even if the economic shock was going to have dreadful global ramifications.

The scandal had never fully come to light at the time: the police knew what was happening, but when they failed to prove it, Oakseed prevented any details of the case from entering the public domain. But now the police *could* prove it, thanks to a quantity of currency turning up that had Miles's fingerprints on it, and there was no Oakseed to suppress it now.

The money in question was one of many off-the-books payments made to Miles by an agent working on behalf of Sunglow. Twenty years ago, when there were still hopes of regenerating London, Miles was appointed head of social engineering, having impressed his superiors with similar work in New Orleans. To this end, he regularly sent in securits to evict squatters. Many of these were sent to prison, and if they had children, naturally they'd be taken into care. At the same time, Sunglow's issues with its accelerated-growth mades were becoming horribly apparent, and while the world at large took little interest, at the other megas it was known that Sunglow was desperate to cover its shortfall of mades, and if the others had surplus mades, it would eagerly buy them.

Miles saw this situation, and he saw the squatters' children being taken into care, and he saw an opportunity. Because after all, these children needed somewhere to go, and Sunglow's nurseries were well under capacity, and if the children were young enough that they wouldn't remember their former lives, was it so bad to send them there? They'd have better lives as mades at Sunglow than if they'd remained with their feckless parents in derelict London.

In a little over three years, Miles had sold a total of seventy-one children to Sunglow. The nursery they ended up in would give them the identity of a deceased made and alter the records to make it appear they'd always been there. Sometimes the kids asked awkward questions, but these stopped after a few months of being told this was where they came from, and the people they thought were their parents had, in fact, stolen them from this nursery. Miles had to pay off a few people, but mostly he was able to funnel the money into a dark wallet of his own.

Eventually, the police got wind that some of Sunglow's mades weren't all they appeared, and began to make inquiries. Sunglow made some unveiled threats in return, making it clear that officers who pursued this line could expect their careers to be terminated. But the investigation did get close to the agent who Miles dealt with, and they successfully marked some of his currency, hoping this would lead them to whoever was selling these kids. Before that happened, the agent skipped the country and Miles opted to quit while he was ahead. The investigation was suspended—but the case was never closed. Now the money had turned up, and it was open again.

As Arlo watched the story emerge, it seemed strange to him how much people cared about it. They hadn't cared what happened to the vagues' children when they were living rough in London. Whenever anyone surveyed the public about the vagues, most people said they should be rounded up and locked away or disposed of. These untouchables had never been considered fully human—yet now it was discovered they'd been treated as mades, the failure to respect their humanity provoked outrage.

"It horrifies them," Loren told him as they ate a meal before boarding their flight out of London, "because suddenly they see themselves in that situation. They never worried about finding themselves in the position of a vague before, but this happens and they see a red line's been crossed."

Arlo agreed. But it threw a lot of things into sharp relief.

There was another part to the story, which broke after it had been in the media cycle for a day or so. Outlets had drilled down into Miles's history with Oakseed, looking for fresh details to capitalize on the public interest, including the spell in New Orleans that had resulted in him being given his position in London. Turned out he'd used similar tactics there, just not for his own personal enrichment. Back then Oakseed was still expanding its use of mades, and would take all they could get. The kids he removed from their parents in New Orleans were sent to a nursery outside Boston. The same one where Drienne grew up.

Arlo did the maths, and it lined up. Maybe she'd been right all along. And he couldn't ever tell her.

Karyn Shaw was a young woman formerly employed by Oakseed as an itemiser. She was based out of Hong Kong and had worked with Miles but had no obvious connection to him. She had not met any of the mades she held and never expected to—they'd all been registered in her name, but she had no involvement in the process. The deeds just turned up in her inbox. So she was very surprised when Loren, Arlo, and Nadi turned up at her home. She recognized them from the pictures on the deeds.

They told her they had a message from Miles. This part was Loren's idea. They figured Miles would not have communicated with Karyn recently, so all she knew would be what she'd seen in the news: that Miles had been charged with kidnapping and trafficking minors. She would be desperate to know what was going on and if she was implicated. The strategy was effective: Karyn invited them inside. Her apartment was small, and it looked like she'd only recently moved in.

"Do you know anything about what Miles sent us to do?" asked Nadi.

Karyn shook her head. She sat down, clearly expecting the others to do the same, but they didn't. Loren went to the fridge and, without asking, got themself a can of M:Pyre.

"It's better you don't know," Arlo told Karyn.

"I figured that was the case, yeah," said Karyn. "From what I heard, I mean."

"The arrangement," Arlo continued in a businesslike manner, "was that if we completed the job we'd be freed."

"And we completed the job," said Nadi.

"But . . ." said Karyn, looking from one of them to the other, "Miles is going to prison."

"We still completed the job," said Loren.

"How do I know you're telling me the truth?"

"The only person who can confirm that for you is Miles," said Nadi.

"And he's never going to make contact with you again," said Loren, "because he doesn't want anyone to connect him to us, ever. That was the point of you being involved in this."

"And *you* don't want anyone connecting him to you."

"Look," said Arlo, kneeling by the chair where Karyn sat, "you just have to file debt cancellation forms for each of us and that's it. You never need to hear about any of us, or any of this, ever again."

"But . . . couldn't I sell you and make some money?" Karyn said. "I don't know if I'll be able to get another job anytime soon, and I could really use—"

"Karyn," said Loren, marching over to her, "we've been fucked around a lot. A *lot*. There were five of us, you remember? You saw the documents?"

Karyn nodded.

"The other two aren't here and that's not because they're off having a fucking pedicure, it's because they're *dead*. And *you*"—Loren jabbed a finger at Karyn, using the hand that held the can of M:Pyre; some of the soda splashed on Karyn's face—"what you've been involved in is some deep criminal shit. You understand that?"

"Y-yes."

"If our debts don't get canned, we stop giving a fuck what happens to us. We'll go to the cops and tell them you were in this up to your neck. So you open up a window right now and file those fucking forms and then we can all move on with our lives. Okay?"

The important part had been not to mention the money to Karyn. If she knew they had the money, she could have claimed it as part payment of the debt, without their permission. But once the forms were filed, anything in their possession was their own. They were free to move as they wished, and had almost as many rights as a nat. They went for cocktails to celebrate. The money wasn't as much as they'd expected, but it was a head start.

And they weren't just celebrating getting free. Nadi and Loren could finally focus on each other, and how they felt about each other. It was a relationship that had been forged in very strange times for them both, and so much was still uncertain—but Nadi hoped that would only bond them more strongly. She'd spoken to Loren of her anger at her old life, how it had kept her from discovering what she really wanted—but Loren was more philosophical. Yes, they had both been ill-treated, but their paths would never have crossed any other way. "So I can't be too mad about it," Loren said. "I've tried, but when I imagine my life being different, you're not there. And I don't like that."

Nadi still felt this let too many people off the hook too easily, but it was a sweet sentiment. Arlo was in the bathroom during this conversation, and the sentiment would not have struck him the same way, so when he returned they changed the subject.

"Do you think we'd have got libbed?" asked Nadi. "If we'd just done the job and handed over the money, I mean?"

"Yeah—or got a share of the money, such as it was?" said Arlo.

"Nah," said Loren. "I think Mia would've either sold us or killed us, on his instructions. And I think Miles was so paranoid about the money he'd have destroyed it."

"I did love that idea of buying Mia's personality."

"'Course you did. We were meant to."

"If we had the money we thought we were getting," said Nadi, "I'd have said let's buy it anyway and make a go of it ourselves."

"What, set up a company of our own?" said Arlo.

"Yeah. Do it our way."

Arlo thought about this—then shook his head. "I think maybe it's over, that whole way of doing things. And if it's not, maybe it should be. I don't think you can change it from the inside."

"I'm not talking about changing it," said Loren. "Just *living*." They smiled at Nadi. "We've got lives now."

Nadi smiled back, then turned to Arlo. "What are you gonna do?" she asked.

Arlo considered for a moment. "I don't know." He laughed wearily. "Being free's harder than I expected."

They were staying in a hostel by the docks. No one was hiring, but Loren was putting it around they could fix janky systems, and there seemed to be a shortage of such skills locally. Nadi got some temp work loading and unloading. They made a strange but charming couple, and insisted they didn't mind Arlo being around, which was nice but made him feel like their adult son who hadn't left home.

They were very kind and patient with Arlo when he suffered a horrific psychological crash shortly after arriving here, as the reality of Drienne's death hit him. Nadi had listened while he'd talked of how he wanted to find out if Drienne really was one of the New Orleans vague kids, and if so, whether her family was still around. It felt like too big a task, and he felt too tired to take it on; but he also felt like he was failing Drienne by not doing so.

"Well, I'm gonna track down that girl I found in that restaurant," Nadi told him. "Still feel bad about that. We can work on your mystery too."

Arlo didn't necessarily share her optimism, but he appreciated it.

He and Loren hadn't fully addressed the odd tension between them during the job. Arlo had tried to apologize, though he wasn't sure precisely what for, and Loren had brushed it off. Once they'd got past that, Loren turned out to have a remarkable, earnest clarity about things that made it easy to be open with them. Not in the way he'd been open with Drienne, but nevertheless, it helped.

"I got her killed," he told Loren. "I convinced Mia to buy her for the job and I led those soldiers to you."

"I mean," Loren replied, "yeah, you can look at it like that, I guess. But she took that risk for you, not telling you what was going on, because she knew how much you needed to be free, and she didn't want you to lose your chance of it."

"I suppose."

"And we got it in the end. I'd have just gone along with the plan if it wasn't for her, I wouldn't have questioned it. And we wouldn't be free. But now we are. She won that for you."

"So did you. Come on, you did a *lot*."

Loren grinned. "Yeah, I did. But what I'm saying is, don't fucking waste it moping around that you got her killed. You didn't shoot her, did you. End of."

"I know, I know. I just don't know what to do now."

They were quiet for a moment.

"Well," said Loren, "you did have that *incredibly* detailed plan to open a bar."

"Yeah."

"I mean, that's what she'd want you to do. Right?"

Arlo couldn't believe this hadn't occurred to him. He didn't feel ready to do it yet, and he didn't know how he'd do it. But he would. As soon as he decided this, he felt a tiny bit better.

Arlo needed to save his share of the money toward this project, but he spent a little of it on one indulgence: a box from RookDivest. Loren had noticed they were selling these "Lucky Dip" boxes of clothing and homeware and worked out what they were and how they'd been serialized, and identified the one Arlo needed.

When it arrived, he opened it up and the scent of Drienne's perfume rose from the clothes inside. All her possessions from Shaw Apartments were there: her scented candles, her animatronic budgerigar, her coffee mug, the Brand Ambassador of the Week award she'd stolen from Roman. Arlo laid all her things out on the floor and felt so sad, he wished he'd never bought it. But the thought of someone else having it made him even sadder.

Their kind was not unique, by definition. And yet he'd never find anyone like her.

He set the animatronic budgerigar singing, and he sang along.

ACKNOWLEDGMENTS

Thanks as ever to my editor, Lee Harris, and all the staff at Tor who helped this book along the way.

Thanks to everyone who chatted through the ideas with me, particularly Andy Diggle. Very late in the process, Laurie Penny asked me a question about how the cloning process works, which was easy to answer but no one had asked it before, and it triggered a train of thought that led me to the idea for what went wrong at Sunglow, enabling me to replace an idea that I knew wasn't working.

Mia's backstory has its roots in a *Future Shock* I wrote for the British comic *2000 AD*, which prompted regular reader Russell T. Davies to get in touch with me out of the blue to say he really liked the idea. So I made a mental note to revisit and expand on it one day.

Biggest thanks of all to my wife, Catherine Spooner. This would have been a different, and inferior, book without her feedback; in particular she saved me from killing off a character who really shouldn't have died. I'm very relieved the original version didn't go out. I must have been in a terrible mood when I wrote it.

ABOUT THE AUTHOR

Sami Kelsh

Eddie Robson's previous novels are *Tomorrow Never Knows*, *Hearts of Oak*, and *Drunk on All Your Strange New Words*. His short fiction has appeared in *Uncanny* magazine. His scriptwriting credits include the BBC Radio sitcom *Welcome to Our Village, Please Invade Carefully*, the Audible rom-com *Car Crash*, and episodes of animated series such as *Sarah & Duck* and *The Amazing World of Gumball*. He has written numerous spin-offs from *Doctor Who* and nonfiction books on film, TV, music, and video games. He lives with his wife and two children in Lancaster, UK.